KERAS

Simon Rae

David Fickling Books
OXFORD · NEW YORK
31 Beaumont Street
Oxford OX1 2NP, UK

KERAS
A DAVID FICKLING BOOK 978 0 857 56034 6

Published in Great Britain by David Fickling Books,
a division of Random House Children's Publishers UK
A Random House Group Company

This edition published 2013

1 3 5 7 9 10 8 6 4 2

The Random House Group Limited supports the Forest Stewardship Council (FSC®), the leading international forest certification organization. Our books carrying the FSC label are printed on FSC®-certified paper. FSC is the only forest certification scheme endorsed by the leading environmental organizations, including Greenpeace. Our paper procurement policy can be found at www.randomhouse.co.uk/environment.

Set in 12/16pt Goudy Old Style

DAVID FICKLING BOOKS
31 Beaumont Street, Oxford, OX1 2NP

www.**randomhousechildrens**.co.uk
www.**totallyrandombooks**.co.uk
www.**randomhouse**.co.uk

Addresses for companies within The Random House Group Limited can be found at: www.randomhouse.co.uk/offices.htm

THE RANDOM HOUSE GROUP Limited Reg. No. 954009

A CIP catalogue record for this book is available from the British Library.

Printed and bound in Great Britain by Clays Ltd, St Ives plc

For the birthday girls,
Beany and Noo

CHAPTER 1

'Settle down. Now, I'd like to introduce our special guest, Mr Finistaire.'

Voices dropped, exercise books and papers stopped being shuffled on desk-tops. Mrs Hinton's class settled down.

Mr Finistaire was a small, rather round man with old-fashioned clothes and gold-rimmed spectacles. Everyone knew who he was and had gazed in wonder as his gleaming Bentley drew up in the middle of the playground, with his chauffeur sitting ramrod straight in the driver's seat, staring out through the windscreen without any sign of seeing any of them.

Mr Finistaire owned the enormous wood that circled one side of the village, and Charnley House, the huge mansion secluded in its leafy depths. He was very seldom seen, and his visit to the school was an event. Mrs Hinton was clearly both nervous and excited.

Jack Henley, sitting in his usual desk right at

the back, was less excited. He didn't expect Mr Finistaire's talk to be at all interesting, and as one of the many village boys who trespassed in his woods, he had no wish to be among those introduced to him. He would keep his head down, as he usually did, and wait patiently for break.

But when the visitor started speaking, Jack looked up. He couldn't help it. All Mr Finistaire said was 'Thank you, Mrs Hinton, and thank *you*' – to the class – 'for listening to what I have to say.'

There was nothing special about the words, but the way they were said demanded attention. Mr Finistaire didn't speak loudly, but he spoke very clearly. Grown-ups rarely seemed to talk to you directly. Teachers were always looking down at a list, or writing on the whiteboard. His mum was the same, talking to him over her shoulder as she did the ironing, stirred the stew or sewed on a button. As for Dad, he was always busy – always cleaning something – his shoes, his gun, his car. And when he finally put down his oily rag, he would sit behind his paper making remarks like 'Villa have slipped down a couple of places.' But Mr Finistaire was different. His voice was warm and friendly, as though he were taking you into his confidence. Despite himself, Jack was all ears.

'I've come to talk to you about something very dear to my heart,' Mr Finistaire was saying. 'I'm sure you are all aware of the issue of endangered species. For lots of reasons, animal populations are being squeezed out of their natural habitats. Can anyone name an animal that's endangered in this way?'

Hands shot up. Harriet Lazenby actually got halfway to her feet from her desk in the middle of the front row, her blonde plaits swinging with eagerness to catch Mr Finistaire's eye.

He nodded at her. 'Yes?'

'Tigers,' she gasped. 'Indian tigers – they're endangered.'

'Quite right,' Mr Finistaire said.

The other hands fell, and there was a resigned sigh. Harriet always got her answer in first. Jack could imagine the smirk of satisfaction on her face.

'Yes, the tiger's natural habitats are seriously threatened,' Mr Finistaire went on. 'Of course, in the past, tigers were hunted. They were hunted for sport, and for their skins. People don't wear fur coats any more, and you're not allowed to shoot them. But tigers are still under threat. In fact, they face extinction.'

Jack noticed a look of sadness passing across his face.

'Can anyone think of another endangered animal?'

Again the hands shot up. Harriet was actually standing up now, and waving at Mr Finistaire as though he were half a mile away and not right in front of her.

'Perhaps someone else would like to have a go?' Mr Finistaire suggested mildly. 'What about at the back?'

Jack's instinct was to drop his head, but he found he had to keep looking up at the visitor. Before he knew it, he was opening his mouth, even though he hadn't put his hand up. 'Rhinos.'

Everyone in the class was looking at him. He felt himself going red.

'Excellent,' Mr Finistaire said. 'And do you know why rhinos are endangered?'

'Hunted. By poachers. For their horns. People grind them up for medicines, although that's stupid because they can't cure anything.' Jack hadn't said that many words in class all year.

'You're quite right,' Mr Finistaire said. 'It's a scandal and a tragedy,' he added in a tone that showed he really meant it. He looked directly at Jack and Jack looked back, ignoring the turned faces, ignoring Mrs Hinton's expression of surprise.

Then he dropped his head. Unlike Harriet, he hated attracting attention. His place was always at the back, away from the limelight.

He started scrawling savagely on a bit of scrap paper. Downstroke after downstroke – a stockade. He tipped each thick black downstroke with a vicious arrow-head. And then, for good measure, he sent a shower of arrows flying over the stockade to keep everyone at bay.

Mr Finistaire continued, but Jack blocked it out. He wasn't going to get sucked in like that again.

He moved on to another piece of paper and drew another stockade. This time he sketched an animal prowling around outside. A tiger perhaps.

Their visitor had asked another question. Hands shot up.

'Dodo!' chorused half the class.

Mr Finistaire had obviously moved on to species that had gone from endangered to extinct.

Jack drew a big-bottomed, ponderous bird with a strange nose-like beak, and then a sailor with a gun. They'd done dodos earlier in the term. He was just putting in the blast lines from the end of the sailor's gun when his attention was dragged back to what Mr Finistaire was saying.

'And how would you describe a dragon?' he was asking.

Harriet's pigtails shot out again. 'Well,' she started excitedly, 'it would have a long scaly tail, and a big scaly body, and a great big mouth with flames coming out.'

Mr Finistaire raised a hand. 'I'm sorry – my mistake. I posed the question wrongly. That is of course a perfect description of a dragon. Very vivid. But what I was after was what *kind* of creature is a dragon?'

A lone hand went up.

Timothy Green was a studious boy with a fringe. Pushing his hair out of his eyes, he said shyly, 'Is it a reptile?'

Mr Finistaire smiled again. 'Well, it might be classed as a reptile. But that wasn't quite what I was after. I mean, do dragons exist? Has anyone ever seen one?' He looked around the room, his face open and inviting.

There was a groundswell of response, and at least one little snigger.

'Well?' he urged gently.

The heads began to shake.

'So what do we call an animal, a creature like that?'

Jack felt the word forming on his tongue, but he wasn't going to say it.

'Is it fairy story?' someone asked.

'You could call it that,' said Mr Finistaire. 'What would another word be?'

Timothy pushed his hair out of his eyes again. 'Is it myth?'

'Yes,' said Mr Finistaire with an encouraging smile. 'Dragons are mythical creatures. Or so we believe – because no one's ever seen one, no one's ever produced a photograph of one, and although there are lots and lots of stories about them, that's all they are – stories. Can anybody think of another mythical creature?'

Once the class grasped what they were being asked, the hands shot up again.

'Mermaids.'

'Centaurs.'

'Yes, yes.' Mr Finistaire beamed.

'Pegasus,' said Timothy.

'Yes, the horse with wings – good. Can anyone think of something very like the flying horse?'

The word formed on the tip of Jack's tongue, but Harriet got in first.

'Unicorn.'

'Unicorn, yes. Very well done.'

And Mr Finistaire closed his eyes briefly, as though he had got to where he wanted to get to. It was only a moment, and immediately after it, he opened his eyes again and looked around the classroom.

'The unicorn,' he said. 'Yes. Of all the creatures you've come up with, the unicorn is my favourite. It's the closest to an animal we know exists – the horse. It isn't a cross between a human and an animal like a mermaid or a centaur; it doesn't fly; it doesn't breathe fire. It is, if you like, the most believable of mythical creatures. And that is why' – he smiled broadly – 'I have decided to make the unicorn the subject for the art prize that I am offering to your class this term.'

He paused to let the idea of the prize sink in. Then he continued: 'And the prize for the winner is a day out at Charnley House which, as I'm sure you know, is not generally open to the public, but which holds much of interest – including a well-stocked larder for a very nice lunch! The winner will be collected by my chauffeur in my car, which you may have seen parked in your playground.'

There was a buzz of excitement.

'And all you have to do,' Mr Finistaire said, raising his hands for quiet, 'is draw or paint a picture of a unicorn as though it were real; as though you'd actually seen it.'

And that was it. Mr Finistaire smiled, and stepped aside while Mrs Hinton thanked him for coming to the school in person, and for offering such a wonderful prize.

'I'm sure everyone will do their very best,' she said with a rather glassy smile.

She was about to usher the visitor out of the classroom when he stopped her and asked a question. Jack saw with alarm that Mr Finistaire was looking at him. Mrs Hinton followed his gaze and then replied. Mr Finistaire nodded and then, with a cheery wave, he was gone.

Everyone crowded to the window to watch Mrs Hinton escort their visitor back to his car. The chauffeur, a tall, thin man with closely cropped blond hair, leaped out to hold the door open for him. And then the beautiful limousine swung round and disappeared through the school gates.

Like a high-speed motor boat, it left a great wash of disturbance in its wake. Everybody was talking about the art prize, and speculating wildly about the day at Charnley House.

'It's got a swimming pool!'

'And a helipad.'

'Who says?'

'Everybody knows that.'

'My uncle did some work there. He didn't see one.'

'How rich do you think he is?'

'Mega. Absolutely mega. My dad says he's richer than some countries,' someone else said.

Jack thought that was silly. Not that he said anything. His own dad worked as a beater on Mr Finistaire's shoots in the winter, taking time off from the grain store. He'd never said anything about a helipad or a swimming pool.

Mrs Hinton came bustling back into the room. Her eyes were bright and her face was slightly pink. 'Well, class, how exciting is that? I want you to work really hard. Do your absolute best, so Mr Finistaire has a really hard choice picking the winner.'

'I've started mine already, miss.'

It was Harriet. Jack could see her bowed over her

desk, busily drawing, rubbing out, re-doing. You could tell she had set her heart on winning. And she probably would. Mrs Hinton always liked her pictures so much they could be seen not only all around the classroom, but in the school hall as well. Harriet got more gold stars in a week than Jack managed in a term.

Dan nudged him. 'Are you going to do one?'

'Jack's rubbish at art,' Luke said from the other side.

It was true that Jack's efforts were pinned up, when they were exhibited at all, at the bottom corners of the display boards, where they would attract the least attention.

However, he did have one advantage as far as Mr Finistaire's prize was concerned.

He had actually seen a unicorn.

CHAPTER 2

All his life Jack had felt at home in the woods – more at home than he felt at home. At home he always seemed to be in the way, somehow. If he was doing his homework at the kitchen table, his mum would find that she had to roll out her pastry or whisk some eggs. If he moved into the tiny lounge and sat on the baggy old sofa, his dad would come in and flap his paper about, and change the television channel to something really boring like horse racing. In his room upstairs there was never anywhere to put anything. But if he left his things out, his mum would tell him to put them away or she'd take them to the charity shop, where she worked two days a week.

If the house was too small, Mr Finistaire's estate was the opposite. Jack loved the sense of space, the high canopy of trees, the ever-changing views between their massive trunks, always pulling his eye deeper into the heart of the woods. He loved to explore, searching for the animals that lived their secret lives under the ferns and bracken, protected by great rolls of bramble, thickets of thorn.

He knew where the badgers lived, and often spent long summer evenings holed up in the tall grass watching them come cautiously out of their setts, the young ones bounding around, clubbing each other with their paws, play-fighting.

Sometimes Dan and Luke came along, and the three of them would crash around pretending to be outlaws setting up an ambush, or cannibals creeping through the undergrowth in search of their next victim.

There was a little sandy cliff where you could slide down on bits of cardboard, though you nearly always got thrown off when you hit one of the gnarled tree roots that had pushed its way to the surface over the years. And there was a derelict woodsman's cottage.

Although the older boys sometimes had parties there, Jack and his friends usually had the place to themselves. They'd get a little fire going and heat up some baked beans. They didn't do this very often, partly because the cottage was strictly out of bounds on account of its sagging floors and the landslide of tiles that had once been its roof, and partly because it was quite an effort smuggling saucepans and cans into the woods.

Of course, the woods themselves were officially out of bounds. There was a lopsided sign saying NO TRESPASSING on the broken-down gate, but Jack's parents didn't bother trying to stop him going in.

'Just don't get caught,' his dad said. 'I don't want Mr Grout bringing you home by your collar – is that understood?'

Mr Grout was Mr Finistaire's gamekeeper, a figure of awe among the village boys. There were dark rumours about what happened to those he did catch trespassing, though Jack had only actually seen Mr Grout once, when he pulled up in the estate Land Rover outside the post office. He was a wiry little man with fierce, sandy-red sideburns, a well-worn countryman's cap, an ancient tweed jacket with bulging side-pockets, and a bone-handled stick.

Jack had no wish to see Mr Grout again, and certainly not in the woods. But although he was always on the lookout for him when he was there, he never saw him. His duties obviously kept him on the other side of the wood, nearer the big house. Anyway, Jack was confident that he would see the gamekeeper before he was seen. He was good at becoming invisible and moving silently so that the animals he wanted to watch didn't know he was there.

It was like being a hunter or a trapper. You needed the same skills. There were deer in the wood, just little ones, and if they caught your scent, they would be off, scampering away through the bracken. But if you stayed downwind of them, and moved slowly, taking care with every footstep, you could get surprisingly close to where they cropped the grass in a rough circle of sunlight filtered through the leaf cover. Then you could raise your gun to your shoulder and take aim.

Not that Jack had a gun. And it would be some time before he got to use his father's shotgun. 'Punch you off your feet, lad,' his dad would say every time Jack pleaded to be allowed a go when they were out rabbiting over the fields.

'What about an air rifle, Dad?' he would ask. Harriet's elder brother was known to have an air rifle.

'When we win the lottery, son,' came the reply, and that was that.

But you could still dream, and when you'd got your target nicely lined up, you pulled the imaginary trigger: *Bang!*

Then one of the deer would look up, stare straight at you with big, anxious eyes, and suddenly it would start, and turn and speed away through the trees, followed immediately by the others, leaving the clearing empty, as though they had never been there. But if you looked closely, there were signs: the little tears in the turf where their strong teeth had yanked at the grass; the divots their hooves had gouged out of the ground; the neat piles of droppings.

Jack knew his patch well and he felt at ease there. But there were times when the woods felt less homely. Sometimes when he went deeper in, beyond the familiar places, they were much less welcoming. The light was almost choked out by the trees. And it was so quiet. The moss under his feet made no sound; the distant traffic noises gradually faded the farther in he went.

He wasn't frightened. But sometimes he liked to pretend to be. He could imagine that instead of being the one slipping unnoticed through the woods, he was the one being watched; the one being foll-owed stealthily, pursued. It made the hair on the back of his neck stand up, and he found himself stealing glances to the left and right, or suddenly slipping behind a tree and peering round back down the way he'd come. He imagined an arrow thwacking into the tree bole just above his head, followed by a panicky chase through the undergrowth as he ran for his life.

Once, when he was escaping from a particularly ferocious tribe, he gave himself a terrible fright. Half crouching as he ran, he was also looking back over his shoulder when there was an explosion of noise right under his feet. He leaped up with a cry, only to see one of Mr Finistaire's pheasants rocketing away through the trees. It was a shock, but it made a good story at break the next day.

'Wicked!' Luke said. 'I know,' he went on. 'We could hunt!'

'Hunt what?' Dan said.

'Anything. Deer. Rabbits.'

'What with – a bow and arrow?' Dan looked scornful.

'We could, couldn't we, Jack?' Luke looked urgently for support.

Dan remained negative: 'What you going to do, creep up on them with a knife?'

'Jack's dad's got a gun, hasn't he, Jack?'

'He'd kill me. Anyway, it's got a kick like a mule. It would take your shoulder off.'

'What about an air rifle? I heard Harriet going on about her brother's.'

'Well, why don't you ask her if you can borrow it, then?' Dan said with a sneer that said it all.

Luke slumped. This always happened. He'd come up with a brilliant idea, and the others would pour cold water on it.

'But it's boring, just going in the wood and heating up some baked beans. If we caught something, we could eat that, cook it over a proper camp fire.'

'D'you fancy skinning a rabbit? All that blood and fur and gristle and bone, and then all the innards. Euuugh!' Dan screwed up his face in disgust.

Luke said: 'I bet Jack's done it.'

Jack hadn't in fact, but he had seen his dad do it, and Dan was right, it was a pretty horrible job.

On the other hand he liked Luke's idea. It would be a challenge.

'We could trap something,' he suggested.

'Brilliant!' Luke said.

'Why didn't you think of it, then?' said Dan.

'How do you do it, Jack?'

Jack wasn't exactly sure. 'Wire hoops,' he said, making vague movements with his hands. 'You have to find where the runs are – I can do that. And then you find a place to hide your' – again he made a loose O with his hands – 'so that the rabbit doesn't suspect anything. And when it comes along—'

Luke interrupted with a strangled death-cry and wrenched his head at a hideous angle with his hands around his neck, before letting his whole body go limp.

'Could we?' Dan asked doubtfully.

Jack nodded. He thought they could.

'I'll get some stuff together. Meet at the oak, Thursday after school.'

Two days later they met under the ancient, once-magnificent tree that had been crippled by lightning.

Jack had an old rucksack over his shoulder.

'Let's see,' Luke said, trying to lift the flap.

Jack shrugged him off, and then led them into the wood. They'd hardly gone ten metres before he stopped.

'Quiet!' he hissed. 'If we're going to do this, we've got to do it properly. We can't go crashing about. We have to think like hunters, act like hunters.'

'I thought we were trappers,' Dan said.

Jack turned his back on him and moved on. Dan and Luke made less noise, though there were still plenty of annoying stumbles, and once Dan got whipped by a branch that Luke had carelessly allowed to catch for a moment on his shoulder.

'Ow! Watch it!'

Jack rounded on them. 'If you two can't take this seriously, I'm going home now.'

'Don't do that, Jack,' Luke pleaded.

'OK,' said Jack. 'But we've got to be really careful. It's not far now.' He was keeping his eyes on the ground, looking for the telltale signs.

He knew where the warren was. He'd often seen the rabbits playing on the little sandy arena that opened out below it. What he needed was to find one of their regular routes as they left the warren to go further afield.

There! He stopped dead, raising his hand at the same time. He crouched down and peered. If you looked closely you could see the bracken stems had been pushed aside.

He carefully lowered himself onto his stomach. There was a sort of tunnel through the bracken. This was what he had been looking for.

As the other two crowded in behind him, Jack raised his finger to his lips, and then put both hands up to the side of his head and waggled his fingers to denote rabbit ears. Luke and Dan looked suitably impressed and sank back onto their haunches.

Jack unbuckled the rucksack.

What followed took quite a long time and involved a lot of fiddly work with wire and the meat skewers Jack had found at the back of one of the kitchen drawers. When he finally finished, he stood up and rubbed the soil from his hands. He inspected his work, both from above, and then, bending down, from ground – or rabbit – level.

'What d'you think?'

'It's great, Jack. You couldn't tell. Nobody could.'

Dan knelt down and squinted along the tunnel through the ferns. 'Not bad.'

'What do you mean, not bad?' Jack whispered fiercely. 'Can you see anything?'

'No.'

'Well, then.'

'But that's not to say a rabbit couldn't.'

Jack gave him a look, but then lay down on the ground once more.

Nothing.

He reached in and smoothed down the frond of bracken he had laid over the buried wire. It looked perfectly natural.

He got up stiffly.

Luke gave him a high-five followed by a big thumbs-up. Dan nodded, impressed despite himself.

Jack shooed them back down the path, and then turned to sweep away signs of their footprints. They circled round and sank into the bracken a few metres away. Jack had little expectation of seeing anything, but the others wanted to stay – just in case.

They weren't very good at keeping still. 'You have to ignore everything,' Jack had told them. 'Even insects.'

But they couldn't. Dan had a good scratch at his leg, and then Luke half rolled over and pawed at his stomach. Jack glared, but it was no more than he'd expected. You had to become part of the landscape; and to do so you had to stop being yourself – or stop being all of yourself. Once you made your body invisible, you simply inhabited it, waiting motionlessly like a sniper.

Eventually he managed to ignore his friends, and sink – or float – into a trance of attention, in which everything fell away, leaving him focused on the tunnel through the grass. When a woodlouse scuttled over the back of his hand, he made no attempt to brush it off. A mosquito whined at his ear. He ignored it. He kept his gaze on the mouth of the rabbit tunnel.

At the same time, another part of his mind opened to the wider life of the wood: the host of different sounds made by the slightest breeze in the boughs far above his head, and the feathery splashes made by wood pigeons among the leaves. The wood was like the sea, ceaselessly, restlessly stirring, creating waves of sound that rose and fell in their own rhythms. Concentrating so intently on the rabbit tunnel turned his mind to a still pond, and the slightest noise sent ripples tripping across it.

In this heightened state of awareness, he seemed to pick up Luke's exclamation of surprise a fraction of a second before he actually heard it. Of course, the little deer that was beginning to make its way down the path immediately turned tail in a flurry of hooves and crashed through the bracken to safety.

'Sorry, Jack,' Luke said as they made their way back out of the wood.

'Loser,' scoffed Dan. 'All you had to do was stay still.'

'It's all right,' said Jack. 'We'd have had to go home now anyway.'

'But he'll have scared off the rabbits,' Dan moaned.

'Don't worry about it,' said Jack. 'They'll have to come out at some stage. They don't have long memories.'

Luke brightened up. 'So we might get one after all?'

'Don't know. That's the first trap I've ever set.'

'It looked great to me,' Luke said.

'Well, you're definitely skinning it, if we get one,' Dan said.

'When will we find out?' Luke asked.

'I'll go and check it in the morning. Before school.'

'Do you want us to come?'

Jack shook his head.

The last thing he wanted was Dan and Luke blundering about in the wood with him in the early morning. It was the time when he felt the wood's magic most strongly; when he felt it belonged to him, and him alone.

CHAPTER 3

Jack was up at five-thirty. He was glad to be awake as he'd been tormented all night by snatches of dreams in which he was moving rapidly through the wood. He was travelling far faster than he could run; it felt like flying. But it was dangerous, as he had to keep ducking branches. Then, without warning, a huge hole opened in front of him. There was no stopping. He fell into the blackness, his arms and legs flailing.

He woke up with his heart racing.

Jack was dressed and out of the house in less than five minutes, picking his way across the dewy meadow. By the time he got to the gate into the woods, his trainers were soaked, but he didn't care. The woods were beautiful. Leaves glistened; his path was barred by spiders' webs silvered with dew and lit by shafts of sunlight.

He was alone in his world, with at least two hours' total freedom ahead of him.

As he plunged into the woods he felt a charge of excitement. Would there be a rabbit in his trap? He hoped so. But what if it weren't dead – if he had to confront an unblinking eye looking up at him over a collar of blood? He felt for the knife in his pocket, but the thought of having to use it made him shiver.

He pushed on down the track they had taken the previous evening. The wood pigeons called sleepily to each other in the branches high above his head. The first insects wove their mazy paths through shafts of sunlight breaking through the leaf canopy. A new day in the woods was starting all around him. There wasn't anywhere he would rather have been.

But when he came to the turn in the path approaching the warren, he stopped dead. Whatever he had been expecting, it wasn't this.

Even from twenty metres away, Jack could see that something had happened to his snare. The bracken around it was trampled down. He went up to it cautiously, and found the earth raw where the wire had been ripped out of the ground.

He squatted down and felt in the exposed soil. What had happened? He thought of Mr Grout angrily beating the bracken with his stick, and shuddered.

He was suddenly convinced that he was being watched, and swung round. But there was nothing – just the silent trees receding into the depths of the wood. He turned back and started to scour the area carefully. *There must be a clue*, he told himself, inspecting every inch of ground. But he could find nothing.

He went back to the path. The soil was packed hard – there had been no rain for days. There were the predictable marks left by the boys' trainer soles, and what might have been a deer's hoof. But there was no sign that the deer had veered off the path to get its foot caught in the snare.

He couldn't make sense of it, and stood rubbing the side of his face, baffled.

Something made him look up – and there, slung from a branch, was the loop of wire. It looked like a stiff lasso. It also looked as if it had been deliberately placed there – to send a message. A warning.

Jack reached up. He could just stretch high enough to unhook it. He passed it through his hands, but there was no hint as to how it had got up there from the rabbit tunnel.

Though his mind was still focused on the mystery, some sixth sense made him look up. A movement, so slight he couldn't have said what it was, caught his eye. It was a long way off, but it had the blood pumping through his veins. Every sense was suddenly alert. He strained his eyes; his ears filtered the wood's soundscape. He suddenly knew what it was to be a deer, or any hunted animal, constantly in fear, ready at a moment's notice to turn tail and escape.

Still holding the wire, he slipped back into the undergrowth and waited, his heart pounding.

Nothing happened. He had made it up, spooked himself. He began to relax, and was thinking about resuming his search for clues in the rabbit tunnel. But then he froze. There was the unmistakable sound of someone making his way through the wood towards him.

With a feeling of dread, Jack recognized the cap and baggy tweed jacket of Mr Grout. It was his worst nightmare – to be caught in the woods by the gamekeeper, caught setting snares, poaching.

The wire burned in his hands. Assuming he'd been the one to pull it out of the ground and hang it on the branch, Mr Grout would know immediately that he had come back to the scene of his crime.

Jack began to panic. There was no chance of sneaking out and putting it back on the branch.

Shrinking down in the bush where he was hiding, he watched in fascinated horror as Mr Grout approached. He had his bone-handled stick in his hand. Jack winced at the thought of that being brought down on his shoulders. But the gamekeeper was not swishing it around in anger. Instead, he used it to part the bracken and probe the grass.

As Jack looked on, he realized that Mr Grout was doing exactly what *he* had been doing – looking at the ground for clues. But clues to what? He was coming from the other side of the wood, the Charnley side. Jack hadn't gone beyond the rabbit warren. Mr Grout would find no signs of his trespassing over there.

Still he came on, and Jack bit his lip as the foxy little man reached the path only a few metres away from him. The peak of his cap was down, masking his eyes, but Jack imagined them burning intensely under the wiry eyebrows.

Jack could hardly breathe as the gamekeeper advanced towards the wrecked rabbit tunnel. He wanted to cry out, turn on his heels and run, break cover and confess – anything to bring an end to this terrible suspense.

The tension became even more unbearable when Mr Grout finally reached the site of the trap. He stepped eagerly off the path and squatted down amidst the disturbed bracken. Jack held his breath. In a moment Mr Grout would look up to check on the wire, and then the trouble would start.

Jack started planning his escape. He could obviously out-run Mr Grout, but he didn't want him to see his face. Perhaps he should go now, while the gamekeeper had his back to him. But something kept him where he was – a curiosity that outweighed even the terror of capture.

The little man took his time. Jack could see him inspecting every inch of ground, just as *he* had done. After what seemed an age, Mr Grout got up and slowly turned. He must have worked out that the trap had been laid by someone from the village, some boy from the village – some boy from the village who was hiding only metres away.

It seemed to Jack that Mr Grout was looking directly at him. He felt completely exposed, as though the bush provided no cover at all.

His nerve broke. With a last look at the gamekeeper's face, set in a grim scowl, Jack broke cover and ran for his life.

There was a shout behind him.

'Oi – you – you come back here!'

This was followed by a torrent of swearing, and dire warnings as to what would happen when Mr Grout got his hands on him.

There was no immediate risk of that: Jack sprinted back down the path towards the village, leaping obstacles and brushing low-hanging leaves out of his face.

As he'd guessed, the gamekeeper wasn't up for a chase through the woods. He heard the stick flail angrily in the undergrowth, but soon the noise of pursuit died away, and he left Mr Grout shouting his threats at the unheeding trees.

When he was sure he was safe, he stopped for breath, his hands on his hips, his head thrown back as he gulped down air. The commotion had disturbed one of the wood's many rookeries, and the great black birds cawed and circled way above him in the high treetops.

Jack moved on more slowly, still fighting for breath. He stumbled up to the sagging gate with its NO TRESPASSING sign. He leaned against the gatepost for support. He had had the fright of his life and he was shaking all over.

* * *

Later, after he'd calmed down, changed into his school clothes and had his breakfast, Jack walked up the hill through the village. Something was worrying him. There was the close encounter with Mr Grout of course, but he was ninety-nine per cent sure the gamekeeper couldn't have seen him well enough to identify him.

The moment he had broken cover and made a run for it had been scary, but also exciting. His fantasies about being chased through the woods had come true, and there was a sense of triumph in having escaped. But what he kept going back to was the way Mr Grout had acted when he was searching the area where the snare had been set. The gamekeeper had not looked up to where the wire should have been – which suggested that he *hadn't* put it there.

So who had?

That was one question. The other was, if Mr Grout hadn't known about the snare, what was he doing in that part of the wood? He was clearly looking for something. But what?

'Well?' Dan caught up with him just outside the school gates.

'Nothing.'

'Nothing?' Luke had joined them. He sounded disappointed.

'What happened?' Dan was inspecting Jack's face.

Jack turned away, aware of the scratches he'd got in his helter-skelter chase through the woods. 'Nothing,' he said again.

'Don't believe you,' said Dan.

'Tough,' said Jack, relieved for once to hear the school bell.

Jack sat at the back of class, even more detached from what was going on than usual. Mrs Hinton did her best to make the Tudors sound interesting. She talked about Henry VIII's six wives and the awful things that happened to them. She talked about the Field of the Cloth of Gold, and of Henry's wars and the huge suit of armour he wore. But Jack took no notice.

He was thinking about what he was going to do. A plan was forming in his mind, a decision that scared him, but the more he thought about it, the more he knew he was going to have to do it. He was going to return to the wood and set the snare again. He wasn't going to be frightened off by Mr Grout. He wanted to see if he could catch something. And if he gave up now, he would never find out how his wire had ended up on that branch.

The question was, when was the best time to do it?

He glanced up, just to suggest that he was paying attention. Mrs Hinton was changing the image on the whiteboard. Jack suddenly *did* start paying attention. There was a long dark picture that he found fascinating.

It showed a forest in which enough huntsmen to form a small army were gathered on horseback and on foot. It was very dark, so it was hard to see the details, and Mrs Hinton explained that it was called *The Hunt by Night*.

'Which is a funny time to go out hunting when you think about it, isn't it?' she added. She then started talking about perspective, and pointed to the lines of trees going back into the picture, drawing the eye in after them. But Jack had stopped listening. He simply stared at the image. It had just made up his mind for him. He too would hunt by night.

At the end of the school day Jack gave Dan and Luke the slip. He couldn't risk keeping them involved. It was going to be hard enough to do what he planned on his own.

Instead of going straight out again the minute he got home, he asked his mum if there was anything he could do to help, and willingly set about peeling the potatoes. Then he went upstairs to his room where he got everything ready.

He heard his dad come in. As usual he clumped upstairs to the bathroom to have a shower. He always complained that the grain dust got 'everywhere'.

Jack guiltily hid the old rucksack under a pillow, though the chances of his dad putting his head round the door to say hello were remote.

Jack was feeling restless. It was still hours before he could make his escape to the woods. When his mum called him down to tea, he found he couldn't stop yawning from pure nervousness.

'Early night for you, love,' his mum said as she dished up.

'Oh Mum,' he said.

'Your mother's right,' his dad said from behind his paper.

After the meal Jack went upstairs again, muttering something about homework. But he couldn't concentrate. 'Why did Henry VIII have Anne Boleyn executed?' It seemed incomprehensible. Surely divorce was enough. Dan's mum and dad were divorced, and they all seemed to get along OK.

He sighed. A page and a half at least, Mrs Hinton had said. He could barely think of a sentence. And it was only going to get worse next term when he moved up to the big school.

Still, before then there were the summer holidays to look forward to. Plus, in the meantime, his own secret adventures in the woods.

He looked at his alarm clock. It wasn't quite nine, but then his mum had said he was going to bed early. He went downstairs to say goodnight.

His parents hardly looked up from the television, and he closed the latched door to the stairs behind him, knowing that he was signed off for the night. He had to stop himself running up to the landing. He wanted to rush to the bathroom too, but told himself to take it slowly. Everything had to seem normal.

He looked out of his window. The moon was beginning to wane, but still gave a strong light as it beamed down from a cloudless sky. Perfect.

After brushing his teeth, he went back to his room and changed. But not into his pyjamas. He'd got out his black jeans, his darkest T-shirt and his top with the hood, along with the rucksack. Then there was the bed. Pillows, his big winter coat rolled up, along with a couple of jumpers to make a bump under the duvet. It was as convincing as he could make it.

Getting out of the house undetected was a challenge, but he'd done it before. He used the window in the spare bedroom to drop gently onto the roof of the extension, and then carefully let himself down onto the top of the water butt, and slipped to the ground. He waited, breathless, for a moment, and then ghosted out of the garden and onto the path that ran along the back of the cottages.

He looked up the hill at the lights in the village. A car made its way along the high street, its headlights playing over the front doors and shop fronts. He imagined people making their last cups of tea and preparing to go to bed.

Then he turned away and faced the woods – a vast impenetrable darkness, waiting for him.

An owl hooted in the distance. He shifted the rucksack on his shoulder and set off.

Once under the trees, he waited for a moment to let his eyes adjust. Beams of moonlight shone down, making everything a silvery grey. Although he had brought a torch, he could see well enough without it.

He had decided not to try the rabbit warren again. This time he was going to drive far deeper into the woods, to a place he had only been to once or twice, but where he had seen rabbits. If only he could find it again.

As he followed the path, his eyes became sharper. Sometimes he stopped to get his bearings. And when he did so, he could hear the night noises the woods made: tiny disturbances in the undergrowth, the barely audible murmur of the leaves. The owl hooted again, and once he heard a fox's bark.

He came to the derelict cottage. The moon shone brightly through the exposed rafters, but the lower windows were dark, and the doorway gaped. Although there couldn't be anyone there, he kept his eyes on it as he skirted round the overgrown garden.

Beyond the cottage there were few recognizable landmarks in the grainy light, but Jack followed his instincts. The contours of the wood helped him. He knew he had to veer to his left, away from the main path, and that there was a gentle incline. Then the way became steeper as you had to negotiate an outcrop of rocks that pushed through the thin soil. It was not a difficult climb, but you had to watch where you put your feet.

The trees were much denser beyond the outcrop, and the light less good. Jack felt his confidence ebb. Even in the day you had to be careful not to lose your bearings. What if he got lost? He imagined his mum going into his room in the morning and finding his coat and the spare pillows under the duvet.

It wasn't too late to go back.

But he went on. He had the woods to himself. He was free to do what he wanted, and in less than an hour he'd be retracing his steps, having passed the test he'd set himself.

The going got harder. There was nothing you could call a path, and the undergrowth between the trees was dense in places. He paused to pull on the old leather gloves he'd had the sense to pack in his bag. These helped when he had to lift brambles away from his legs or push his way between bushes, but his progress was slow.

Then there came a point when the going seemed to get easier. The ground cover thinned out, and the trees grew further apart. He stopped for a minute, breathing hard. He could hear a stream, which he remembered from the previous times he'd come this far. It would guide him to where he was trying to get to, so he began to make his way down towards it.

The stream became more audible and it wasn't long before he reached it. It was shallow and not very wide, and he soon found a convenient stepping stone to help him cross to the other bank. He walked along beside the stream for a while, and cut off to his right.

The trees now were beeches, their smooth tall trunks rising like columns all around him. It reminded him of the picture Mrs Hinton had shown them in class. He smiled. No one at school would believe what he was doing. And he would never tell anyone. It was his adventure, and his secret.

And then the trees suddenly opened out to form a great glade in front of him. It was bigger than he remembered – like an arena. The moonlight made it almost as bright as day, and he stood for a moment, stunned by the beauty of the place, looking around at the ring of trees gathered as if for some solemn ceremony.

Jack felt as if he had intruded on a holy place where he didn't belong. Although he was alone, he sensed he was being watched. The moon was like a brilliant, all-seeing eye. He looked up and it held his gaze, until he had to force himself to look away. He shivered, although he wasn't cold.

He had to stay focused, he told himself, and

started edging round the glade, flitting from tree to tree, keeping to the shadows. There was an area of dense ferns to his right. That's where he'd seen the rabbits, and it would be the perfect cover for his snare.

He felt a rush of nervous excitement as he reached the first fronds of fern and began very gently to push them aside, looking for the telltale signs. It didn't take him long to find what he was after – neat little droppings nestling in the grass.

He crouched down and opened his bag. Out came the wire and the skewers again, and the gardening knife to grub up the soil. He pushed forward on his knees, choosing his spot. When he found it, he set to work, easing the soil aside with his blade, and then carefully positioning the wire and covering it up again.

He wasn't thinking of the rabbit, caught by the neck, screaming in panic and pain. He was simply working out methodically the best way to set the snare, so that his prey would suspect nothing until it was too late.

He reached out for the skewers. As he did so, he felt a sudden unease, as though a cloud had passed over the face of the moon. But the moon was still shining steadily down. He glanced out across the grass arena to his left, but there was nothing there. All the same, he wanted to get the job done and be on his way back home as soon as possible. He just needed to set the skewers and secure the wire.

He plunged the first one in, as deep as it would go. Then, as he picked up the second, he froze. He knew, absolutely *knew*, that he was not alone after all. He was so terrified, he didn't dare turn round. He wanted to cry out, and opened his mouth. But no sound came. And then he felt a prod in his back.

Mr Grout's stick. Somehow the foxy gamekeeper had crept up and was now standing over him. He felt faint with fear. Caught red-handed, trespassing in Mr Finistaire's woods in the middle of the night, poaching. There would be no escape this time, and he could only guess at how awful his punishment would be.

CHAPTER 4

Jack remained in his crouched position, overcome with dread, too frightened to move. Then he heard a noise that surprised him: a sort of breathy snuffle. Next there was a soft thud beside him. He turned his head slightly and gave a startled cry. Mr Grout on horseback? That hardly seemed possible. He half turned to get a better look.

What he saw was the most astonishing thing he'd ever encountered in his life. Poised only centimetres above his face was what he'd thought was the gamekeeper's stick. But it wasn't a stick – it was a horn, nearly half a metre long, ivory white, and delicately spiralled. On either side of it were two large eyes, staring at him fiercely.

Jack fell back to one side, his mouth open in terror.

The creature took a half-step closer. *Don't hurt me*, he wanted to cry out. *I'm sorry*.

Suddenly the extraordinary horn jabbed down.

Jack flinched out of the way and shut his eyes, preparing himself for a stab of burning pain. He felt hot breath on his face, and heard an angry snort, but the horn was not aimed at him.

He heard a ripping noise by his head, and opened his eyes to see the wire uprooted from the soil, and dangling from the end of the horn.

So that was what had happened to his first snare, he thought.

But nothing could explain how he found himself sprawled between the forelegs of a mythical beast who didn't – who *couldn't* – exist.

Jack looked at them, strong, sturdy, set firm on the ground. They seemed real enough. His mind must be playing tricks on him. It was a horse. The horn was a trick of the moonlight. Or he was dreaming. But he wasn't in bed. The ground beneath him was hard. He dug his fingers into the ferns, and the soil was cold and gritty under his fingernails. And there was his snare, hanging inches from his face. This was no dream.

He looked away, avoiding the huge, angry eyes. As he did so, he saw that the hooves planted on either side of his body were not like a horse's hooves, an unbroken round; they were cleft, like a goat's.

And when he looked up again, he noticed that the great beast had a long, straggly goat's beard.

It was definitively not a horse.

It could be only one thing: a unicorn.

Alongside the terror, Jack now felt a sense of wonder. Whatever the extraordinary creature decided to do to him, this was a totally unique experience.

For a moment the unicorn stood still, as if he too were wondering what to do next.

Then, with a brusque neigh, he jerked his head and sent the snare flying off over the ferns. Jack heard it fall metres away. He remained on his back, propped uncomfortably on his elbows, wishing he were back in the safety of his room, but at the same time electrified by being in the presence of a creature whose existence no one in the whole world believed in.

Would he be killed? The beast only had to butt his head down and the horn would pierce his skull like a spike through an eggshell.

Jack bit his lip as the great head dropped. The horn lowered until it was pointing at his chest. He tried to squirm away, but then the beast's eyes locked onto his, and he stayed still.

Although the horn was not touching him, he was pinned by that unwavering gaze. He had never felt so exposed, so vulnerable, as under this terrible, silent interrogation. He felt shame as an image of a rabbit struggling in his snare formed in his mind. He tried to look away to escape the judgement he knew he deserved, but he couldn't. Tears blurred his vision, but still the two dark eyes bored into him. Jack's chest started to heave. He was sorry, he was sorry. What more could be asked of him?

Suddenly, with a shake of the head which flashed the horn alarmingly close to Jack's chin, the unicorn took a step back. Jack pushed himself up into a sitting position.

Then the magnificent creature reared up on his hind legs, his front hooves pawing the air high above Jack's head. For a frozen moment, the unicorn held his heraldic pose. Then the hooves crashed down. Jack stifled a cry as, once again, the gleaming horn was aimed straight at his chest.

But then the unicorn turned and, with a flick of his tail, galloped off across the glade.

No, Jack wanted to shout. *Come back!*

But the unicorn was away, great haunches rippling in the moonlight.

Jack got to his feet and took a step or two onto the turf. His relief at being released was overshadowed by a far stronger emotion. Watching the ghostly form galloping away from him, he felt a wrenching pang of loss. It was as though he had found the most precious thing in the world, and then had it taken away from him almost immediately.

Come back! Please! the voice in his head wailed.

Another few strides and the unicorn would be lost in the trees at the far end of the glade. Lost for ever. He couldn't bear it. He felt the start of a terrible sorrow, which he knew would remain with him always. He took a few faltering steps, his arms stretched out before him.

To Jack's amazement, he saw the fabulous beast suddenly stop, digging his hooves into the turf and kicking up his hind legs and swinging round, all in one breathtaking movement. And then, from a distance of nearly two hundred metres, the astonishing animal charged.

Jack felt an ecstatic moment of joy, but then, as the hooves drummed over the glade and the powerful shoulders drove the unicorn towards him at a terrifying speed, he felt his legs growing weak. The silvered horn was aimed like a lance. Jack wanted to run for the safety of the trees, but he couldn't move. There was no escape. He had wished for the unicorn to come back. Now, alone and defenceless, he had to face the ordeal.

Closer and closer beat the hooves. Jack's eyes were fixed on the horn. He knew that if he closed his eyes, if he ducked or flinched, he was doomed. He would fail the test, and the unicorn would power past him and gallop off into the woods, never to be seen again.

When he was only a matter of metres away, the unicorn seemed to pause; but he was only gathering his strength. As though leaping a fence, he soared into the air, landing with his hooves digging into the turf right in front of Jack.

The eyes were looking into his again. But this time Jack sensed the gaze was kindlier than before. He didn't feel he was being judged now. Or rather, he felt as if he had already been judged, and had passed the test.

The great head dropped down, bringing the horn to the level of Jack's heart, which was thumping uncontrollably. Jack was completely drained, helpless and powerless. He could only wait for the unicorn's next move.

Nothing happened for a long moment. Then the

unicorn took a step forward, very gently prodding him with the tip of his horn.

Jack didn't know what to do. There was another, slightly harder prod.

Very slowly Jack raised his hand and touched the horn. It was cool and smooth.

But before he could do more than feel its spiral groove, the horn moved. The unicorn turned his head and at the same time took a step away. He seemed to want Jack to follow. Jack hesitated, but an impatient stamp and an urgent snort made him take a step himself.

The unicorn led him off across the glade, and then stopped. He dropped his head and the horn pointed to a shape in amongst the bracken: a log.

Jack wasn't sure what was expected of him. The horn swung round at him and then dipped to the log again.

What could he want? Jack wondered.

The unicorn gave him a shove with the side of his head. Jack stumbled forward and nearly fell over the log.

The unicorn came and stood right in front of him. He pawed the ground once more and turned one large eye on Jack.

Jack suddenly saw what he wanted – but he couldn't believe it. It was only when the unicorn rubbed up against him that he was sure he was being told to climb up onto that broad strong back.

He stepped onto the log, but the unicorn still seemed impossibly tall. There was nothing to hold onto – no saddle, no reins. He took a deep breath, and reached forward, taking a grip on the white mane. Then, in an ungainly scramble, he threw his leg up and over, and clung on as best he could.

He felt panicky at being so high off the ground. His only riding experience had been years before, sitting on a donkey at the beach – a docile beast, with a saddle like a small armchair. How could he ride something larger than the greatest racehorse? He'd be flung off with the first stride.

But it was too late to worry about that. Jack felt a lurch as the unicorn moved off, and all he could do was dig his fingers into the coarse hair of the mane and hold on as though his life depended on it.

They started slowly, but were soon gaining speed. At first Jack bounced about, feeling his bones jar with every stride. He was certain he was going to be tossed to the ground, and tensed against the inevitable fall. After a while, though, he managed to relax a little. He felt his body finding the rhythm of the hooves. And with that came a surge of exhilaration that made him want to whoop.

They cantered down the glade. Jack felt the breeze blowing through his hair. It was like flying – it was like his dream. Only, in his dream there was no moon-silvered horn rising and falling ahead of him.

When they reached the end of the turf, the unicorn stopped. Jack was breathing hard and he could feel his blood pumping. It was like life itself coursing through his veins. He had never felt so alive. He was proud of himself for having stayed on, but was still nervous, sitting so far above the ground. He was wondering whether he should call it a day and slip down, but just as he was trying to make up his mind, the unicorn pawed the grass playfully, and then set off back the way they had come.

They went faster this time, and Jack had to hold on even tighter, gritting his teeth and closing his eyes. It was like being strapped to an express train – whipped by the wind and driven on by an unfathomably powerful engine. It was the most frightening experience ever, but he never wanted it to end.

Gradually he summoned up the courage to open

his eyes. Seeing the ground rising and falling beneath him was scary, so he looked further afield. The towering columns of the beech trees were flying by, and as they galloped on, Jack felt his terror gradually ebbing to exhilaration. He wanted to cry out in triumph, but still felt as though they were in a sacred place. He was there as the great beast's guest. He should take no liberties.

They were approaching the end of the glade from which they had started, and Jack expected the unicorn to slow down. But he didn't. He sprang off the turf and headed straight for the trees. Fortunately the beeches had few branches at Jack's level, but he had to keep his wits about him as they twisted their way through.

Jack thought again of *The Hunt by Night*. What a crazy idea. But at the same time it was brilliant. It was dangerous – if he fell, or was struck by a branch, he could be seriously hurt. And yet, with his hands buried in the unicorn's mane, and the hugely powerful body driving forward effortlessly beneath him, he wanted the journey to go on and on.

They splashed through the stream and flew up the incline beyond. For a moment Jack thought they were going to gallop straight into the undergrowth of brambles he'd had to pick his way through, but at the last minute they veered off to the right.

Jack was straining to see where they might be going when he suddenly saw a huge branch hanging low, right in their path, and he had to duck. He felt a spasm of fear. It was a warning that he was expected to look out for his own safety.

They were now careering through parts of the woods he had never explored and he had no idea where they were going. The pace never dropped, and he had to stay alert. But he didn't want to stop.

After a while they started going downhill once more. Jack noticed a change in the trees. They were in an area of regimented firs, and the hooves made hardly any noise on the carpet of pine needles. The moonlight barely struggled through, and Jack felt a chill running up his arms and the sweat on his back cooling.

For the first time the unicorn slowed his pace, and Jack sensed a wariness as he picked his way through the pines.

They came to a low wire fence. The unicorn stood absolutely still, moving his head slowly from side to side. The silence was broken only by a distant owl. Then, with a single blow of his hoof, the unicorn stamped down the wire and walked on.

Jack felt uneasy. It was as though they were entering hostile territory. And in a little while it became clear why. The fir trees thinned out, and in the gloom Jack could see little wooden coops surrounded by low wire fences. The pheasant pens! This was Mr Grout's realm, and here the birds were reared for the autumn's shooting.

Jack wondered why the unicorn had brought him to this grim place when they had the rest of the wood to roam in. He soon had his answer. Beyond the pheasant runs stood a low wooden hut, its window shuttered. It was just an ordinary hut, but in the shadows cast by the firs it looked sinister, part pillbox, part sentry box, staking out Mr Grout's claim to the clearing – and to the woods beyond.

Beside the hut there was a strange structure made of crudely nailed logs and planks. Jack shuddered as he realized what it was: the gamekeeper's gallows.

He knew about these. Men like Mr Grout would display the creatures they shot – 'vermin', they called them: foxes, crows, weasels – to warn off others who were tempted to trespass on forbidden territory.

Jack felt uneasy, especially as the unicorn was walking deliberately towards the gallows.

As they got nearer, Jack could see the bedraggled bundles of feathers hanging down, and other grim shapes nailed alongside them. He looked away; it was enough. He wanted to stop. But the unicorn was not going to let him off lightly. He moved on, one hoof after another, closer and closer, until suddenly he bowed his head.

Jack lurched forward, scrabbling for a grip in the mane.

He found himself face to face with a fox. It must have been dead for a while. Its jaw sagged open in a sorry grin, and where the eyes should have been were only two black holes.

Jack cried out and tried to flinch away, but there was no escape. Slowly the unicorn moved his head, and Jack had to confront the other exhibits in Mr Grout's grisly trophy cabinet: fur and feathers, bones bleached by the sun, washed by the rain. Small wild lives of fear and subsistence ended in a blast of shot, before suffering this last indignity.

Jack thought of the rabbits he had set out to catch – the pain he would have inflicted, and the long slow hours of suffering as the wire bit mercilessly through the soft flesh into the aching bone below. He felt ashamed.

'I'm sorry,' he whispered into the ear nearest his face. 'I'll never try to kill anything again.'

The unicorn remained motionless. Jack looked again at the fox grimacing up at him. There was no forgiveness there, just the outrage of the victim, burning fiercely even in death. Jack felt sick and his head swam. He took a firmer grip on the mane to stop himself falling off.

At last the unicorn moved. He backed away from the gallows, turned, and started to make his way back through the pens of doomed game birds. Jack had been taught his lesson. He felt drained, and realized for the first time how tired he was. But he didn't want to go home to bed.

He revived rapidly as they put Mr Grout's grove of death behind them. He could sense the unicorn's playfulness returning as well, and soon their speed increased again. The gloomy firs gave way to the traditional woodland mix of oak and ash, hornbeam and chestnut. They swerved round ancient trunks, avoided sweeping branches, breasted their way through bushes, leaped over fallen trees. Jack clung on, loving every minute of it, happy in the knowledge that he had been forgiven.

The incline grew steeper and the ground stonier.

They were climbing an escarpment which, Jack realized, would give a wonderful view of the estate when they reached the top. Suddenly the trees thinned out and he saw a little grassed promontory in front of them. The unicorn seemed to accelerate, as though intent on jumping over the edge, and Jack buried his face in the wiry white mane and clung on more tightly. At the last minute the unicorn dug his hooves into the chalky ground and came to a dead stop.

Jack cautiously opened one eye – and gasped. Immediately beneath him the escarpment fell away like a cliff. He quickly looked further away, and there, down below, to the left, was Charnley House, its stucco façade making it look like an elaborate wedding cake in the moonlight.

Jack tried to take it all in as he got his breath back. There was an ornamental pond at the front, reflecting the moon like a mirror. The drive finished its journey from the village road with an impressive sweep to the grand entrance. To the side lay walled gardens, in one of which glinted a large glasshouse, and at the back was a stable block and a small field that ran up to the woods.

It was like looking at a model village, perfect in

every detail. It was almost impossible to believe that it was a real house with bedrooms and kitchens and bathrooms. Jack tried to count the windows, but there were too many. He had just turned his gaze to the roof, which was crowded with chimneys, when the unicorn bowed his head slightly, and began to turn.

Jack stole a last look at the house, trying to fix it in his memory, to be explored later when he was back in the real world of cars and homework and washing up, where people didn't live in fairytale houses, and certainly didn't spend their nights riding through moonlit woods on the backs of unicorns.

CHAPTER 5

Jack spent the next days reliving every minute of his adventure. It was all he could think about; he just wanted to get back into the woods and experience it all again.

But would that happen? He went over the moment when the unicorn stopped in the glade and let him slide to the ground. He had stood awkwardly, his whole body beginning to stiffen after his hour's ride. The horn swung round slowly, and he looked into the beast's eyes once more.

The unicorn breathed a gentle whinny into his face. It was warm and friendly, encouraging him to be brave for the final leg of his journey home. Jack already knew that he had been forgiven, but he had no idea whether he would ever be allowed to ride the unicorn again. He wanted to ask, but didn't know how to. He longed to put out his hand, but he was sure you didn't pat a unicorn.

After a long moment during which he tried to

communicate all he was thinking through the intensity of his gaze, Jack had to be content to take a step back.

The unicorn looked him up and down and very gently rested his horn on his shoulder. Jack felt as though he were being knighted, and made an awkward little bow in acknowledgement of the honour. Then the fabulous creature swung round, reared up on his hind legs and, with a snort of farewell, flicked his tail and galloped away down the length of the glade, disappearing among the trees at the far end.

Jack had made his sad way home and wearily climbed back into the house. It was only after he had tiptoed into the sanctuary of his room that he realized he hadn't got the rucksack – or his gloves – or his torch. In all the excitement everything had been forgotten. His heart sank at the thought of Mr Grout uncovering these obvious clues that the trespasser had been out and about in the woods once more. All he could do was hope there was nothing that incriminated him personally.

He went over every item he had had with him – the knife, the wire, the skewers. No, none of those would lead a vengeful gamekeeper to the cottage door. But what about the rucksack itself? It was Dad's; the one he used to keep his sandwiches in when he went beating. Mr Grout couldn't possibly remember that, surely? But fear tormented him, and he was determined to go back and retrieve the missing items before Mr Grout had a chance to find them. The trouble was, he couldn't go back into the woods after school the next day because his mum was taking him into town on a big shopping trip to get new clothes for the summer. He groaned at the thought.

And at school he had Dan and Luke badgering him. He nearly had to punch Luke when he blurted something out about the snare within hearing of some classmates at break. Harriet Lazenby gave him an odd look that made him feel foolish. This, along with the horror of imagining Mr Grout holding up the rucksack at the end of his stick, and the almost irresistible urge to fall asleep whenever he was sitting down, made for a testing day at school. He went off shopping with very bad grace.

When he did finally go back to the woods the following afternoon, and retraced his steps to the great glade, he could see no sign of the rucksack or any of the other missing items.

It was two days after this that Mr Finistaire visited the school. When Jack heard the details of the art prize, he felt sure it couldn't be a coincidence.

He didn't believe that Mr Finistaire had actually seen the unicorn, or was even sure he existed, but he sensed that the secret was in danger. But what was Mr Finistaire's game? He hadn't come across as sinister. Odd, certainly. But Jack had been drawn to him. He was so open, and hadn't talked down to them. And he seemed very passionate about endangered species. It was hard to imagine that he had bad motives.

On the other hand, the art competition was obviously an attempt to see if any of them had seen the unicorn. Jack, of course, was not going to give anything away. He'd do the standard unicorn picture, little more than a horse with a horn. It wouldn't be any good, and Harriet Lazenby could win the prize and have her day of glory at the big house. That wasn't something he was interested in at all.

'There's not much time now before your pictures have to be in,' Mrs Hinton said a few days later. 'We're going to spend this morning on them so you can do some really nice work for Mr Finistaire.'

The girls in the front row were very excited, and even the boys thought messing around with paint was more fun than doing maths.

Mrs Hinton came round, handing out two sizes of paper. 'Don't start on your big sheets – do some sketches first.'

Jack picked up his pencil and drew a very unconvincing outline. Although he was deliberately doing it badly, he still felt frustrated. He couldn't talk to anybody about his night in the woods. Not that anyone would have believed him if he *had* told them. And once he'd told one person, it would be round the school in no time, making him a laughing stock.

He soon moved on to his big sheet, and made a thorough dog's breakfast of it. His unicorn looked like something someone had knocked up using a random assortment of plywood off-cuts. You could just about see that it was meant to be an animal of some sort, but that was it. Jack finished long before everyone else. Looking up, he saw Harriet Lazenby working intently, kneeling on her seat with her hair falling to within centimetres of her picture.

He pretended he needed to sharpen his pencil and stole a glimpse as he went up to Mrs Hinton's desk. It was exactly what he'd have expected – good in its way, but horribly cute. And nothing like the real thing.

He went back to his seat and sat tapping his teeth with the pencil. Then he started doodling on his piece of rough paper. Memories of the other night flooded through his mind, and he started playing a game. He would try to draw something accurate, but would disguise it so no one would know what it was.

He started with the horn, which he managed to blend in with dagger-like blades of grass. Then he did the hooves with their distinctive cleft. He couldn't think of anything to disguise them as, so when he'd finished, he rubbed them out. He moved on to the view he'd had when he was on the unicorn's back: the ears, the mane, and again, the horn pointing the way like a wand. He was enjoying himself.

'Right, that's just about time now, so finish off, and I'll come round and collect them. And I'll take in your sketches as well.'

There was a chorus of protests.

'Mr Finistaire was very clear on this. He said it's important to see the development of your inspiration.'

'Mine's awful.'

'I don't want him seeing mine: it's rubbish.'

'Do we have to, miss?'

'Yes you do,' Mrs Hinton said. 'You'll only be judged on your painted work, but you can't win the prize without your sketches.'

Fine, thought Jack. *I don't want to win the prize.* And he scrumpled up his rough paper and flung it accurately into the big bin in the corner by the door. Then he looked at his watercolour. It had to be the worst picture of a unicorn ever painted. He smiled again. Mr Finistaire wasn't going to get any clues from that.

'Where's your sketch, Jack?' Mrs Hinton was standing at his desk, her arm draped with damp sheets of paper.

'Didn't do one, miss,' he said.

'Yes he did, miss,' Luke chipped in. 'I saw him.'

Jack glared at him.

'Where is it, then?'

'He threw it in the bin, miss. I'll get it.'

And before Jack could stop him, Luke had rushed over and retrieved the scrumpled piece of paper.

'Thank you, Luke,' Mrs Hinton said, straightening it out. 'You'd do a lot better in school if you listened to what people told you, Jack.'

And she added the sketch to the others.

* * *

'Ouch! That hurt.'

'It was meant to.'

Jack had Luke in a half-nelson in a quiet corner of the playground.

'Why can't you ever keep your mouth shut?' he asked, with another jerk of Luke's arm.

'Leave off,' Dan said. 'What's all the fuss about a silly sketch? It was rubbish.'

There was some consolation in that, Jack thought, but he was still furious – more with himself than with Luke. Why had he done it? Why hadn't he ripped it into a hundred pieces? Perhaps, he thought, he might get it back, and then destroy it.

But before he could even begin working on a plan to do that, he was distracted by a commotion at the school gate. Everyone stood aside to let Mr Finistaire's Bentley purr into the playground.

The car eased to a standstill, and the chauffeur leaped out and went round to open the passenger's door. Mr Finistaire got out, smiling broadly. Jack was reminded of the man he'd seen on the news standing outside a boring-looking black door with the number 10 on it, waving to a cheering crowd.

Mrs Hinton was suddenly there to escort the

visitor into the school. Jack scowled. Now there was absolutely no chance of getting his sketches back before Mr Finistaire saw them.

He kicked viciously at a stone. It was a stupid thing to do. He knew that the moment he made contact. It could have hit somebody.

Instead, it hit Mr Finistaire's car. Jack watched in horror as it struck the front passenger door like a bullet and ricocheted off across the playground.

The chauffeur, who had resumed his place behind the steering wheel, reacted immediately, jumping out of the car and crouching down to inspect the damage. Then he stood up and turned menacingly.

A silence had fallen as word of what had happened ran like wildfire through the playground. Everyone gathered at a safe distance while the chauffeur stood looking at them as though trying to divine who the culprit was. Jack briefly met the man's eye but dropped his gaze immediately.

'You aren't half going to cop it for that,' Luke muttered out of the side of his mouth.

'I suppose you're going to go over and tell him it was me, are you?' Jack whispered back.

'Well, you're going to have to own up, aren't you?' Dan joined in. 'I mean, lots of people saw you do it.'

'But we're not going to grass you up,' Luke said, ''cos we're your mates. Here – catch.' He backed away from Jack and threw him the ragged old tennis ball they always kicked around at break.

It was too wild a throw, and Jack missed it. The ball bounced across the playground. It was heading directly for the Bentley.

The boys watched, fascinated, as it bobbled along and eventually came to rest against one of the chauffeur's immaculately polished shoes.

The man seemed not to notice, but then put his foot on the ball. There was tension in the air as everyone watched to see how he would react. The chauffeur's eye scanned the crowd once more, and then finally fell on the three boys. Jack felt sure he was being singled out as the most likely suspect.

'I think he wants you to go and get it,' Dan said softly.

Jack stared at the chauffeur. He was tall, quite young, and had closely cropped blond hair. But there was something remarkable about him – the way he seemed to hold himself aloof from everything – and everyone – around him. Jack had noticed it on Mr Finistaire's first visit, and had found it creepy then. Now, he found the man positively sinister as he waited, motionless, by the damaged car with the tennis ball under his foot.

'Well, go on,' said Luke.

'Remind me to break your arm next time,' Jack whispered back. And then, with a growing sense of dread, he started to walk forward.

What was he going to say? *Can we have our ball back, mister?*

The man would probably seize him by the collar and frog-march him into the school building to report the damage to the car.

With everyone looking on, Jack felt like a condemned felon making his way to the gallows. It was a very long twenty metres. The chauffeur was looking directly at him with an unblinking stare. He stood with his foot still on the tennis ball, waiting.

Jack faltered to a halt.

He had no idea what to expect, but what did happen took him completely by surprise.

With a speed and deftness that was almost too quick for the eye, the chauffeur suddenly got his shoe under the tennis ball and flicked it up into the air. Then, with a graceful swing of his leg, he kicked it straight over Jack's head.

Everyone in the playground swivelled to watch it. It seemed to go for miles, soaring over the old bike shed and disappearing into the trees beyond.

There was a gasp of astonishment, mixed with laughter, because the stupendous feat made Jack look very stupid indeed.

But there was no flicker of triumph or pride on the chauffeur's face. He simply continued to look straight at Jack.

Jack was rooted to the spot, seemingly powerless to look away. He was close enough to inspect the chauffeur's face a little more closely. Apart from its lack of expression there was something else that was unnerving. Jack struggled to identify it, but then he realized what it was: eyebrows! The man's hair was so fair that it looked as though he didn't have any eyebrows.

Jack was saved from having to decide what to do next by the bell marking the end of break.

He turned away gratefully and joined the jostling over-excited crowd pushing through the doors.

'You won't get that back!' someone said to Jack, and he felt himself going red as the laughter rose.

It was almost a relief when Mrs Hinton called out

his name and told him to go and see Miss Hubbard.

But once he started down the carpeted corridor to the Head's office, he realized that he was almost certainly heading for the biggest telling-off he'd ever had in his life.

CHAPTER 6

It was just his luck. Some member of staff must have glanced out of the window and seen him kicking the stone against the Bentley. That's what this was about. Miss Hubbard would be looking at him over her spectacles with that pained look, and beside her, no doubt, Mr Finistaire would be fuming with rage.

Dad'll kill me, Jack thought moodily. He looked out of a window. The sun was shining. A car went past the school gates. Out there it was a normal day. If only he could escape back into it . . .

He walked slowly on down the corridor and turned the corner.

Miss Hubbard's door was slightly ajar. He lifted his hand to knock, but then let it drop. It was too much effort. He felt as if he was about to faint. Perhaps that would get him off the hook.

But he knew it wouldn't.

He took a deep breath and pushed the door open.

The first thing he noticed was that Miss Hubbard's big swivel chair was empty. The second was Harriet's unicorn displayed on an easel. The other attempts were spread all over the big table in the middle of the room.

Jack looked at Harriet's picture. She had lavished a lot of care on it, painting the surroundings in sickly day-glo colours. The unicorn itself was ridiculous – My Little Pony, with an ice-cream cone stuck to its forehead.

'Ghastly, isn't it?'

Jack spun round. There was Mr Finistaire, smiling at him from the corner of the room. He gave a chuckle and came forward, pushing the door shut.

Jack hadn't anticipated finding Mr Finistaire on his own. He'd expected Miss Hubbard to be there as some sort of buffer against their visitor's understandable fury. He felt himself going red with guilt, and opened his mouth to say something.

But Mr Finistaire wasn't looking at him. Instead he was looking at the easel. 'There's our winner!' He laughed, appearing much more interested in Harriet's terrible picture than in what had just happened to his car. If anything, he seemed in rather high spirits. Jack still had his mouth open, but couldn't think of anything to say.

'It's all right,' said Mr Finistaire, in a conspiratorial voice. 'You don't have to be polite. I know it's frightful, but it's the best of the frightfuls, if I may put it that way. She has tried, bless her. She's done her best. And for that she deserves the prize, don't you think?' He beamed encouragingly, and again Jack felt the openness, the warmth that he had been so drawn to on Mr Finistaire's first visit.

'I suppose so,' he said.

'You don't sound convinced. You're welcome to go through the rest, but Mrs Hinton and I couldn't find anything better.'

He took a pace towards the table and began to lift up one painting after another, dropping them back on the pile as Jack looked on, more and more bewildered. Why was he here? Why had he been summoned, if not because of the car?

'Take this one, for instance. A bit slapdash, wouldn't you say? Nowhere near capturing anything anyone could remotely believe was a real unicorn.'

Jack blushed. It was his.

Mr Finistaire let it fall. 'Whereas this . . .'

Jack felt his heart suddenly start thumping in his chest. Mr Finistaire was holding his sketch.

'This – despite being scrumpled up and thrown in the waste-paper basket . . .' Here he smoothed the sheet out firmly. 'This is the real thing, isn't it?' Mr Finistaire's eyes behind his spectacles were bright. His eyebrows puckered, almost as though he were pleading with Jack.

'Oh, I know you've disguised it all – very clever – you're an exceptionally intelligent boy. But we know, don't we? The two of us. And just the two of us. It's our little secret, isn't it? Except of course' – and he glanced at the door and dropped his voice – 'it's not a *little* secret at all. It's a huge secret. The most important secret either of us will ever have.'

He pointed at the sketches again. 'It's as though you wanted to share it, but only with someone who could believe. In other words, me!'

Jack couldn't answer. His worst fears had come true, and yet now that Mr Finistaire knew, he found he didn't wish for things to be different. To be able to talk, at last, would be wonderful – even if all his instincts told him to keep his mouth shut and pretend he didn't know what the man was talking about.

'You're not going to deny it, are you?' Mr Finistaire was smiling at him.

Jack slowly shook his head.

'Good lad, good lad! What a day! It has exceeded my expectations a hundredfold. The best I thought I could hope for was a glimpse through the trees, some hint that I was right to hope. But you – you've seen him, haven't you? You've *ridden* him.' Mr Finistaire's voice had sunk very low. It was as if he were in awe of Jack's experience. No grown-up had ever taken Jack as seriously as he was being taken now.

Under that unwavering gaze there was no possibility of playing dumb, let alone of lying outright.

'Yes,' Jack said.

It was little more than a whisper, but it sent Mr Finistaire's eyebrows shooting up in delight. He clasped Jack's sketches to his chest and closed his eyes. 'Yes, yes, yes.'

Then he opened his eyes again and blinked, as though making sure it was true, before beaming once more. Jack found himself smiling back shyly.

'Good man,' Mr Finistaire said. 'Now, sit down and tell me all about it.'

There were two chairs in front of Miss Hubbard's desk where countless parents had sat to hear good or bad things about their children. Mr Finistaire took one and waved Jack to the other.

Jack was pleased that the visitor hadn't chosen to sit in the Head's chair to quiz him. But in a way that made it harder, because Mr Finistaire could lean across with his encouraging smile, eyes wide with the intensity of his interest, and prompt Jack whenever he was at a loss for words.

'I want to know everything – even the smallest thing. You can't know how important it is.'

It was hard to know where to start. Jack thought Mr Finistaire would be angry about his unsuccessful attempts at setting snares. But he waved that away with a laugh.

'Don't worry about that. I know you boys like to get into my woods, and if you wanted to try your hand at a little poaching, what do I care? It was very brave of you, going out at night like that. And look what came of it! Go on!'

So Jack took up the thread again, and told everything he could remember.

He was hesitant at first, but gradually he grew more confident. Mr Finistaire sat listening more intently than anyone had ever listened to Jack before. And the few questions he asked all showed how keenly he was paying attention, how hard he was working to follow everything that Jack told him.

'So he didn't like Mr Grout's gibbet?'

'No,' said Jack, remembering with a shudder his close encounter with the dead fox.

'I can't say I care for it much myself, and I doubt very much whether it works. But gamekeepers have their traditions, and Grout's a good man on the whole. And his wife is a splendid cook. Go on.'

So Jack did.

At the end, Mr Finistaire let out his breath in a low whistle. 'Quite extraordinary . . . quite extraordinary.' Then, looking straight at Jack, he said, 'You are the luckiest boy in the world. I can't tell you how much . . . how much . . .' The sentence petered out. He had a faraway look in his eyes, and a smile played around his lips.

Suddenly he darted a glance at Jack. 'And you've told nobody?'

'No – no one.'

'Good. Keep it that way. If this got out . . .' Mr Finistaire shook his head at the thought.

'Does Mr Grout know?' Jack asked timidly.

'Mr Grout knows what it is necessary for Mr Grout to know. What we need to decide is what is to happen next. Now that we have proof, we need a plan.'

'What sort of plan?' Jack asked anxiously.

'A plan that will protect and preserve the rarest creature on the planet.'

'But what can we do?'

'We have to find out more about him – as much as possible. If you want to save tigers, you have to understand them – their habitats, their diet, everything. If we're going to protect him, we have to *know* him. And you're the key. You already know him and, most importantly, he trusts you. You will help, won't you?'

Jack looked into Mr Finistaire's face. It was charged with enthusiasm. It was difficult to hold onto his own thoughts against that powerful current of urgency.

'Yes.' He nodded.

Mr Finistaire went on, 'Good. I knew I could rely on you. There's so much to think about, so much to do. Our first duty, as I've said, is to keep our secret. He must be protected from the outside world. And so must you.'

'Me?' said Jack, genuinely surprised.

'Why, yes. Can you imagine what the newspapers and television would make of your experience? A boy riding a unicorn – on every screen across the land? It would be around the world in a day. My woods would be seething with cameramen; hordes would descend on the estate and the village. Life would be made hell – your life would be impossible, and he would be in such danger I'd have to hire a small army to protect him. We must defend his privacy at all costs and, at the same time, discover as much as we can about him – to help preserve his way of life. Think tiger!' Mr Finistaire spoke with absolute confidence that he was right.

'So,' he said, looking Jack in the eye, 'we'll do this together, yes?'

'Yes,' said Jack.

'Excellent! You must come over to the house – as soon as possible – and we'll hold a council of war.' Mr Finistaire had a steely look in his eye. He suddenly looked formidable – not a man to be denied.

Then Jack remembered the awful thing he'd done to the Bentley.

Mr Finistaire picked up on it immediately. 'What's wrong?'

Jack couldn't speak, he felt so bad.

'Come on, out with it.'

So Jack told him.

Something very strange happened to Mr

Finistaire's expression: the eyes that had twinkled with such warm friendliness changed in an instant. Jack flinched away from their burning intensity.

Mr Finistaire stood up. It seemed as though he would go on rising until he hit the ceiling. 'You dented my car?' he shouted. 'YOU DENTED MY CAR BY KICKING A STONE AT IT?'

Everyone in the whole school must have heard.

Jack tried to say sorry, tried to explain, but Mr Finistaire strode to the door and called down the corridor: 'Miss Hubbard!'

The Head appeared within seconds, looking flustered.

'This boy' – Mr Finistaire was pointing at Jack like a prosecutor in court – 'this boy dented my car. By kicking a stone at it!'

'Jack!' Miss Hubbard looked appalled. 'What were you thinking of?'

'I'm sorry, Miss Hubbard,' Jack said. 'I didn't mean to hit the car. It was an accident.'

'Even so, it was a stupid thing to do,' she said severely. 'I'm so sorry, Mr Finistaire.' And then, after a brief pause, she went on: 'Is it not insured?'

'Insured? Of course it's insured,' Mr Finistaire retorted. 'It is insured against almost anything you can imagine – but there happens to be something called an "excess". This is a ploy to save insurance companies wasting their time with petty claims. The excess on my policy is particularly high, so if I put in a claim to my insurers, they'll charge me several hundred pounds.'

Miss Hubbard looked crestfallen. 'Oh dear, Jack,' she said. 'Look what a mess you've got into.'

'Yes,' Mr Finistaire said. 'A big mess. Someone is going to have to pay for the damage.'

'I'm afraid,' Miss Hubbard said, turning to him, 'Jack's family aren't very . . .'

'Are they not? Well, they should steer their son away from kicking stones at other people's cars. It's a very expensive hobby.' Mr Finistaire paused. 'Do they live in the village?'

'Yes, at the bottom. Isn't it your father's afternoon off, Jack?'

Jack nodded. He couldn't speak, and it was all he could do not to cry.

'I could give Mr Henley a call,' the Head offered, picking up the phone.

'No, don't do that. I'll drive down now – strike while the iron's hot – and he can see the damage for himself. You'd better come too,' he added, giving Jack a cold look.

Under the baleful eye of Miss Hubbard, Jack walked miserably out into the playground.

The chauffeur was waiting by the passenger door, and pointed a bony finger at the coachwork.

There was definitely a dent, and the paint had been scratched off too. Jack put his head on one side in the hope that a different angle would make it look less bad. It didn't.

Miss Hubbard launched into an apology, saying she hoped Mr Finistaire would not stop taking an interest in the school because of the thoughtless, stupid, destructive actions of one of its pupils. She was just getting into her stride when Mr Finistaire raised a hand.

'Fear not, Miss Hubbard. I will not hold it against the school. Look, I am taking away some of the children's work for further examination . . .' He held up an untidy bundle of sketches he had swept up from the table in the Head's study. 'I am sure things can be sorted out with Jack's father. But time presses. You must excuse me.'

With that, he signalled the chauffeur to open the door and lowered himself into the back seat.

Jack stood by awkwardly, not sure what to do.

'Get in, boy,' Mr Finistaire said crossly. 'You know where you live, don't you?'

The chauffeur shut Mr Finistaire's door and walked round to the other side of the car, indicating the rear door to Jack. He didn't open it for him, but instead got into the driver's seat and reached over for his cap.

Jack pulled the door open for himself and gazed into the interior. He couldn't believe he was being ordered to sit next to Mr Finistaire. He glanced back at the school buildings. Rows of faces were pressed against the classroom windows.

'Do get in, boy. We haven't got all day,' Mr Finistaire said impatiently.

So Jack climbed into the Bentley, and pulled the door closed.

CHAPTER 7

The drive couldn't have taken more than a minute or two, but for Jack it seemed to last for ever. His dread of his dad's reaction cancelled out any thrill he might have felt at being driven through the village in the most luxurious car he'd ever seen.

'Left here,' he said as they reached the bottom of the hill. And then they pulled up at the end of Meadow Lane.

The car stopped, and Mr Finistaire and Jack got out.

'It's that one,' Jack said, pointing at the middle cottage. As they walked up the garden path, he thought how shabby it looked.

Mr Finistaire seized the knocker and rapped it two or three times. The was a long pause, and Jack could imagine his dad lowering his paper, heaving himself out of his armchair and making his way grumpily down the hall. He prayed that he had his shirt on. He was glad his mum was at the charity shop.

'Yes? What do you want?'

Jack's dad stood in the doorway in his vest, looking down at Mr Finistaire. When he saw who it was, his demeanour changed. His eyes narrowed and he glared at Jack. 'What's going on? What have you done, Jack?'

It was soon explained to him what Jack had done. Yet again the dent was inspected. Jack's dad put his finger in it and whistled between his teeth. 'How much?' he asked in a low voice.

'Can't say, but coachwork on these things isn't cheap,' Mr Finistaire told him. 'I'll need to get an estimate. Perhaps we could go inside and discuss the matter.'

'Come into the lounge,' Jack's dad said, leading the way. 'And you,' he hissed to Jack, 'get out of my sight. Go into the kitchen. Make yourself useful. Do the washing up. You're in so much trouble, my boy.'

Don't I know it, thought Jack as he stared miserably at the saucepans and crockery piled in the sink. But the worst thing, he realized as he turned on the tap and waited for the ancient boiler to produce some lukewarm water, was how hurt he felt at Mr Finistaire's reaction. Obviously he was cross – who wouldn't be? – but they had been getting on so well;

there had seemed a genuine warmth between them when Jack had shared the secret of his ride. Mr Finistaire had entered so sympathetically into his adventure, clearly believing everything Jack told him – unlike pretty much any other grown-up you could mention, who would have assumed that it was all one big leg-pull.

Given that, Jack thought, moodily dumping a pile of crockery in the washing-up bowl, you'd have thought Mr Finistaire might have cut him a bit of slack over the car. Obviously Jack didn't do it on purpose. It was a mistake – a stupid mistake, true, but surely something that could have been treated a little more discreetly. It was humiliating, being marched off the school premises like a common criminal.

But although his feelings were hurt, that wasn't the only thing getting to Jack. The yellow sponge scourer was on its last legs, and as he started to smear it across his dad's dinner plate, he wondered how on earth they were ever going to pay for the repair to Mr Finistaire's car.

He also wondered what was going on in the lounge. To begin with, he had heard his dad's voice, but then it went quiet. Perhaps Mr Finistaire was spelling out some repayment scheme stretching away into the future, making their lives even more difficult.

What would his mum think? She was more worried about money than his dad, always scheming to cut the shopping bills, always putting a little bit aside 'for a rainy day'. But this wasn't the sort of rainy day she'd had in mind.

Jack shook the grey suds off the last bowl and placed it in the rack. Then he reached for the threadbare towel and dried his hands. After that he sat down. All he could do was wait to find out what his fate would be.

It seemed an age, but was probably only five minutes before the lounge door opened, and his dad appeared at the kitchen door. He jerked his head. 'Come on, you. Out here.'

Jack got up and went into the hall. Mr Finistaire was pretending to study a faded print of a hunting scene. He turned to Jack.

'Your father and I have come to an understanding. You will pay for the repairs.'

'Me?' Jack said. 'How?'

'With the sweat of your brow, son,' his dad said. 'You can go over to Charnley and work it off.'

Jack wasn't sure what that meant.

Mr Finistaire broke in to explain. 'Instead of having to find the money to pay for the repairs, you can come over to my house and help in the gardens – weeding the vegetables, that sort of thing. Your father and I have agreed an hourly rate, and when I get the bill for the car we'll know how much work you'll have to do, and when you've done it, that'll be that – all done with and forgotten. We thought this the best solution.'

'And it's very generous of you, Mr Finistaire.'

'Not at all, Henley. Don't mention it.'

'What do you say, Jack?' Jack's dad gave him a prod in the back.

'Thank you,' he stammered. He could see why his dad was so pleased about the plan, but *he* wasn't the one who was going to have to spend his summer pulling up weeds.

'As I say, it seemed the best solution,' Mr Finistaire said, adding, 'And, with your father's permission, we're going to start today.'

'So go upstairs and get changed,' his dad said.

Jack did as he was told, though not with good grace. He hated gardening at the best of times. Having to spend long hours slaving away in Mr

Finistaire's vegetable plot was pretty much the worst punishment he could think of. And then there was Mr Grout. Jack could just see him looking on. He'd enjoy that, wouldn't he? The thought made him groan aloud as he pulled his oldest T-shirt over his head. Why had he kicked that stone?

Thinking of the conversation in Miss Hubbard's office also made him feel bad. He'd told Mr Finistaire his secret, and although he'd seemed friendly at the time, his rage over the car showed a different side to him. Jack stabbed his feet into an old pair of trainers and dragged himself downstairs.

There was an uneasy silence in the hall, and his dad was obviously eager for them to get going. Mr Finistaire shook hands with him, and said: 'I'll have someone drop him back this evening, Henley.'

That was the second time Mr Finistaire had called his dad simply by his surname. Jack looked from one man to the other: his dad towered over Mr Finistaire, but there was no doubting who was in charge.

Jack's dad said, 'Thank you,' and then told Jack: 'Put your back into it, son. I'll explain what's happened to your mum.'

And with that they were away. Jack sat in the back seat behind the driver. Mr Finistaire sat in the next seat, divided from him by a broad elbow rest.

At first Jack was tense. He was still resentful about being forced to work as a gardener's boy, and felt bruised by Mr Finistaire's sudden anger. But after a while he began to relax a little. After all, it wasn't every day that he got a lift in a Bentley. The interior was upholstered in soft cream leather and the seats were wonderfully comfortable. He nestled down and gazed admiringly at the walnut cabinets set in the back of the front seats. They were as shiny as mirrors, and he could only guess at what they might hold – cold drinks, delicious food. It was more like being on a luxury yacht than in a car.

Mr Finistaire sat staring out of his window, obviously in no mood to talk. Having caught the unblinking eye of the chauffeur in the rear-view mirror once, Jack didn't want it to happen again, so he turned to his own window.

They passed the school and the empty playground. Jack closed his eyes, but found his mind replaying the incident in all its vivid horror. He could almost hear the dull clunk of the stone hitting the bodywork. If only he'd resisted the temptation to kick it. If only he had kicked it in any other direction . . .

He opened his eyes again. At least he would be missing French, and he couldn't pretend he wasn't enjoying the drive. They were now out of the village, moving sedately along the back road that skirted the Charnley estate.

Jack looked out over the densely packed trees and wondered what it was like owning such a huge amount of land, not to mention a mansion and a beautiful car. Even if, by some miracle, his mum's weekly attempt at winning the lottery came off, they would still be poor compared to Mr Finistaire.

He risked a glance to his left. Mr Finistaire still had his head turned away, but Jack noticed an odd thing: something was happening to Mr Finistaire. His shoulders were moving gently up and down. Jack watched in fascination. Now they were going up and down even more. There was no doubt about it: Mr Finistaire's whole body was shaking.

Jack wondered what was going on. He wasn't working himself into another rage, was he?

There was a noise like a whimper. Perhaps Mr Finistaire was about to burst into tears.

Then came the explosion. A prelude of squeaks and wheezes suddenly rose to something like a scream, and Mr Finistaire burst out laughing. Huge panting gusts of laughter rocked him to and fro. He clutched his stomach. His knees rose. And, when he finally turned his face towards Jack, it was a dark puce, and tears were pouring down his cheeks.

'Stop the car! Pull up anywhere. Oh dear! Oh dear!' And with that he succumbed to another fit of hysterics.

He was just recovering when the car rolled to a stop on a broad verge. Mr Finistaire caught Jack's eye, and that set him off again. 'Your face . . .' he managed to blurt out, but it was too much for him. He groped blindly for the handle and swung open his door. He stood beside the car, doubled up with spasms of laughter.

Jack sat looking out at him, utterly mystified. Had he gone mad?

Eventually Mr Finistaire stopped heaving, and motioned for Jack to get out and join him.

Jack stood on the grass, looking on, bewildered.

'Oh dear,' Mr Finistaire said, wiping the tears off his glasses. 'I haven't laughed so much in years. Your face! Perfect – fooled everybody!'

Jack had absolutely no idea what he was talking about.

Mr Finistaire looked at him, his face gradually

coming back under control. 'I'm sorry,' he said, looking genuinely regretful. 'I'm so sorry I put you through all that. But it was the only way.' He saw Jack's bewilderment. 'Don't you see? It gives us the perfect alibi!'

Jack tried to grasp what he was saying, but ended up even more sure that he'd gone mad.

'I'm not explaining myself . . .' Mr Finistaire tried again: 'Through a stroke – or rather a kick – of genius on your part, and a bit of pantomime overacting on mine, we have now got exactly what we want – what we need.'

Jack blinked at him.

Mr Finistaire threw his arms wide. 'You – at Charnley. Think what that means!'

Pulling up weeds in your vegetable patch, Jack thought crossly.

As though reading his mind, Mr Finistaire shook his head. 'You're not going to have to lift a finger in the gardens, young man. No, no, no – that's just the cover story. We've got far more important things to do.'

Jack frowned. The penny was beginning to drop. But what about the car? Mr Finistaire really had seemed upset; very upset indeed.

There it was now, the dent. Mr Finistaire followed his glance.

'Do you mean . . .' Jack started: he really wanted to get it straight. 'Do you mean you weren't angry . . . ?'

'I wasn't angry at all, dear boy. I was ecstatic! The plan came into my head fully formed the instant you made your confession. My only fear was that you hadn't done enough damage to justify dragging you over to Charnley to slave amongst the weeds. And my only regret is that I couldn't let you in on the plan and had to make you undergo what must have been a horrible half-hour.'

Jack looked Mr Finistaire in the eye. It certainly *had* been a horrible half-hour.

Mr Finistaire looked steadily back at him. 'You were perfect, Jack. Every reaction to a T. But you couldn't have *acted* that. It had to be for real, so I had to let you believe I was furious and determined to make you pay for the car.' His mouth formed a rueful little smile. 'Can you forgive me?'

He looked almost comical. Of course Jack could forgive him. He smiled, and then found he was grinning. All of that, every last bit of it, had just been play-acting.

Mr Finistaire nodded – and then mimed Jack's kick, watched the imaginary stone make its imaginary contact with the car, and then threw up his hands in mock rage.

Jack started laughing. He caught Mr Finistaire's eye, and *he* started laughing again too. They stood beside the road and, under the cold gaze of the unsmiling chauffeur, laughed and laughed and laughed.

Eventually they stopped. Jack was gasping for breath, and brushed the tears away with the back of his hand. Mr Finistaire had taken his spectacles off and was wiping them with a large coloured handkerchief.

The chauffeur got out of the car and held the door open for his employer. Then, to Jack's surprise, he walked round to the other side and opened *his* door too.

'Thank you, Sefton,' Mr Finistaire said when they were all buckled into their seat belts. 'Straight back to the house now, please.'

Turning to Jack, he went on, 'You must be hungry. I'm sure there'll be something in the kitchen for us. Mrs Grout makes an exceptional game pie – and the finest lemonade known to man.'

The pie and the lemonade sounded very welcome, but mention of the gamekeeper's wife cast a shadow over Jack's suddenly buoyant mood. He hoped profoundly that his visit to Mr Finistaire's mansion would not involve meeting the wiry, whiskery little man with his bone-handled stick.

Mr Finistaire was right about the lemonade. It was delicious. They were sitting on a terrace looking out over the ornamental lake. A fountain played from the statue of a scantily dressed female figure rising out of the water.

'Do you know who she is?' Mr Finistaire asked him. 'The Greek goddess Aphrodite. Lovely name, isn't it? Far better than Venus, which is what the Romans called her. Names are so important, I think, don't you?'

Jack's mouth was full of Mrs Grout's pie, so he could only nod. He looked away from the Greek goddess, and glanced up at the gleaming façade of the house. It was almost impossible to believe that he was sitting here having lunch with its owner, less than an hour after being publicly paraded as a vicious vandal.

Mr Finistaire smiled at him, and took a sip from

his wine glass. From the moment the chauffeur had parked the Bentley in front of the grand entrance with its pillared portico, Jack had been made to feel a hundred per cent welcome. He sat in the warm sunshine feeling he could begin to congratulate himself on this unbelievable turn of events.

Mr Finistaire's next remark, however, reminded him of the more challenging side of the situation.

'And talking of names,' he said casually, 'what do you call him?'

Jack swallowed effortfully. Mr Finistaire could only be talking about the unicorn.

'I – I don't,' he said, brushing a crumb from the side of his mouth. It had never crossed his mind that he could presume to name the extraordinary creature who had given him the most magical night of his life.

'He should have a name,' Mr Finistaire went on. 'After all, we're going to be talking about him rather a lot, aren't we?'

Jack eyed the remaining portion of pie on his plate but thought it would be inappropriate to carry on eating while they considered such an important issue. But how could you name a unicorn? He was too real, too powerful, too awe-inspiring. What name could possibly be adequate?

There was a pause. Mr Finistaire watched him as he struggled to sort out his thoughts. Then he spoke. 'What about Keras? *Keras* is Greek for "horn". No one else would know that, so if we were to be overheard, it wouldn't give the game away. Not that I worry about that. I only employ people who are very discreet – almost, you could say, with a talent for silence. Think about it – Keras. But meanwhile, keep eating. I wouldn't want Mrs Grout to think you didn't like her pie. And while you do, I'll tell you a little about Sefton . . . talking of unusual names.'

Jack gratefully returned to his pie.

'Sefton . . .' Mr Finistaire said, in a measured tone. There was a hint of sadness in it, Jack thought. 'Hardly ever speaks. Taciturn to a fault, some would say, but there are reasons for that – rather tragic reasons, in fact.'

He took a sip from his wine glass before going on. 'Sefton's not his real name. It's where he came from. Sefton. In Lancashire. He doesn't like to use his real name, for reasons that I'll explain. Of course, you won't mention any of this to another soul, will you?'

Jack shook his head.

'Of course you won't. I'm only telling you so you

can understand if Sefton seems rather aloof, rather cut off from the rest of us.'

He paused and took another sip of wine. 'He hasn't had a happy life. His whole existence has been overshadowed by a tragedy that struck him when he was a young man.' Mr Finistaire lowered his voice. 'Yes – when he was really quite young, he killed someone.'

Jack's mouthful of pie suddenly thickened unpalatably. He took a gulp of lemonade.

'Of course, he didn't mean to, and it wasn't his fault, and nobody blamed him. But it was still a terrible thing to have happened – for both of them.'

Jack swallowed his mouthful, but didn't feel like eating any more. The thought that he'd met, stared into the eyes of a person who had killed someone was a shock.

'It happened in a cricket match. Sefton was a very promising fast bowler. He had worked his way up to a first team place in one of the Lancashire League sides – they take their cricket very seriously up there. There was talk of him playing for the county, and even, looking further ahead, for England. On this occasion, the county had sent a scout to the game, so he was obviously keen to do his best and bowl his fastest.'

Mr Finistaire paused again. Despite the warm sun, Jack felt a chill. Perhaps a breeze had blown over the lake. But none of the leaves on the trees stirred.

'It was all going very well,' Mr Finistaire continued. 'Sefton had taken two or three wickets, and a new batsman was at the crease. Sefton bowled him his fastest delivery. It was short, and far too quick for him. It struck him here . . .' He thumped a hand on his chest. 'Right above the heart. And down he went, poor chap. They did everything they could for him, of course. There was even a doctor on the ground, and the ambulance was there in minutes. But it was no good. He was dead on arrival at the hospital.'

He sighed. 'As you can imagine, Sefton was shattered. He'd done nothing wrong. He'd just tried his best. He wasn't to know that the man had a weak heart. The man himself probably didn't know. It was just fate. But of course it was the end for poor Sefton. He never played again. Couldn't bear to. His career as a cricketer was over almost before it had begun.'

Jack imagined the awkward group around the ambulance as the stricken batsman was taken away, and the young, tall fast bowler standing on his own, hoping against hope that the man would survive.

Mr Finistaire resumed the story: 'I heard about it from a friend of mine – a member of a very select circle of people who share certain interests. We gather from time to time in one place or another: indeed, I've got a big party of people coming this month. But that's by the by. This friend mentioned the circumstances, and said that Sefton was devastated and was looking for a completely new life away from it all. The press had really gone to town and he couldn't walk down the street without people staring at him. All he wanted was to get away and live quietly out of the public eye. As it happened I was looking for a new chauffeur, and my friend made contact for me. Coming down here was perfect for him, and he's a very good driver. He's a bike enthusiast – used to compete at motor cross when he wasn't playing cricket. He still likes to scramble around the estate on his bike – and although we take it more steadily in the Bentley, he has an uncanny road sense.'

Mr Finistaire drained his wine glass. 'He still misses his cricket, so we put up a net for him in one of the back gardens, and he likes to take his exercise knocking the stumps out of the ground. He really is a great loss to the game, but he'll never bowl another ball at a batsman. I think he may be having a session this afternoon. We'll see when we walk round. Which, if you've finished, we may as well do now.'

Jack had finished, and felt much better for his late lunch. He made to pick up his plate, but Mr Finistaire stopped him with a slightly raised hand.

'Leave it. Mrs G will clear away. She disapproves of guests doing her work. Now for the grand tour.'

Later Jack found it hard to sort out the jumble of impressions of the house. Each room was like a gallery in a museum, filled with exquisite exhibits – ornate furniture, cabinets containing porcelain and silver. Every table displayed some treasure – a bowl, a statuette, a vase – invariably filled with flowers that could only have come from the house's own gardens.

And on the walls, painting after painting hung in gilded frames – landscapes, still-lifes and portraits.

'There he is,' Mr Finistaire said. 'Sir Archibald, founder of the family fortune.' He pointed at a portrait above the mantelpiece in the morning room.

Jack looked up at a forbidding figure staring down at him with hooded eyes. The face was lean, and framed by two ferocious white sideburns that stopped just short of forming a beard over the sharp chin. The cleanly shaven mouth was sternly unsmiling.

'My great-grandfather,' Mr Finistaire continued. 'Self-made man. Pulled himself up by his boot-straps. Hard as nails. Factories all over Scotland and the north of England. Ruled with an iron fist. Strikes broken, trouble-makers hounded out. Rode the tidal wave of the industrial revolution to fame, fortune – and Charnley House. Never met him, of course; but I do remember my grandfather.' He indicated another unsmiling Victorian on the wall. 'Chip off the old block. As tough as they come. When I knew him, he was an old man being wheeled around in a bath chair. But he was still terrifying. Big hunter in his day. Used to go out to India to shoot. Tigers – by the score – alas! He was a one-man extinction engine. Shot anything that moved.'

Mr Finistaire sighed. 'They did things differently in those days.' He gave a little shrug. 'The height of the Empire – unlimited wealth, boundless power. They had the world at their feet. It was their plaything; they felt they owned everything in it.'

He shook his head sorrowfully, but then moved on to a picture of a magnificent racehorse. 'That's a

Stubbs. Possibly the most valuable thing in the entire collection.'

Jack looked at the gleaming haunches, and the look of almost human pride in the horse's expression.

'It's a shame we can't have a painting of Keras by Mr Stubbs. Not that Mr Stubbs would have believed in unicorns. But I'll show you what we *have* got.'

Mr Finistaire led the way back to the grand entrance hall, from which a massive flight of steps rose to the floor above. Leading off the hall towards the back of the house was a long corridor. Several rooms opened off it to the left, but to the right there were no doors at all. Halfway down there was a vast tapestry that hung from the ceiling right down to the parquet floor.

'There!' He stood back and flung up his arm.

The colours were faded, and it looked to Jack like an enormous carpet. He probably wouldn't have given it a second glance. But now that he'd been made to look at it, he could see that it was special.

It showed a hunting scene. The huntsmen were surrounded by hounds, looking eagerly for their quarry. A magnificent antlered stag stood surveying them from a safe distance.

But the hunt, Jack realized, was just the backdrop

to the main subject. In the foreground there were two figures, a man and a woman. They were both dressed in hunting clothes of the finest quality, but seemed much more interested in each other than in the hunt. The man's doublet was spangled with stars. He had a neatly pointed beard and was very handsome. His pretty companion wore a magnificent riding dress.

'It's known as *The Lovers' Hunt*,' Mr Finistaire said. 'And there's Cupid.'

Jack saw a ridiculous baby figure with no clothes on, holding a bow and arrow, hovering above the couple.

'But that's not what's important to us. Look up there.'

Jack tilted his head back. Then he gasped.

In the top corner of the tapestry there was a scene that set his pulse racing. A unicorn stood beside a lake. Kneeling in front of him, on the shore of the lake, were two figures, a man and a woman. From their clothes it was clearly the same couple who featured in the foreground. The unicorn had reared up on his hind legs, as though giving them some kind of blessing.

Jack looked intently at the scene, trying to take in every detail. Behind the unicorn there was a rocky hill with what looked like a cave. Above the dark entrance, a lone tree grew out of the stony ground. It looked a magical place, but somehow Jack felt sure that it wasn't just made up by the artist; that it really could exist.

'Fascinating, isn't it?' Mr Finistaire said softly.

Jack nodded, still gazing.

'It's very old. They certainly believed in unicorns in those days – but no one seems to know anything about it. We don't know who designed it, we don't know who commissioned it; we don't know who the lovers were. And, crucially, we don't know where the scene with the unicorn is. But I've always believed it must have been here on the estate. The tapestry came with the house. My grandfather found it rolled up in an attic, and decided to get it out and hang it here. My father loved it, as I do. We've had countless experts in, and they've told us one or two things. It was probably made in Belgium. That's where the great tapestry factories were. But of course they worked from the designs they were given, and we still have no clue who the artist was. Or why he chose to pop a unicorn into his picture.'

They both gazed up at the tapestry, as though looking at it could solve its mysteries.

Then Mr Finistaire started speaking again. 'My nurse was absolutely certain that the story was set here, and she was a local woman whose family had lived in the village for generations. Her mother had told her that the couple in the picture were ill-fated. She didn't know what the story was; only that it was terribly sad. There was also a strong belief that the descendant of the unicorn still lived secretly on the estate, somewhere within five miles of the house.'

A strange look came into Mr Finistaire's eyes. 'I used to spend hours roaming the woods looking for him. As I grew older, I realized that a belief in unicorns was impossible in the modern world. But . . .' And here a shadow passed over his face. He hurried on – though not, Jack thought, with what he had been going to say. 'Anyway, something made me take a less sceptical view, and ever since, I've always had an open mind about it. And now you – you've proved me right. Keras *does* exist, and you have seen him.'

He smiled again, his good humour restored. 'Come on, let's finish the grand tour.'

Jack could hardly tear his eyes away from the tapestry, but he went on down the corridor until Mr

Finistaire stopped to fling wide double doors that opened onto an enormous space.

'Here's the ballroom!'

The high mirrors lining the walls made it seem even bigger. Jack caught sight of their reflection – two small figures dwarfed in the doorway.

Mr Finistaire pirouetted onto the floor. 'One, two, three; one, two, three,' he called out as his feet glided to and fro. He was multiplied in the mirrors, small twirling figures all moving in perfect time. It reminded Jack of a mechanical toy he had once seen in a toy museum – ballerinas, he remembered, who turned and raised their arms as the handle was wound.

Mr Finistaire spun round one last time and stopped, panting slightly. 'My mother would invite a hundred people – more, probably. The whole house came alive with music and conversation. The staff moved through the crowds of guests with trays of champagne, and everything glittered in the light of the candelabra. I was only allowed to stay up for a little while, but of course when they sent me to bed I couldn't sleep. I used to creep down the stairs as far as I dared and gaze down. The men all looked the same in their dinner jackets, but the women were stunning!'

He stood there, lost in the memory. More to himself than to Jack, he murmured: 'Dear dead women, with such hair too – what's become of all that gold . . . ? Come on,' he said, smiling once more. 'Leave the dead to bury the dead. It's the present we should be interested in, not the past. Let me show you around outside.'

Chapter 8

'We'll go out through the kitchen,' Mr Finistaire said over his shoulder.

The kitchen was enormous. Jack had a fleeting impression of gleaming pans hanging in orderly rows, along with ladles, sieves, knives and a host of other implements, some of which he couldn't even name. There was a vast ancient oven, and a great array of hobs.

He was glad there was no sign of Mrs Grout. He had seen her briefly when they arrived – a sour-faced woman who had looked him up and down and made him feel self-conscious in his scruffy clothes.

'More than we need these days,' Mr Finistaire laughed as he led the way through. 'Normally, that is. It'll be working to capacity for the gathering.' He flung open the door.

Steps led down to a walled and cobbled yard. There were two archways, to the left and right.

'Stable yard through there . . .' Mr Finistaire

pointed to the right. 'And through there . . .' As he indicated the gateway on the left, they heard a terrific crack. It sounded as though something wooden had been hit very hard. 'Ah-ha, as I thought . . .' He beckoned Jack to follow him.

They went through the gateway into a much bigger space dominated by a cricket net. The stumps were at the end nearest them, and one of them was lying on the ground some distance from the others. A cricket ball rested against the back of the net. In the distance they could see Sefton just reaching the end of his run-up. He turned and charged in to bowl.

The ball flew down the net, just missing the two remaining stumps, and made the net bulge.

'I told you he was quick, didn't I?'

Jack nodded, wide-eyed. He hadn't known a cricket ball could travel that fast.

Sefton had seen them now, and stood with his hands on his hips, breathing hard.

'Don't mind us,' Mr Finistaire called out to him. 'I'm just showing Jack around. You're quite safe on this side of the net,' he added to Jack.

But their presence had obviously broken the chauffeur's concentration; he looked around for his cricket sweater and started packing the scattered balls into his bag.

'He doesn't like to be watched,' Mr Finistaire said in a low voice, 'but I'm glad you saw that one ball. The best fast bowler England never had.'

Jack looked on in awe as Sefton marched down the net in his flannels and white shirt to retrieve the balls. Apart from a brief nod to his employer, the man made no acknowledgement of their presence, but simply went about scooping the last few balls into his bag.

There was something slightly robotic about his movements, Jack thought. Everything was direct, deliberate and efficient. His run-up and delivery had been like a piece of well-designed machinery. Jack felt a shiver of fear at the thought of having to face him, and couldn't help thinking of the poor batsman he'd killed. Having rounded up the balls and replaced the fallen stump in its hole, Sefton turned and started making his way back up the net away from them.

Jack thought he'd never seen anyone look so solitary; he felt as though they had trespassed on a jealously preserved privacy. Mr Finistaire seemed to intuit what he was thinking and, touching his arm, led the way back through the arch and across the kitchen yard to the gateway on the other side. Opposite them was the stable block. It had a run-down, neglected air. A door stood open, giving a glimpse of cobwebby darkness beyond.

The stables formed the far side of a square, abutting at right angles onto a gatehouse, whose heavy double doors were open, giving onto a paddock beyond. The gatehouse in turn met a nondescript, windowless wall, which Jack assumed was an extension or annexe to the original house.

He was going to ask what it was and what it was for, but just as he was opening his mouth, Mr Finistaire directed his attention to the vehicle drawn up by the gatehouse. It was an open-topped buggy with surprisingly large tyres.

Mr Finistaire walked over to it. 'Hop in,' he said, climbing into the driver's seat. Jack got in beside him.

'I don't do a lot of driving,' Mr Finistaire said as he turned the key, 'but I do enjoy this.' And with a clumsy lurch they were off.

They turned in the stable yard, then shot out under the gatehouse and were soon bouncing across the field, heading towards a track that led up into the woods.

'Better than weeding?' Mr Finistaire smiled at him.

Jack nodded vigorously. He couldn't think of anything he'd rather be doing – other than riding Keras, of course.

The track into the woods was rough, and the buggy bucked as it negotiated the incline. Jack clung onto his seat to stop himself being thrown about. They were soon climbing steeply. The trees crowded in, filtering out the sun and blocking the view.

Jack gazed into them, trying to penetrate the kaleidoscope of leaves as they darkened into deep shade. What was he hoping to see – the flash of a white flank, or a tail flicking through the undergrowth? Hardly. And anyway, would he have wanted Keras there in the undergrowth, watching him in the buggy with Mr Finistaire?

He felt a momentary twinge of doubt, but quickly suppressed it. He was having fun, and now that he knew Mr Finistaire's fit of rage had only been play-acting, he felt comfortable in his company. It was just a shame he employed such dour people as Sefton and Mr and Mrs Grout.

The track became less steep, and they soon crested the hill. Jack worked out where they must be, and realized why they were there. Suddenly the vehicle lurched to a halt. Mr Finistaire said, 'We'll go on foot from here.' He spoke quietly, and there was a tremor of excitement in his voice.

Jack felt excited too, as they walked onto the open grassy space leading to the edge of the escarpment. It seemed very different in daylight, with the buzz of insects in the background, and the woodpigeons calling monotonously through the afternoon haze. But Jack felt his skin prickle with every step as he remembered cantering across the same stretch of turf in the moonlight, and the vista of the estate stretching out below them when they reached the edge.

Mr Finistaire turned to him. 'It was here that he brought you, wasn't it?' he asked.

Jack nodded.

Mr Finistaire led the way across to the vantage point Keras had chosen the other night. When he got to the edge, he lowered himself carefully onto his hands and knees. He looked like a slightly portly detective searching for clues, Jack thought.

It didn't take him long to find what he was

looking for. Suddenly he signalled Jack to join him.

Where the grass gave way to the bare chalk of the escarpment there were two indentations. Jack remembered with a shudder how Keras had suddenly dug his hooves in just as they reached the brink. Jack thought Mr Finistaire might have suspected he was exaggerating, but now he had the proof. They both looked hard at the two deep nicks in the chalk. Mr Finistaire ran a chubby finger round them, and Jack could see he was noting the faint cleft in the hoof marks.

'You did come close to the edge,' Mr Finistaire murmured. Then, looking Jack in the eye, he asked: 'Weren't you frightened?'

He *had* been frightened, but at the same time he had felt safe; absolutely confident that no harm would come to him. Somehow he couldn't find the words to explain that.

Mr Finistaire looked at him sympathetically. 'You're a gutsy boy, Jack . . . Well,' he went on, standing up stiffly, 'it's been quite a day – a day of dents!' He seemed ridiculously pleased with his little joke, and laughed while brushing off his trousers. 'We'll go down and take stock. And then we must get you home – with enough soil on your hands to prove you've been working hard.' He clapped his hands together to shake off any dirt, then smiled, and Jack smiled back. They would fabricate this harmless deception together. Jack would go home with soil on his palms and tales of back-breaking labour in the Charnley vegetable plot. Nothing could be easier.

He could only hope it was for the best.

'This is the map room,' Mr Finistaire announced. 'And this is where we will plan our campaign.'

By the standards of the rest of the house, it was a small room, shelved from floor to ceiling. The shelves were crammed with ancient leather-bound volumes of all shapes and sizes. Laid out on the table there were maps which Jack could see at a glance were of the estate.

'These are all the ones I have found so far. The earliest dates back to the fifteen hundreds. Barely recognizable now, of course. There have been so many changes over the centuries.' Mr Finistaire leaned over and pulled one of the maps over to the middle of the table. 'This is the best, I think.'

It was large, and had obviously been rolled up for a long time. Mr Finistaire weighted down the four corners.

Jack peered at it, recognizing several features. There was the old woodsman's cottage, with a track leading to the village. Other routes through the woods were clearly marked, as well as contour lines to show how the land rose and fell.

Mr Finistaire opened a drawer and produced a sheet of adhesive coloured dots. 'You met him here, I think . . . ?'

He peeled off a red dot and placed it at the end of the open space labelled *The Great Glade*. More followed as they traced Jack's ride over to Mr Grout's pheasant runs and up to the escarpment.

Jack felt excited as his extraordinary night extended over the map, but he was uneasy too. Riding Keras had been so personal, so private, and now here was the route of his ride being charted on the estate map.

He stole a glance at Mr Finistaire, who was poring over the map intently.

'And you finished where you started?' he said, with a last dot poised on the tip of his forefinger.

Jack nodded.

'And then you walked back through the woods this way . . .' A stubby finger indicated Jack's journey home. 'Did you see which direction Keras went?'

Jack remembered the unicorn cantering back up the glade, head high, tail flicking his great haunches. And then the moonlit moment was over, and Keras disappeared into the shadows at the far end.

Jack was about to put his finger on the map, but stopped himself. 'No,' he said.

'No?' Mr Finistaire looked at him closely. 'What do you mean?'

'He waited . . . for me to go.' Jack worked desperately to imagine a new reality for their parting. There was Keras, standing stock still in the moonlight while he set off for home. 'I looked back – and waved,' he said. It didn't sound convincing. He hurried on, 'And when I next looked back – he'd gone.'

'And where do you think you were then?'

Jack stared at the map. His finger hovered, but it was difficult to gauge where he might have been. How soon did the trees become impenetrable? Where did the ground dip down towards the stream? 'I'm not sure,' he said. 'It can't have been far.'

Mr Finistaire looked hard at the map. The red dots showed the route Jack and Keras had taken. It started at the glade, ran over to Mr Grout's hut, up to the escarpment, and then, more directly, down to the glade again. But that was all – it was a closed circuit, like a carelessly discarded necklace.

'And you didn't see what direction he came from either?'

Jack was on safer ground with that – the truth. 'No,' he said, remembering that first awful prod in the back while he was crouched over his snare.

'He came up behind you, yes . . .' Mr Finistaire acknowledged. 'Well, he must have come from somewhere. We need to know where.'

Jack looked at the area beyond the glade, but the map gave no details – just unbroken woods. It would seem the most likely place to look. But he hated the thought of trying to track Keras down.

Yet again, Mr Finistaire seemed to read his mind.

'We have to find out as much about him as we can – in order to protect him. You understand that, Jack – don't you?'

Jack nodded, but his doubts remained.

'Well, we're not going to find out any more today. Good heavens, is that the time? We must take you home. I'll get Sefton under starter's orders. You carry on looking at the map – just in case anything occurs to you.' He gave Jack a friendly look, and went out into the corridor.

But Jack didn't want to look at the map any more. With all its dots, it reminded him of a plan for a military campaign. It depressed him. Instead, he went over to the shelves and started inspecting the titles embossed on the leather spines.

They all seemed pretty boring, until one leaped out at him. Pausing to listen for noises outside in the corridor, Jack cautiously eased the large volume off the shelf. It was heavy and rather dusty. He put it gently down on the table and opened it. The title page read: *Charnley House: Its History, Architecture and Estate. With 20 Plates, including Plans of House and Outbuildings.*

Jack turned the ancient pages and looked at the tightly packed print. He saw a few names and dates; it looked like a history book. He was just about to close it and put it back on the shelf when he came to the first plate: it was a picture of the house at an earlier time. It was recognizably the same house, but something was different. The picture showed the front elevation, and a couple of figures were posed on the steps up to the main door, having just got out of a carriage.

Jack bent down to look more closely. The house was smaller. He tried to work out what the difference was. Then he realized: the wing that now joined the house to the stable block wasn't there. As he'd guessed, it was a later extension.

He turned some more pages. They were stiff and gave off a dusty, musty smell. He felt nervous even touching such an old book. But then he came to another plate, which showed the house a century after the first one. The missing wing was now there. Well, houses did get added to. He thought with a smile about the decision to build the extension to their cottage. His mum and dad had argued for weeks before finally deciding to go ahead with it.

Mr Finistaire would return soon and Jack knew he ought to put the book back, but when he turned another page he found a floor plan of the house, and stopped to look at it. There were the rooms he had been shown: the morning room, and other reception rooms; the ballroom; the kitchen. He could even see the little room he was now standing in, just up the corridor from the kitchens.

But there was something puzzling: the new wing was there, marked *Banquet Hall.* A banquet hall sounded rather grand, but Mr Finistaire hadn't shown it to him, or even mentioned it. Nor had Jack seen any door that might lead to it.

He was still puzzling over this when he heard footsteps in the corridor, and Mr Finistaire calling his name. He quickly shut the book, which gave off a damp puff of ancient dust. What use would there be now for a banquet hall? It was probably full of old furniture under dustsheets, he thought as he slid the heavy volume back in its place and moved across to the table to pretend that he had been looking at the map all along.

'Any joy?' Mr Finistaire said as he came back in.

Jack shook his head.

'Not to worry. Sorry that took so long. Something needed my attention. Sefton will bring the car round in a minute.'

Back out in the corridor, Jack looked at the great expanse of wall to their left. Apart from the tapestry, it was completely blank. He could have asked Mr Finistaire about it, but his host was obviously preoccupied with whatever it was that had cropped up. He was hurrying ahead now, his shoulders slightly hunched. This was not the moment to start asking questions. Jack gave the top corner of the tapestry a glance, but the light was not good and the unicorn was shrouded in shadow.

'Here we are,' Mr Finistaire said, holding open the

front door. Jack could see the Bentley drawn up outside, and the chauffeur waiting for him. He must have hesitated slightly.

'Don't worry about Sefton. Perhaps I shouldn't have told you his story – but there are no secrets between us, are there, Jack? You couldn't be in safer hands, I assure you. Now, off you go – oh, and remember to rub some soil into your hands.' He indicated a neatly trimmed holly tree standing in an urn at the top of the steps. 'Just to keep up appearances.' He smiled, but Jack thought he suddenly looked tired.

'We've had a wonderful day – made some real progress. But there's so much more to do. Can you come over again this week? I'll ring your father to arrange it. Goodbye, Jack – and thank you; thank you very much indeed. You have no idea how important all this is. And I must remind you, it is absolutely vital that no one – no one at all – gets to know. It's our secret. And Keras's, of course.'

He put a hand fleetingly on Jack's shoulder, and then pushed him gently in the direction of the urn. Jack felt foolish scrabbling in the soil around the base of the holly tree, and he was very careful to brush it off on his trousers. He didn't want to get dirt on the immaculate leather of the Bentley's interior.

He could feel Sefton's unblinking gaze on him, but the chauffeur gave no sign of what he was thinking when Jack walked down the steps and got into the car.

He looked back up at the house, but Mr Finistaire had gone inside and the great front door was shut. He turned his attention to the car, marvelling again at how sumptuous it was. You could hardly hear the engine as they moved off, and Sefton changed gear with the minimum of effort.

Jack stole a glance at him. He sat rigidly in his seat, staring fixedly ahead of him. It was like being driven by a robot.

CHAPTER 9

Jack had gone to bed as soon as he could, but inevitably there had been talk when he got home.

'He kept you a fair while,' his dad said.

'Look at the time,' his mum joined in. 'Six hours – that's too much. It's exploitation.'

'Jack's just paying his dues. Teach him to go kicking stones at expensive cars.' Jack's dad had retreated behind the paper again.

'It's all right, Mum. It was OK.'

'Let's see your hands. They must be torn to shreds.'

'They're fine.'

And Jack had held them out for inspection, silently giving thanks for Mr Finistaire's attention to detail.

When he got to bed, he found he couldn't sleep, even though he was exhausted. He had spent more time with grown-ups in a day than he usually would in a month, and they wore you out. You had to be constantly on your guard because they picked up on everything – like his mum wanting to see his hands. Fortunately they could also out-think each other. Not that he liked the idea of Mr Finistaire pulling the wool over his parents' eyes. It all seemed less of a joke now.

He lay there, trying to sleep, but found a succession of images, snatches of the day's events, swimming into his mind – and they all seemed to be focused on one person: Sefton. Jack saw the stone hitting the car, and then Sefton kicking the tennis ball into orbit; Sefton looking on unmoved as Jack and Mr Finistaire laughed hysterically by the roadside; Sefton knocking cricket stumps out of the ground in the net; and Sefton watching him as he delved into the urn to get soil on his hands before the drive home in total silence. The last thing Jack was conscious of as he finally dropped off was Sefton's impassive face, with its invisible eyebrows and unwavering stare.

He dreamed. It was the same dream as before: he was flying through the woods again, but this time he was riding Keras. They went fast, terrifyingly fast, though Jack wasn't frightened. He felt safe; he felt exhilarated: it was the best thing, just the best. And then, suddenly, a great pit opened up before them. Keras couldn't stop, couldn't help but leap into it, and down they fell together into the darkness.

Jack woke with a cry. His pyjama top was soaked with sweat, and he was gasping for air. He turned on his light and checked the time. It was early, very early, but he knew he wouldn't get back to sleep.

Instead he lay there, watching the light creep across the ceiling, wondering what the dream meant, and whether he was right to be going along so readily with Mr Finistaire's plans. What were those plans, anyway, and what was his part in them?

He didn't come up with any answers, and eventually pulled open the curtains and got up, even though it was ages before school.

School. In all the extraordinary events of the previous day, he'd forgotten about school. Or at least, had not thought about the furnace of curiosity he would have to face when he rejoined the ordinary world of hands-up and 'Yes, miss'.

'There he is!' someone shouted as Jack walked up the hill. He was mobbed as soon as he went through the playground gates. It was like being a film star or a footballer. Everybody had a question, everybody wanted his attention. If being rich and famous was like this, he didn't want it. It was horrible.

'Has he got a swimming pool?'

'Has he got a helipad?'

'Has he got gold taps?'

He was rescued by Dan and Luke, who forced their way through to him and made a pretty good job of keeping the others at bay until Mrs Hinton came out with the bell and everyone surged into the school buildings.

'Welcome back, Jack,' she said, when they were all in their seats and the hubbub had died down. 'I hope you had a productive afternoon over at Mr Finistaire's house?'

When Jack said nothing, she prompted him: 'Tell us what you were doing?'

'I had to do some weeding,' he muttered.

'Speak up, Jack: everyone wants to hear.'

'Weeding,' he repeated, still addressing the top of his desk. 'I had to work in the vegetable plot.'

There was a groundswell of suppressed laughter, and he was aware that every face in the class was turned towards him.

'And why did you have to do that, Jack?'

When he failed to respond, she answered for him: 'Because, when we had our most distinguished visitor, you, Jack Henley, kicked a stone at his car, doing so much damage that your parents couldn't afford to pay for it. And that is why you had to spend yesterday afternoon – with quite a few more to come, I imagine – working in Mr Finistaire's gardens. I just hope you worked hard. And learned your lesson.'

'He still got a ride home in the Bentley, miss. I wouldn't mind doing an afternoon's work for that.'

'Don't call out, Martin,' Mrs Hinton said with a warning frown.

A hand went up.

'Yes, Giles?'

'If I scratch his car when he comes next, can I go over there too?'

Mrs Hinton cut through the swell of laughter. 'But he won't be coming back. Because, as I announced yesterday, we have chosen the prize-winner in the art competition, and Harriet is the one who will be spending a day over at Charnley House. And I only hope she conducts herself in such a way as to prove to Mr Finistaire that this school can produce well-behaved pupils.'

'Will she go in the Bentley, miss?'

'I'm sure she will, but we haven't discussed the details with Mr Finistaire yet.'

Harriet now put up her hand.

'Yes, Harriet, what is it?'

'Do you know when it'll be, miss – my prize day?'

Mrs Hinton smiled at her. 'I don't, I'm afraid. As I said, we still have to discuss it all. But I'm sure it will be very soon.'

'Thank you, miss. It's just that my mother asked me.'

'I quite understand. And you'll be the first to know when the date is decided. Now, class, let's get our maths books open at page thirty-eight please.'

'Jack . . .'

He felt a tug on his sleeve. It was Harriet. They were pressed together in the crowd at the end of school.

'I need to talk to you,' she whispered fiercely.

His expression must have showed his surprise.

'I mean it,' she said. 'Meet me . . .' She paused. 'Meet me at the back door of the church in five minutes. It's important.'

Then she was gone, mingling with Jacky and Becky and Naomi, and all the other girls who sat at the front of the class and always had their hands up when Mrs Hinton asked a question.

'Ooo-oo.' Dan sidled up to Jack with a big grin on his face. 'Who's got a girlfriend?'

'Shut up,' said Jack.

'I *saw* you . . . Luke,' he called out. 'Guess what I just saw— Ow!' He suddenly doubled up, clutching his leg. 'That really hurt.'

'Sorry,' said Jack. 'I'm not in the mood.'

Luke came up. 'Walk down the hill?'

Jack shook his head. 'Gotta get something at the post office for my mum,' he said, pushing through the crowd. He felt bad about kicking Dan, but he'd had enough. And now he had to meet Harriet, of all people. What could that be about?

He set off down the high street, and then slipped up one of the many paths that wound their way round the backs of people's gardens to get to the churchyard.

No Harriet. Was she trying to wind him up like everyone else? He scowled. A stone was lying invitingly on an ancient flagstone, and he drew his foot back to kick it.

'Don't you kick that at me!'

Harriet had appeared round the corner, and she

was right – it did look as though that's what he was intending.

'I wasn't going to,' he said. And as though to prove it, he put his toe to the stone and deftly scored a goal with it against the back door of the church.

'Boys,' said Harriet with a sigh of assumed female superiority. Then she smiled at him.

It wasn't what you'd call an honest smile. It was a winsome, little-girlie smile that obviously meant she wanted something.

'What do you want?' Jack said guardedly.

'Look, it's really important. To me. I'm sorry about . . .' She waved vaguely at the church. 'I thought this would be better than . . . You know what they're like.'

'It's OK,' Jack said, deciding to give her the benefit of the doubt. 'It's like . . .' He hesitated, and then suddenly ducked down behind a tombstone.

'What are you doing?' Harriet asked.

'. . . a secret rendezvous,' Jack said, slipping back into view and giving his best shot at a Sean Connery impersonation. 'Double-o-seven at your service . . .'

For a moment he thought Harriet was going to go 'Boys' at him again, but then her face split into a genuine smile. 'That's a terrible accent,' she said.

'Do you have the secret codes for me?' Jack asked. His accent was getting worse, and they both burst out laughing.

Suddenly Harriet grew serious again. 'Look, it's no laughing matter. It's about the prize – and going to Mr Finistaire's house, and my stupid, stupid mother—' Then she burst into tears.

This took Jack completely by surprise. He watched, appalled, as Harriet stood with her head in her hands, sobbing uncontrollably. *Girls*, he thought, desperately wondering what he ought to do.

'Don't cry,' he said uselessly. He reached out a hand, but then withdrew it. 'It's all right.'

'It's *not* all right – it's not all right at all,' she said fiercely, looking up at him with her eyes still welling.

'What's the matter?'

'She won't let me go! Of all the mean and horrible things she's ever done, this is the worst.'

Harriet stamped her foot. Jack was rather impressed with this. He'd read about people doing it in books, but had never actually seen anyone do it in real life.

Something must have shown in his face, because Harriet tore into him.

'*You're* all right – you kick a stone at his posh car

and you're chauffeur-driven around the village like . . . like a lord. Whereas I actually do something good, like win an art prize, and I'm not allowed to go. And it's just not fair!'

'Why won't she let you go?'

Harriet looked at him to check that he was taking her seriously. 'I don't know,' she said. 'She wouldn't say, wouldn't explain. She just said she didn't think it was right for me to go over there for a whole day – on my own.'

'But I'll probably be there.'

'Exactly! I *said* that. I said you'd be there, and it would be OK. But then I had to explain why you'd be there and she got all funny about that as well. But it's OK, isn't it? I mean, they're not . . . being horrible to you, are they?'

Jack had to fight back a smile. Horrible? Far from it. 'Course not. It's great. I mean, obviously I have to do stuff. But it's not slave labour. And it's an amazing place. And Mr Finistaire is really nice.'

'Is he? He didn't half blow his top at you yesterday. Everybody in the school heard it.'

As they were meant to, Jack thought. 'He said sorry later on. When he'd calmed down.'

'So he's not weird or anything?'

'No. A bit strange perhaps, but not weird. I mean, where did your mum get that idea from?'

'Like I said, she won't really say. She just said no one knows very much about him. He's a recluse, living out there in his big house all by himself. So why is he giving an art prize to the school and inviting the winner over on their own for the day?'

'Why shouldn't he? It's a nice thing to do.'

'Exactly! That's what I said. But Mum – do you know what I think? I think she's jealous. She's jealous because *I've* been invited and not her. But I want to go. I deserve to go.'

'You'd love it,' said Jack. 'You'd have a wonderful time. The food's amazing.'

'They fed you?'

'Yes. I mean, just a snack. Cold pie and lemonade – the best I've ever had. So if they do that for me, you'll get something really special.'

'That's what I *said*,' said Harriet. 'I said Miss Hubbard would never allow you to go over there if it wasn't all right.'

She shook her head in frustration; it made her plaits go to and fro across her face. Then she looked up, the tears still sparkling in her eyes. Jack felt suddenly nervous.

'Jack?' she said.

He waited.

'You couldn't—' She broke off and scuffed the flagstone of the porch with her shoe. 'This may sound a bit strange, given that we're not exactly – well, you know, friends or anything . . .'

It was coming.

Harriet took a deep breath. 'Look,' she said, 'you've got to tell her – my mum. You've got to convince her it'll be OK. Will you?'

Jack had only the vaguest impression of Harriet's mum. She drove up to the school in a huge four-by-four, and always looked very smart on the few occasions she actually got out of the car. He couldn't see how he could walk up to her and start telling her about Charnley House.

'I'll invite you over to tea, and you can tell her then. You will, won't you? Jack?'

There was a tremor around Harriet's chin. If he said no, she'd burst into tears again.

'Sure, Miss Moneypenny,' he said, reverting to his Sean Connery accent.

She gave him a watery smile. 'Great,' she said. 'We'll pick you up at the end of Cobbs Lane after school tomorrow.'

'But—' Jack started.

'It's all right. I can invite anyone I like. And Mum makes delicious cakes. I gotta dash.'

And with that she was gone. Without even saying thank you. But as he made his way thoughtfully home along the back lanes, Jack didn't hold that against her. He was, however, extremely anxious about the invitation to tea.

CHAPTER 10

After school the next day, he again gave Dan and Luke the slip – even though, as far as his mum was concerned, he was spending the afternoon with them. He didn't know why he couldn't tell her about Harriet's invitation. Perhaps because he didn't fully believe in it himself. Harriet was quite capable of cancelling it. If she managed to get her mum to change her mind about the visit to Charnley, she wouldn't need him.

There was no communication at all during school, not even eye-contact. Which was fine by Jack. Dan and Luke were watching him like hawks, even though they both had the sense not to say anything. But as he loitered at the end of Cobbs Lane, waiting to be picked up, he felt bad about neglecting them, and promised himself he would find time to make it up to them.

He was just beginning to wonder if he would be collected after all, when he heard the throaty rumble of the powerful engine, and there, squeezing its way between the stone walls of the lane, was the enormous black car.

Harriet's mother was sitting stony-faced at the wheel, with Harriet looking very small beside her. Harriet gave him a funny little low-level wave as they approached, but Mrs Lazenby hardly glanced at him as the vehicle drew up.

Jack pulled open the back door and climbed up into the roomy interior of the car. They started moving as soon as the door shut, leaving Jack scrabbling about for his seat belt.

'This is Jack, Mum,' Harriet said.

'Hello, Jack,' Mrs Lazenby said, without enthusiasm. Jack caught her eyes in the rear-view mirror. They were not friendly.

Jack prepared himself for an uncomfortable afternoon.

To give Harriet her due, she half swivelled round in her seat to give him an encouraging smile, but was immediately told to 'turn round and sit still'. They drove on in silence.

Eventually they swung off the road down a gravelled drive. It was nothing like as grand as the approach to Charnley House, of course, but it was still impressive. As was the house, which was surrounded by lots of outbuildings.

Mrs Lazenby drove round to the rear and stopped near the back door. Harriet leaped out, to be greeted by two large dogs. Her mum went straight into the house, muttering something about tea, and leaving Jack fumbling awkwardly to undo his seat belt. He eventually released it and dropped down onto the pristine gravel.

Harriet gave a sort of helpless shrug as the dogs continued to leap up and lick her. They then turned their attention to Jack. They certainly made up for Mrs Lazenby's lack of friendliness, and Jack nearly lost his footing as they jumped up at him.

'Down, Dorry,' Harriet said, 'and you, Mungo. Down. Don't worry about them. They won't eat you. Come on, let's go and have tea.'

Tea at Jack's house was the evening meal – meat and two veg, with a dessert to follow. Tea at Harriet's was going to be different, he could tell.

It was a big kitchen, four or five times the size of the one at the cottage. It had a huge cooker, and a large dresser with lots of nice-looking plates, and mugs hanging from little hooks.

Harriet's mum was taking something out of the oven, and it smelled delicious.

'Show Jack where he can wash his hands,' she said over her shoulder.

'This way,' Harriet said, leading him into a spacious hallway and pointing to the downstairs cloakroom.

When he returned to the kitchen, there was a handsome cake sitting on the table. Mrs Lazenby had made herself a cup of tea, and after she had served up slices of the cake, she sat down and took a long sip.

Then, looking Jack straight in the eye, she said: 'Well?'

Jack had just taken a very large bite of cake. Playing for time, he managed to get out a rather cake-muffled 'Very good.'

Harriet gave a little snigger, but her mum looked at him severely.

'I don't mean the cake,' she said. 'Didn't Harriet tell you? I want to hear about Charnley and Mr Finistaire.'

Jack's mouthful was now down to manageable proportions. He nodded, partly to help get more cake down his throat, partly in answer to the question. 'What do you want to know?' he asked.

Mrs Lazenby looked at him. Didn't she ever smile?

'Everything. How you were treated, what they made you do – everything you can remember.' She had the same grating, superior voice as that woman on the telly who humiliated contestants in the game show Jack's mum sometimes watched.

'Mum,' said Harriet.

'Be quiet, Harriet.'

There was a pause. Jack felt his mouth go dry, and took a sip of lemonade. It wasn't nearly as good as Mrs Grout's.

'Well?' Mrs Lazenby urged again.

He gulped, started to wipe his mouth, and then decided against it. 'It was OK,' he said. 'Really. I just . . .' He paused. Harriet's mum's gaze was unwavering. Stumblingly he started to talk about his fictional weeding tasks. He supposed if he told a lie often enough, even he would come to believe it.

'And they gave you something to drink?'

'Oh yes,' Jack said. 'And food. It was really very nice. I mean' – he paused to get it right – 'I had to do the work. But that was only fair because of what I'd done to Mr Finistaire's car. But they weren't nasty to me.'

' "They"?'

Jack took another sip of his drink. 'Mr Grout,' he said.

'The gamekeeper? Yes, we know Mr Grout – Colin's been on one or two of the shoots over there.'

'That's my dad,' Harriet said helpfully.

'I'm surprised Mr Grout gave up an afternoon to supervise you.'

'He wasn't there all the time. I mean, he was hardly there at all. He really just showed me where I was to work, told me what to do, and left me to it.'

'And what vegetables were you weeding?'

Jack's head was beginning to spin. What had he been weeding? The only vegetables he could think of were potatoes and sprouts, but he wasn't sure if sprouts were in season.

'Mum . . .' Harriet came to the rescue.

'What, Harriet?'

'Well, it's a bit embarrassing. For Jack, I mean. He's being punished. Don't go on about it. It's my day out at Charnley we're meant to be talking about.'

Jack gratefully took up the baton. 'I'm sure Mr Finistaire will put on something special when Harriet comes over.'

'*Comes* over?' Harriet's mum's eyebrow was raised enquiringly. 'You think you'll be there, do you?'

'Mr Finistaire did say. I'd be doing my work, of course, but I'd be there – someone Harriet knows. But I wouldn't spoil anything,' Jack added quickly.

Mrs Lazenby looked thoughtful, though it was impossible to guess what she was thinking. 'And what's he like, Mr Finistaire?'

'Very nice,' Jack said. 'Really, really nice.'

'Harriet said he shouted at you.'

'He was pretty cross about the – about my . . .' Jack abandoned the sentence and felt himself going slightly pink. 'But he knew I didn't mean to, and he said he was sorry for losing his temper.'

'And what's Harriet going to do all day? If she goes.'

'Oh, lots of things. Mr Finistaire will show her around the house, and the gardens are fantastic. And then there are the woods. He's got this little buggy he uses to ride around the estate. It's—'

Fortunately Mrs Lazenby interrupted him before he could say it was a bit bumpy but a lot of fun. 'Well, it does sound as though—'

Harriet seized her chance. 'So you *are* going to let me go!' She jumped up and gave her mum a big kiss. 'I knew you would!' As she sat down again, she flashed Jack a smile and mouthed 'Thank you' at him.

'I'll have to talk to your father,' Mrs Lazenby said grudgingly.

'Dad'll be all right. I'm so excited! It'll be wonderful – I can't wait. Thanks, Mum.'

Mrs Lazenby looked slightly wrong-footed. 'You can't be too careful these days,' she said darkly.

'It'll be fine, Mum. Honest. I'll have a lovely time – won't I, Jack?'

Jack nodded.

'So, that's settled. Can I show Jack around outside, Mum?'

'All right, but I've got a lot to do this afternoon, so I'll need to take him back soon.'

'Come on.' Harriet was on her feet, and Jack got up too.

'Thanks for tea,' he said, remembering his manners.

But Mrs Lazenby gave no sign that she'd heard him.

With a brief flick of her head, Harriet indicated the kitchen door. The dogs suddenly sprang up from their baskets, and in a moment they were out in the bright sunshine in the yard.

'Thank you, Jack. You were brilliant. Absolutely brilliant.' She gave him a huge smile.

'Any time, Miss Moneypenny, any time,' he said in his bad accent.

'Oh, stop it,' she said, but he could see that she was happy and wanted to be nice to him.

'Do you want to see my pony? He's the cutest thing ever. He's called Seth, and I love him more than anything in the world!' She set off without waiting for a reply, the two dogs bounding along beside her.

When they reached the stable, Harriet threw open the top part of the door. 'Seth! Come and meet Jack,' she called into the darkness.

Jack had to agree that Seth *was* quite cute. He was a light biscuit colour, with a sweep of forelock falling down over his eyes. And he was quite obviously the model for Harriet's unicorn picture. Just without the ice-cream cone stuck on his forehead.

'I don't suppose you ride . . . ?' she said.

Jack allowed himself a little unseen smile. 'No,' he said. 'But I'd like to.'

Harriet wasn't listening. 'We should have brought some carrots or something.' She frowned. 'Silly old Harriet, forgetting your carrots,' she added, tickling Seth's ear.

She seemed so absorbed in her pony that Jack was surprised when she swung round and smiled at him.

'Thanks again, Jack. You didn't have to do that. You don't know how much it means to me.'

'That's OK. I'm glad she said yes.'

'So am I. I just wish I knew when it was going to be. He didn't say, did he?'

'No,' said Jack; 'but I'll try and find out.'

Harriet's smile broadened. Then the smile vanished. Her mother was calling them.

'You don't have to take me back to the village. I can cut across through the woods if you drop me round this corner.'

'Are you sure?' Mrs Lazenby asked, but Jack could tell she would be as relieved as he was to end the painfully silent car journey.

'I'll be fine – really. I love the woods.'

The huge vehicle was already slowing down. Mrs Lazenby was obviously keen to get back to the house, where she'd left Harriet doing her homework at the kitchen table.

She pulled in at a gateway, and Jack jumped out. The four-by-four swung round and shot off in a cloud of dust.

'Thanks for having me,' Jack said as he watched it disappearing round the bend.

He felt sorry for Harriet. For all her advantages, he could see that her life was not without its problems. He was glad he had helped to make sure she got her day out at the big house.

He looked both ways and crossed the road. The trees came right down to the hedge, and he climbed over a little stile.

It was good to be back in the woods. No one knew where he was. He was on his own. He was free. He set off into the trees.

After a while the ground started to rise. The sounds of passing cars back on the road faded, and Jack was able to pick up the rhythms of the wood – the soughing of the breeze in the branches, the hum of insects, the wood pigeons keeping up their monotonous calls. He began to feel part of his surroundings, to blend in. Not that he was expecting anyone else to be around. He reckoned he was as far away from Charnley as he could be. He had the woods to himself.

He was startled by a crash in the undergrowth. He froze, but then relaxed when he saw the flanks of a deer flitting away between the tree trunks. He also disturbed a squirrel, which gave him a beady look and darted up into the branches to safety.

I'm no threat, he wanted to say. *I'm just here, like you, minding my own business*.

The painful memory of his attempts at setting snares flashed through his brain. He shook his head. What could have possessed him? Now he could walk through the woods with a light heart and a clear conscience.

He came to a great up-ended ash. Its branches lay sprawled for metres on either side of the trunk, and its roots had torn a wide crater in the earth. It seemed incredible that a tree that had stood for perhaps a hundred years could be plucked out of the ground like one of Sefton's cricket stumps by a violent gust of wind.

One branch, which must have been ten or twelve metres above the ground when the tree still stood, arched invitingly, and Jack climbed onto it and balanced his way along it like a tightrope walker.

But time, he knew, was passing, and he soon jumped down to resume his journey home.

The going was easy to begin with, but then the ground ahead rose steeply, and he was faced with a smaller version of the escarpment on the other side of the estate. He walked along the bottom of it for a while, hoping for a path, but started worrying that he was losing his sense of direction. He would have to climb it.

It was almost vertical, but there were exposed roots and some hardy shrubs to hold onto, though the last couple of metres posed a serious challenge. He lost his footing when a stone he was stepping on gave way, leaving him clinging with both hands to a wizened old thornbush. Eventually he scrabbled his way to the top, dragged himself over the edge and lay panting, face down on the grass.

He could feel the sweat cooling on his neck. Something buzzed annoyingly in his ear, and he slapped at it. The palms of his hands were stinging, and his right knee had taken a knock during his climb. He was so absorbed in his body's sensations that it took him a moment to decode the sharp pain in his back.

But then he turned his head.

'Keras!'

There he was, far bigger than Jack remembered, his head lowered and the two huge eyes gazing into his.

Jack felt a surge of joy. He had only suggested walking home through the wood to avoid spending another moment with Harriet's mother. He hadn't allowed himself even to think about seeing Keras. And now here he was.

Jack scrambled to his feet and stood before the unicorn. He wanted to step forward, and half raised his hand. But Keras was no tame pony to be patted and stroked. He had been no phantom in the moonlight when they first met, but now, in daylight, Jack could see more. The horn, that extraordinary ivory wand with the spiral groove running its entire length, drew his eye of course, but he also took in the oddness of the goat's beard and, dropping his gaze, the cloven hooves standing foursquare on the turf. The unicorn was completely other, utterly unique. No one would ever throw a saddle over that broad back; no one would ever dare to approach that head with a bridle. Keras was untameable, gloriously and irresistibly free.

It was a freedom that had to be preserved at all costs.

A shadow passed over Jack's thoughts: was he in danger of jeopardizing Keras's freedom? He wished he hadn't got involved with Mr Finistaire; wished he hadn't drawn those stupid sketches; wished he could go back in time and rip them to shreds and just play dumb, as he'd intended. And he wished he hadn't kicked that stone at Mr Finistaire's car. Keras might be free, but he wasn't.

The unicorn was looking at him steadily while these regrets clouded his mind. Jack looked ruefully into the dark eyes, and seemed to find sympathy and understanding there. He suddenly felt tired. The stress of the last few days seemed to flood through him, draining the energy out of his body. He felt a tear welling and wiped it away.

Keras snorted gently and moved a step forward, presenting his neck to Jack.

'Oh, Keras,' he said, reaching up and resting his head against the unicorn's warm, wiry coat. Immediately he felt his strength returning, and with it a sense of hope and the simple joy of being alive – alive, in a wood on a summer's day, with the most magnificent creature on earth.

He wanted the moment to last for ever, but he knew it couldn't. Keras shook his arm off his neck. Jack stood back, and the unicorn swung his head round, leading the way to a boulder a few metres away. With a dip of his horn, he indicated that this was to be Jack's mounting block.

He was being offered another ride – something that, since the first time, he had longed for, without knowing if he would ever experience it again. He leaped onto the boulder and hoisted his leg over Keras's back.

He had hardly settled before the unicorn moved off. Jack lurched forward and nearly fell, only saving himself by burying his hands in Keras's mane. The going was rough and there were a lot of low branches to duck under, but Jack soon regained his confidence, and began to enjoy himself – the sheer thrill of speed, and the breakneck changes of direction. The thud of Keras's hooves was like the beat of a song – a brilliant song, a song of joy; limitless, boundless joy. Once he had attuned himself to the rhythms of Keras's stride, he felt as if they were one and the same, galloping effortlessly through the trees in complete harmony.

Jack was so happy he didn't care where they were going, but after a while he started to get his bearings. They had returned to familiar reaches of the wood. Suddenly they burst into the clearing with the derelict cottage and, with a sinking feeling, Jack realized that the ride was nearly over.

Keras slowed his pace. He was noticeably less relaxed now. His ears pricked up, and he kept looking from side to side. When he stopped to let Jack slip to the ground, it was obvious that he was eager to get away. Jack wanted him to stay, but he knew he mustn't try to prolong the leave-taking.

He put his hand up to Keras's neck to say thank

you. The unicorn acknowledged his gesture with a gentle snort of warm sweet breath, and then tossed his head back and launched himself away through the bracken.

Jack watched the white haunches for as long as he could, but they soon melted into the dappled shadows of the woods, and he was alone again.

He felt sad, deflated. But he wouldn't have traded those precious twenty minutes for anything in the world.

CHAPTER 11

Jack hadn't meant to tell Mr Finistaire about his second meeting with Keras, but he did. It just happened.

He was talking about his tea at Harriet's house, though playing down how anxious Harriet's mum had been. He tried to make it sound as though she were more concerned with the date of Harriet's visit to Charnley, and what kind of excitements would be laid on for her.

Mr Finistaire listened sympathetically. At the end, he said: 'I see. Thank you, Jack. That is most interesting. So, the Weirdo in the Woods – that's how I'm regarded by the wider community, is it?' He laughed to show that he didn't take it all terribly seriously, before asking, quite casually, 'And then she drove you home, did she, Harriet's mother?'

Jack should have said yes. He meant to say yes. He should just have said it, and looked away. But he hesitated, and then it was too late. 'No, I— She dropped me off, and I walked back through the woods.'

With Mr Finistaire's eye on him, it was impossible to pretend nothing had happened. And anyway, Mr Finistaire was the only person he could talk to about Keras.

So out it all came – the unicorn's sudden appearance and his second glorious ride.

Jack shifted in his chair. He wasn't as stiff as he had been after the first ride, but he was still feeling it.

'How marvellous,' sighed Mr Finistaire, after listening intently. 'What an extraordinary boy you are.'

He took off his glasses and rubbed his eyes. 'Did he – did Keras . . . ?' For once he needed to search for the right words: 'Did he *want* something, do you think?'

It was a new thought. Jack had just accepted Keras; accepted him as the most wonderful thing that had ever happened. But why should Keras have chosen him? Was there a purpose to his making contact?

'He did . . .' Jack felt embarrassed to say it, but Mr Finistaire gave him time. 'He did catch me trying to set those snares. And he showed me Mr Grout's gallows. He seemed to be saying he didn't like things being killed.'

'Yes,' said Mr Finistaire; 'but Grout has been shooting stoats and weasels and crows and nailing them up all over the estate for years. And no unicorn has appeared – to Grout or anyone else.'

Jack smiled. The idea of Mr Grout meeting Keras was too ludicrous.

Mr Finistaire smiled too. Then he suddenly looked serious. 'I don't like the shoots, and rearing the birds for sport, and all the rest of it. The trouble is, it helps maintain the estate. You cannot believe what it costs to keep it all up – the house, the gardens, the woods themselves. Guess how much I spent on guttering last year? You can't, can you?'

Jack shook his head.

'You're lucky you don't have to worry about that sort of thing. But I do. I have to find ways of making the estate pay for its upkeep. And there's the village to consider. Your father's a beater – and he enjoys it, doesn't he?'

Jack nodded.

'They all do – guns and beaters alike. As I say, I don't. I sometimes plod around with a gun over my arm – people like to see the owner out and about. But I never fire a shot in anger, and I'm always happy to see them climb into their ridiculous off-road troop-carriers at the end of the day.'

Jack allowed himself an inward smile at the thought of the Lazenbys' huge four-by-four.

Mr Finistaire for once wasn't looking closely at him. Instead he leaned back in his chair, putting his fingers together and gazing up at the ornate ceiling in the morning room.

'But maybe it's time for a change. Just because something has been going on for over a hundred years doesn't mean it has to go on for ever, does it? Hunting, shooting and fishing aren't the only things to do in the countryside. Not that I have ever allowed the hunt on the estate. Imagine all those horses and hounds crashing about in the woods.' He shuddered.

Then he looked at Jack. 'Perhaps he's chosen you as a messenger, a harbinger of change.' His eyes drifted away again and he seemed lost in thought.

After a moment he leaned forward in his chair and said: 'Jack, how would you like to stay late tonight? I thought we might try an experiment, and who knows, we might end up having an adventure. What do you say?'

Jack was taken aback. The intensity with which Mr Finistaire was looking at him was uncomfortable. But still he said: 'All right.'

'Wonderful. I knew you'd be up for it. It might not come to anything, but we can only try.' The excitement seemed to propel him out of his chair. 'Will anyone be at home now?'

'Mum will be,' Jack said.

'I'll phone her immediately,' Mr Finistaire said, getting up and leaving the room.

Jack looked about him – at the exquisite furniture, the pictures on the wall, the glossy magazines laid out on the table in front of him. When Mr Finistaire was there, Jack was fine, but as soon as he was left alone, he felt intimidated by the treasure trove of antiques. He was terrified of brushing against a priceless ornament and smashing it to pieces, or getting dirty marks on one of the silk cushions surrounding him on the sofa.

The portrait of Mr Finistaire's great-grandfather didn't help. Jack looked up at the forbidding features and found he was unable to meet those fierce, hooded eyes. You'd have had to be a brave mill-hand to stand in his presence and ask for a pay rise. Even when he looked away, Jack felt the disapproving gaze boring into him.

'Good news,' Mr Finistaire said, coming back into the room. 'I have got you a late pass.' His eyes were bright and kindly – nothing like his great-grandfather's.

Jack felt at ease again.

Mr Finistaire put his hand to his mouth to cover a little cough. Jack thought he looked slightly embarrassed.

'I confess I wasn't entirely frank with your mother – very nice to talk to her for the first time, by the way. She sounded very pleasant, and has your best interests at heart, as a mother should, of course.'

'What did you tell her?' Jack couldn't imagine the conversation.

'White lies, white lies,' Mr Finistaire said. 'Not really lies at all. I said some extremely nice things about you: you have an aptitude, I told her – a great and surprising talent for gardening.'

'I haven't done any gardening.'

'But your mother doesn't know that. We could hardly tell her that you come over here in search of unicorns.' Mr Finistaire raised an eyebrow and smiled, as if asking for Jack's indulgence.

'Anyway,' he went on, 'the important thing is, I told her that we have to transplant a very rare plant – an orchid from the farthest reaches of the rainforest – from its current bed to the urn in which it is to be exhibited. This much is true. The rest was rather an embellishment, I'm afraid. But sometimes you have to fall back on poetic licence!' He shot Jack a quick glance. 'The orchid is so delicate that it can only be moved in the right conditions. Its roots are sensitive to daylight. The best light is moonlight, and as there's a nearly full moon, and a clear night forecast, I said that we'd be doing it this evening. And that you had an important part to play.'

'Me?' Jack asked, genuinely shocked.

Mr Finistaire made his mouth do a sort of upside-down smile. 'Was I very wicked?'

His expression was so funny that Jack laughed as he shook his head. 'But she'd never believe that. I'm hopeless at gardening!'

'People believe what they want to believe, Jack. And good news, however unexpected, is always welcome.'

Jack could believe that. He remembered vividly

his dad's joy when he had a small win on the lottery. 'Well, you never know your luck,' his mum had said, all smiles. Perhaps she saw Mr Finistaire's interest in him in the same light.

Mr Finistaire was looking at him and, as though reading his thoughts, went on: 'Your mother believes in you, Jack. Deep down, all mothers believe in their sons; and she wants the best for you – rightly so. And it's not a lie to say that you're doing brilliantly; that I foresee great things for you. That's the absolute truth. And it's also true that we will be transplanting the orchid. You won't, of course, be involved, but for the sake of our cover story, I'm going to show it to you now. Come on.'

Mr Finistaire took Jack out through the kitchen again. They went past Sefton's cricket net and through a gate into a second, larger walled garden. Jack found himself in an aisle of beautifully shaped yew trees, which eventually opened out onto a lawn with copiously filled flower borders. And there, forming the corner of the garden's outer wall, was the huge glasshouse that Jack had seen gleaming in the moonlight from the top of the escarpment. He remembered a school trip to some botanical gardens:

this glasshouse was just as big as the ones they'd been led round by their guide.

Mr Finistaire fished a key out of his pocket, unlocked the door and slid it open.

Jack was immediately struck by the temperature, and the moist, sticky atmosphere.

'A little bit of rainforest, here in the heart of England!' Mr Finistaire said as he slid the door shut.

Wherever you looked there was a riot of growth: exotic trees decked with luridly coloured creepers reached up towards the roof, and gigantic ferns spread their fans as though forming a guard of honour.

Immediately in front of them was a platform reached by wooden steps, and from this they stepped out onto a walkway. Jack looked around, astonished. You really could be in the middle of the jungle. He felt like an explorer, pushing the giant leaves out of his face, breathing in the warm, soporific air.

There was a pond in which huge golden fish swam lazily. As Jack was staring down at them, he heard a soft whirring noise and, looking up, saw a tiny bird in a blur of wing-beats just ahead of him.

'Hummingbirds . . . Beautiful, aren't they?'

Mr Finistaire let him gaze for a few moments, then

indicated that they should push on. 'This is what we came to see . . .'

They had come to a little clearing, in the middle of which stood the orchid in splendid isolation. It was enormously tall, and looked, Jack thought, more like a statue than a plant.

'The Lady of the Moon,' Mr Finistaire said quietly. 'Come and meet her.'

There was another flight of steps, and they went down.

The orchid was nearly as tall as Jack. It had a slim stem, but it was perfectly proportioned to carry the weight of its flowers. These were lantern shaped, and Jack stared at them, transfixed. Tinged with pale golds and mauves shading out from creamy alabaster, they seemed to radiate a light of their own; but it wasn't a warm glow, more a cold, moon-like gleam. He could see how the plant got its name.

'Beautiful, isn't she?' Mr Finistaire said in a hushed voice. Then he reeled off a long Latin name, adding: 'That's the finest specimen in the world – outside the rainforest. And here she is safe. However much of the rainforest goes under the chainsaws, she will always have sanctuary here at Charnley. But she has to be handled with extreme care. Hence our little subterfuge, which I hope you'll agree is justified, because exactly the same applies to Keras. Except he's even more magnificent and rare and important, of course.'

Jack could only nod in agreement.

'Good lad. Now, take a last look. You'll remember her when you get home, won't you? Because, whatever else we see tonight, this is what you'll be telling your parents about.'

Jack could imagine the hushed group of gardeners delicately scraping away the soil, delving like surgeons to expose the tendril-like roots, and then, at a signal from Mr Finistaire, easing the treasure out of its soil and into its next resting place.

They climbed back up onto the walkway and retraced their steps to the glasshouse door. Mr Finistaire locked up.

'We'll go back to the house and have a bite to eat. It may be a long night.'

Jack was beginning to realize what Mr Finistaire had in mind. He'd known all along really: it was obvious. But he'd been fighting against acknowledging it because it made him feel bad. Mr Finistaire wanted to see Keras for himself, and was trusting Jack to bring him out of hiding.

It felt wrong, but there was nothing Jack could do to get out of it, not now Mr Finistaire had persuaded his mum to let him stay late.

'Into the map room,' Mr Finistaire said brightly, after they had helped themselves to some cold meat from the larder.

Jack glanced quickly at the shelf where he'd found the history of Charnley, but couldn't see it. It was the estate map spread out on the table that demanded his attention. He saw that more red dots had been added, showing the path of his second ride with Keras. It made him feel very uncomfortable, as though he'd been spied on – even though he was the one who had volunteered the information.

Mr Finistaire leaned over the map like a general in one of those old war films Jack's dad liked so much. 'There's our best bet, don't you think?' he said, looking up intently at Jack with his finger planted firmly on the Great Glade.

It was a straight question, but Jack hesitated.

'What's wrong?' Mr Finistaire asked.

'Nothing.'

'Spit it out. Got to share your doubts at the briefing, otherwise we'll jeopardize the whole operation.'

'It just that . . .' Jack paused. 'Well, he won't be expecting . . .'

'Me. No, of course he won't. And he certainly won't want to give me a ride.'

Once again, Mr Finistaire had found the right note, making a little joke at his own expense. 'Jack, don't worry. I won't embarrass you. I don't intend him to see me. It's *me* that wants to see *him*.'

He was serious again. Jack looked into his face. There was a faraway look of hope, anticipation; you could almost call it yearning.

'I have waited all my life for this, Jack. It's the most important thing that's ever happened to me. The last thing I want to do is spoil it. I'll keep in the background, and if he wants to give you another ride, off you go – nothing would make me happier! You're the one he has chosen to make contact with. I don't want to get in the way of that. Not at all.'

He looked so earnest, Jack felt reassured.

'Come on, off we go.' With that Mr Finistaire opened the map-room door and ushered Jack down the corridor.

CHAPTER 12

Jack couldn't help but feel excited as they made their way out through the kitchen. They could almost be a pair of adventurers, strapping on their flying helmets before taking off in search of lost treasure hidden deep in desert caves. He smiled at the thought of Mr Finistaire heaving his portly frame into the pilot's seat.

The smile was soon wiped off his face, for there in the stable yard was the grim figure of Mr Grout.

'Evening, Grout,' Mr Finistaire said as they came up to him. 'You've brought the buggy round – thank you. Just taking our young friend for a moonlit jaunt.'

Mr Grout nodded but said nothing. He didn't have to say anything to Jack: his look said it all. It seemed to penetrate Jack's defences, turning over all the secret parts of his mind, exposing his thoughts, his desires, his intentions.

As Jack slunk past him, he couldn't help noticing

how white Mr Grout's knuckles were as they grasped the bone handle of his stick.

It was a relief when Mr Finistaire started up the buggy and they jolted off through the archway. Jack didn't look back, but he could sense Mr Grout staring balefully at him. Jack shuddered at the thought of finding himself alone with the man and his ever-present stick.

'Cold?' Mr Finistaire asked, looking at him anxiously.

'I'm all right,' said Jack, but he still drew his top tighter about him.

They bumped up the path to the top of the escarpment and parked near the little clearing.

'On foot from here, I think,' Mr Finistaire said, hopping out.

Jack got out of the buggy slowly. The encounter with Mr Grout had darkened his mood. Quite apart from the gamekeeper's animosity, he was deeply worried about the plan to lure Keras into the open. There was something underhand about it; it felt like a betrayal. Though as Mr Finistaire was always pointing out, they were only working to protect Keras and preserve his way of life, so what harm could there be in Mr Finistaire seeing him for himself? Keras wouldn't even know he was there.

Jack looked at the dark shape pushing on ahead of him. Mr Finistaire was so enthusiastic, so committed to helping Keras, to saving him from the awful things that could happen if the secret got out. By his own account, he had dreamed all his life of seeing the unicorn. Who was Jack to begrudge him the chance now?

Keras probably wouldn't show up anyway, Jack thought.

The path led downwards and took them steadily further into the heart of the wood. The light grew dimmer, but they could still just see.

An owl hooted, answered by another across the woods. Jack suddenly shivered and realized he was nervous. What if Keras did appear, saw Mr Finistaire, and then turned tail and vanished – never to be seen again? Jack felt he was risking the most precious thing in his life, and the thought made him sick with worry.

But as they got closer to their destination, he started to concentrate on the immediate present. He heard the stream, and soon they reached it and walked along its bank for a while. It was much darker now. The tree cover filtered out most of the moonlight.

Then they branched away from the stream. Jack knew where they were going, but was still surprised when the trees started thinning out on the approach to the Great Glade. Suddenly they saw the moon hanging, brilliant, above the wood, bathing everything in its silvery light. It was much brighter than it had been the night he first encountered Keras. He felt excited once more. It was too late for second thoughts. He just wanted to see Keras again.

Mr Finistaire stood at the edge of the grassy arena, his face turned up to the sky, the moonlight glinting on his glasses. Then he took a step back, motioning for Jack to stay beside him.

They took up positions on either side of a great beech tree, which commanded a view down the length of the glade.

Jack felt edgy. On the two occasions he had encountered Keras, it had been the unicorn who had found *him*. There was something unsettling about lurking in the shadows, lying in wait for him.

There were a lot of noises in the woods – indefinable scratchings and skirrings, rustlings, sighings. It was as though every woodland creature was taking it in turns to come and inspect them.

Mr Finistaire was completely motionless. It was as

though he'd become a tree himself. Jack found it hard to settle. He wanted to scratch his leg. He felt an urge to cough, and nearly made himself sneeze suppressing it. Then he was certain that something had dropped into his hair, but couldn't put his hand up to brush it away.

It was anxiety, he realized, and tried to pull himself together. The trouble was, Keras could approach from any direction and without warning, without a sound. Jack allowed himself to turn his head and look behind him. As he did so, he half anticipated finding himself looking into those deep eyes, finding Keras's horn pointing enquiringly at his chest. He felt a charge of fear. But there was nothing – just the great trunks of the beech trees thickening into impenetrable darkness.

Keras might be there, standing as still as they were, watching the watchers. But if that's what he intended, thought Jack, that's what he'd do, and he turned his head back to face the Great Glade.

It was like water in the moonlight. You could almost imagine that you were standing at the edge of a lake. And it relaxed him. As the minutes passed, it seemed more and more probable that Keras wouldn't come. Jack yawned. He felt his eyes closing. It was only standing up that prevented him from dropping off to sleep.

But then, suddenly, he was wide awake, all his senses on red alert. He scanned the far end of the glade. There was something there, he was sure of it, though he couldn't have sworn he had actually seen anything.

He sensed that Mr Finistaire had picked up something too – or maybe he was just responding to Jack's tenseness.

Calm, he told himself. *Stay calm. Keep looking. Don't move.*

And then – there! There he was – a glimpse, a distinct flicker of a lighter shade among the darker shadows. Keras! It *had* to be.

'Is he there?' Mr Finistaire's whisper was barely audible, but Jack could sense the excitement in his voice.

'I – I think so,' he whispered back.

'Where?'

'Far end of the glade: straight ahead.'

Then, unmistakably, Keras showed himself.

'There, now. He's coming out! He's coming down the glade!'

He heard a gasp of breath from the other side of

the beech tree. 'How marvellous . . .' Mr Finistaire said.

But Jack was hardly listening. All his attention was fixed on Keras, cantering through the moonlight towards him.

'Show yourself,' Mr Finistaire whispered urgently. 'You've nothing to fear. Just walk out and he'll come to you. I'll stay here. Go on.'

Jack peeled himself away from the trunk and stepped hesitantly out into the moonlight. He stole a glance back. Mr Finistaire's face was partially in shadow, the moonlight glinting on the lenses of his spectacles.

Keras was halfway down the glade, his hooves thrumming on the turf. Jack stood exposed, a shiver of fear running through him. Just like the first time, the unicorn seemed to be coming straight for him, horn aimed at his heart like a levelled lance. What if Keras was angry with him and was going to punish him? Jack was completely defenceless. He knew he had to stand his ground, face the ordeal without flinching.

The sound of Keras's hooves grew like soft thunder. A divot flew up from the turf. The horn caught the moonlight. The great eyes were in shadow, but Jack knew that their penetrating gaze was fixed on him.

And suddenly he was there, with a snort and a duck of the head. Jack's resolve broke, and he flinched. Immediately he felt a stab of pain in his side, and cried out. But even though he was hurt, he still felt giddy with joy. He clung onto Keras's neck for support, fighting back tears and trying to assess the extent of the damage. He put his hand to his side, but there was no blood. It must have been a glancing blow. He'd be bruised but nothing worse.

He felt the strength returning to his legs, and the pain became more manageable. He stepped away from the unicorn and gave his side a proper rub.

Keras looked at him as though asking, *Are you all right?*

Jack forced himself to smile. He *was* all right. The pain was dying down – to be replaced by a sense of shame. At the last minute his courage had deserted him. He had failed the test and paid the price. The least he could do now was put a brave face on it.

He held his arms out, even though it hurt, and smiled.

Keras seemed pleased. He looked at Jack and breathed wonderful sweet, warm breath into his face.

And then, with a snort, lurched to his knees. Jack had never seen this before, but its meaning was obvious. Rather gingerly he threw his leg over the unicorn's back, and held on tight.

There was just time to glance over at the beech tree where Mr Finistaire was hiding. Jack caught a glimpse of his pallid face peering round the trunk, his glasses shining.

The pain in his side had dulled to an ache, but Jack was still tense, not sure whether he would be able to cope with one of Keras's wild gallops.

As though sensing this, Keras started off slowly. Even so, it took Jack a while to relax. He bounced around as he had the first time, and felt the unicorn's impatience at having a sack of potatoes on his back. Jack forced himself to concentrate, and eventually managed to fall in with the rhythm of Keras's hooves.

As soon as he did so, their pace quickened. Jack felt the wind in his face, and the sensation of flying over the turf returned. For the brief moment it took to cover the rest of the glade, he forgot everything, lost in the wonder of riding the unicorn.

But as Keras slowed to pick his way through the trees, the doubts and worries returned. What would Mr Finistaire do? Would he wait by the beech tree, and if so, for how long? Jack needed to go home at some point, and it was getting late. And then he wondered what Keras would do. They seemed to be heading in a new direction, into unfamiliar territory.

A low branch forced him to duck. Staying on Keras's back was his first priority, and that became more challenging as they drove on through the undergrowth.

After a while Jack noticed that the going was getting harder. The trees were closer together, and great banks of bushes loomed above them. Keras had slowed his pace to pick his way through this labyrinth, and Jack had to put one hand up to protect his face from the low-hanging branches.

The moonlight only penetrated in patches, and it was very hard to see more than a few metres ahead. Then they came to what appeared to be a wall of shadow, an impenetrable barrier of utter darkness. They couldn't possibly get through that, Jack thought, expecting Keras to veer to one side or the other. But to his surprise the unicorn carried on, now at a slow walk.

Jack bowed his head and pulled his hood up for protection. It was like forcing a way through a very tight tunnel. The backs of his hands were being scratched, and he tried to cover them with his cuffs. His legs were getting the same treatment and something caught at his ankle through his sock.

The air was close and musty, and as they proceeded they seemed to disturb all sorts of insects, which rose in resentful swarms around his nose and eyes. Jack was beginning to feel panicky and wondering how long he could bear it when, suddenly, they were out in the open again, and the air miraculously sweetened.

He pushed his hood back, relieved to be able to breathe freely once more. The moon shone down unimpeded, and as he looked around, Jack saw another moon reflected in the small lake ahead of them. The water was so still that the reflection was looking-glass perfect.

He sat on Keras's back, the twigs in his hair and the thorns in his jeans forgotten, and tried to take in the extraordinary beauty of the place. This was obviously Keras's home, his sanctuary, an undiscovered spot – certainly unknown to the estate's map-makers, because there was only one lake shown on the maps he had seen, and that was the one in front of the big house.

Jack managed to drag his eyes away from the

moon's reflection, and as he scanned the shore of the lake, he suddenly felt his heart lurch with shock. It was the shock of recognition. Because over to his right was the outcrop of rock with the dark gash of a cave's entrance. There was even the little tree growing out of the rock above the cave.

It was astonishing! It was just as the tapestry showed it. Which meant that someone had been here before Jack – centuries before him – and seen exactly what he was seeing! It was the most exciting discovery in the world.

But his contemplation of the unicorn's cave was interrupted by Keras taking a lurching step towards the edge of the lake, and then dropping his head. Jack gave a startled cry and leaned back to save himself from slipping into the water.

He peered down between Keras's ears and caught his own reflection with a comic look of alarm still on his face. He thought at first that the unicorn was drinking, but Keras didn't disturb the water, not even with the tip of his horn. Jack realized that he was studying their reflection, drinking the image in, fixing it in his memory. Although Jack was sitting at an uncomfortable angle, he tried to compose himself, as though for a photograph, and for a moment the strange pair – the unicorn and the boy – gazed at themselves in the looking-glass lake.

Then Keras shifted his footing, and in doing so let one of his hooves disturb the water. Immediately unicorn and rider disappeared in a flurry of ripples, and the moon became crinkly like a scrumpled piece of paper.

Keras lifted his head, allowing Jack to slip back into a more comfortable position on his back, and started picking his way along the strand towards his cave.

At the entrance, Keras stopped. Jack looked into the darkness but could see nothing. He wasn't sure what was expected of him. With a shiver of his huge shoulders, the unicorn made his wishes clear. Jack slipped off his back and dropped onto the pebbles of the little beach.

With a nod that seemed to mean *Wait here*, Keras disappeared into the cave.

Jack strained his eyes, but could see nothing beyond the rocky mouth. He was excited, but he was also cold, and the pain in his ribs, forgotten during the ride and the excitement of discovery, had returned – an angry ache that flared whenever he moved a muscle.

He rubbed his side and winced. He was exhausted.

It was as though all the adrenalin had changed into some other chemical that flowed leadenly through his veins. A breeze blew across the water, sending chill little ripples whispering among the pebbles at his feet. The moon didn't look so friendly now, and stared stonily down on him, coldly indifferent. He thought longingly of his own bed. How long would this amazing – but testing – night go on?

There was a rattle of pebbles at the mouth of the cave, and there was Keras again. Jack noticed something hanging from his horn, a small object on a chain that glinted dully in the moonlight. The unicorn stopped in front of him and moved his head, making the object swing gently to and fro, inviting Jack to take it.

Jack reached out his hand, and felt the cold metal of a locket between his fingers. Keras dropped his head and stepped back, leaving it in Jack's palm, with the chain trailing from his fingers. Jack looked up, and Keras nuzzled him gently on the shoulder. He obviously wanted Jack to have it.

Jack started to investigate his gift, feeling for the catch. But Keras stamped his foot impatiently. He shook his great head and then pushed his horn up against the back of Jack's hand. *Not now*, he seemed to be saying. Then the horn described a circle in the air, before pointing at Jack's throat.

Slowly, in case he'd misinterpreted Keras's meaning, Jack put the chain around his neck and then tucked the locket down inside his shirt. The metal felt cold against his skin; it also seemed to burn with mystery.

But Jack would have to be patient. They needed to be off. Keras indicated a nearby boulder, and Jack quickly scrambled up again. He took one last look at the cave mouth, and at the wizened tree above it. He couldn't wait to compare it with the scene in the tapestry, but it had to be the same. There could be no doubt.

Then, with the moon gliding along beside them in the water, they set off. Keras headed unerringly for the hidden tunnel through the lake's sheltering stockade, and once again they pushed their way through, leaving Jack spitting insects out of his mouth and brushing them away from his nostrils.

Then they were back in the woods, making for the Great Glade.

Jack found this ride far less enjoyable than the others. The unicorn's stride seemed less regular, and he bounced about uncomfortably. Each jolt jarred his ribs. He wanted to put his hand to his side, but didn't dare let go of the mane as they twisted through the trees.

It was perhaps a good thing that he was distracted by the discomfort, because whenever there was a more open stretch of ground and Jack didn't have to duck and weave under branches, his head was deluged with thoughts.

How late was it, and how was he going to get home? Would Mr Finistaire still be waiting for him? Would he insist on taking him back to the big house and interrogating him before sending him back? And if he did, how much should Jack tell him? More than anything, he wanted to be alone, to inspect the locket and try to work out why Keras had entrusted it to him.

They were cantering up an incline now, but it was not one that Jack remembered from their outward journey. The next minute they were splashing through the stream, which they had certainly not crossed earlier.

Perhaps Keras was trying to confuse him, or cover their tracks. Jack suddenly felt afraid. The stakes had got higher, he felt sure of that. But he was uncertain what the game was, and what part he had to play in it.

After splashing through the stream, Keras tacked round. The trees became more stately and more widely spaced, and the going became easier. A few more swerves, and a last duck under a particularly low branch, and they were entering the glade. They galloped so smoothly over the springy turf that Jack felt a flicker of his previous exhilaration. But it wasn't enough to outweigh his anxieties, or dull the pain in his side.

Keras charged to the village end of the glade, and then stopped with a snort. Jack dismounted, the final jolt as he landed causing him to wince. He put his hand on Keras's neck for support, then looked anxiously towards the tree where he had left Mr Finistaire. He thought he could see a dark shadow, but there was no movement.

Keras showed no sign of having seen anything.

Jack kept his hand on the unicorn's warm neck, and then pressed his face against it to say goodbye. He wanted to say so much, to ask so many questions, but he knew that was impossible.

Then, with a shake of his head and a whinny, Keras turned and started to gallop away down the glade.

Jack stood and watched him.

'Magnificent . . .' Mr Finistaire had left his cover

and was standing close by. Jack looked at his face, expecting it to be lit by a smile, but it wasn't. He was simply staring down the glade after Keras.

Jack turned to take a last look at the unicorn, who suddenly veered off to the right, as though he'd changed his mind about going back to his cave.

Jack swivelled to follow the new direction he was taking. As he did so, something very strange struck him.

Mr Finistaire hadn't moved his head at all. He was still looking fixedly towards the far end of the glade.

Jack stared at him. And then he realized something extraordinary: Mr Finistaire couldn't see the unicorn at all.

CHAPTER 13

'He's right here. Would you like a word?'

Mr Finistaire was coming into the kitchen, where Jack sat in front of a plate empty apart from a few scattered crumbs of pie-crust.

'It's your mother. She says it's fine for you to stay over, if you'd like to.'

Jack took the phone, glancing down at his jeans, filthy with mud and grass-stains from the scramble back up to the buggy. His mum would be mad at him.

But when they spoke, she sounded surprisingly relaxed. She started talking excitedly about the orchid. Mr Finistaire had obviously prepared the ground with his customary charm and attention to detail.

'It sounds as though you were really helpful, love. Mr Finistaire says you've got the touch. I can't wait to see it.'

'See it?' Jack said, startled. He had a vision of his

mum and dad appearing at Charnley in the middle of the night.

'Yes, love. He's invited me over to tea tomorrow. Isn't that nice of him? Now you get off to bed. You must be exhausted. And Jack?'

'Yes, Mum?'

'Well done. I'm proud of you.'

Proud of me? Jack thought. *But all I've done is go along with Mr Finistaire conning you*. He felt a sudden surge of guilt as he handed the phone back. But then his mouth was wrenched wide by an irresistible yawn.

'Come on, I'll show you to your room,' Mr Finistaire said. 'You'll be tucked up in bed in less than five minutes.'

Jack got up to follow him out of the kitchen and into the long corridor. There weren't many lights on, so though he glanced up at the great tapestry as they passed it, he couldn't make out the unicorn or the cave. But he would look carefully in the morning.

The bedroom was the largest Jack had ever seen. The bed, with its covers folded back revealing crisp white linen sheets, looked so inviting, he wanted to throw himself down on it just as he was, unwashed and fully clothed.

'Bathroom's through there – there should be a toothbrush, face-cloth, towels, et cetera. Oh, look – Mrs Grout has managed to find some pyjamas for you.'

Jack saw them laid over the back of a chair, along with a pair of slippers on the seat. It was like being a guest at a five-star hotel.

'I hope you'll be comfortable. Sleep well – I'm sure you will. And Jack' – Mr Finistaire looked into his eyes – 'thank you for a quite extraordinary evening. We'll talk in the morning.' And then, with a cheery 'Goodnight', he was gone.

We'll talk in the morning.

That would mean Mr Finistaire asking him where he'd gone with Keras. But would it also mean his host owning up to the fact that he hadn't actually seen the unicorn? Jack doubted that. And if Mr Finistaire wouldn't tell the truth, why should he?

He felt inside his shirt and pulled out the locket. It bound him even closer to Keras. That had to be his first loyalty.

It didn't look anything special as it rested in his hand. He guessed it was made of silver, but it had tarnished with age. He held it up to the bedside light. It had suffered some blows during its existence, and there was a big dent on the lid.

But Jack had been given it by Keras, so it had to be special. His fingers trembled as he felt for the catch. Slowly the lid opened. And something fell out.

It was a lock of hair. In fact, it was two locks of hair. He scooped them up from the bedcover and examined them. One was dark, the other one lighter, and they had been loosely twined together. His fingers tingled as he touched them. He was probably the first person to do so in hundreds of years.

He put the locks of hair carefully down on the bedside table, and turned his attention to the locket itself.

It contained a tiny picture – in which a couple knelt facing each other. And behind them, as though blessing their union, stood a unicorn. Jack stared and stared. The picture was beautifully coloured and exquisitely detailed. And it had to be the same people as those in the tapestry – it just had to be.

But who were they? What had happened to them? And why did no trace of them or their story survive? Their story was obviously part of Keras's story – or that of his forebears. Jack's tired brain struggled to make sense of it all, but his eyes were closing and a huge yawn engulfed him. He was just about to shut the locket and force himself to get ready for bed, when his eye caught something on the inside of the lid.

There was an engraving in the silver. He brought it closer. It looked like a couple of snakes entwined with one another, but then he realized it must be lettering – highly elaborate, and very difficult to make out. But he guessed it was the initials of the two lovers. The locket was obviously a love token, but how it had ended up in Keras's cave was a mystery.

He yawned again, then replaced the locks of hair in the locket and closed the lid, which gave a satisfying little click. Putting it back around his neck, he went into the bathroom.

There was a huge mirror above the basin. He stared at himself and was shocked at how knocked about he looked. He undid his shirt to inspect his side. It didn't look too bad. There was a bruise coming up, and it was very tender to the touch, but he didn't think anything was broken. He shook his head, disappointed in himself. If he hadn't flinched, the horn wouldn't have caught him. It wasn't Keras's fault.

As Mr Finistaire had said, there was everything he

needed – a brand-new toothbrush, a clean flannel, a fresh cake of soap, and the most wonderfully soft towels. He washed, and brushed his teeth, then went and got into the pyjamas laid out for him, and climbed into bed.

He only just managed to turn the light off before he fell into a very deep sleep.

'Ah, the old tapestry!'

Jack gave a start. He had been so absorbed in studying the top corner of the vast hunting scene that he hadn't heard Mr Finistaire approach.

'It's strange that they put the unicorn out of the way up there, isn't it? Far more interesting than the couple of lovebirds in the foreground. But then, they are almost certainly real people, while the unicorn – well, the artist probably thought of it as a decorative flourish, something to fill an awkward gap in his picture.'

Mr Finistaire must have caught the shadow of doubt that crossed Jack's face. 'You disagree?'

Suddenly he was leaning down, looking directly into Jack's eyes. 'Tell me.'

'He knew.' Jack felt confused. He hadn't meant to say anything.

'Knew what, Jack?'

Jack found he couldn't meet Mr Finistaire's eye. He looked down at the parquet flooring of the corridor. 'He knew . . . he was real.'

'Yes,' said Mr Finistaire, looking up at the tapestry again. 'I do believe you're right. And I'd very much like to know why you're so sure. But now, it's time for breakfast. Come on, let's see what Mrs Grout has laid on for us.'

He led the way into the morning room, where there was a table set for two.

'Ha!' exclaimed Mr Finistaire. 'I should invite visitors more often – I don't normally get this sort of spread.'

There was fruit juice, yoghurts, toast, three types of marmalade, and, under silver salvers, a choice of bacon, sausages, tomatoes, mushrooms, and two perfectly poached eggs.

'Tuck in. We're in good time to get you home and changed for school, so don't stint yourself.'

Jack didn't. It was the best breakfast ever, and Mr Finistaire kept him company by loading *his* plate as well. They ate in silence for a while.

'Anything your mother particularly likes? For her tea?' Mr Finistaire enquired after a while.

Jack stopped to think. He could only think of his mum as the provider of food. She was the one bringing hot dishes from the hob, serving out the vegetables, asking his dad if he wanted more. She was always last to sit down and first to get up from the table, clearing the dirty dishes, spooning out tinned apricots and custard.

'Cake,' he said. He couldn't remember ever seeing his mum eat cake, but everybody liked cake.

'Oh, there'll be cake,' Mr Finistaire said with a smile. 'We'll put on quite a spread. But now, young man, we'd better get you off to school.'

He stood up. 'I think we want to draw as little attention to last night as possible, don't you? I'll get Sefton to take you back in the Land Rover. But I'll send him over in the big car to collect you for tea. Your mother would like that, wouldn't she?'

Jack nodded.

'Good. I thought so. Right, off you go. And' – here his voice became more solemn – 'thank you again for last night, Jack. Thank you very much indeed. We'll see you later. Have a good day at school.'

'What's that round your neck?'

Jack put a telltale hand up to conceal the chain.

Luke reached his hand up, but Jack slapped it away.

'Go on, show us.'

'It's nothing,' Jack said sullenly. He'd known it would be risky keeping the locket around his neck, but he couldn't bear to take it off.

'Did you steal it from the big house?' Luke asked. 'I bet it's a diamond.'

'It's a love-token,' said Dan, with a challenging smirk; 'from Harriet.'

'Mind your own business,' Jack said, feeling his face going hot. He walked away from them.

'Not good enough for him now,' Dan said pointedly to Luke.

Jack wanted to turn back and explain, but he knew it would be useless.

He was sad as well as angry. He hadn't seen much of his friends lately, but it wasn't his fault – there'd just been too much going on. But he couldn't talk to them about any of it. It would have been good to see them after school, but with his mum being invited over to Charnley, there was no chance.

He banged his way into the boys' toilet, and looked in the mirror. His face was hot and sweaty, and the chain was just visible under his collar. He took off the locket hurriedly, pausing to enjoy the feel of it in his palm before thrusting it into his pocket. Then he turned on the cold tap and splashed cold water all over his face and round the back of his neck.

That helped a bit, but it didn't solve the problem of how to keep on side with his two best friends. And it certainly didn't help with the problem of Mr Finistaire. Or with working out what Keras wanted of him, and what he was to do about it all. He also felt a sense of dread about going back to Charnley; he just knew his mum would be embarrassing. His face was going hot again.

The bell rang for the end of break. Well, at least the horrors of French would keep his mind occupied for a bit.

'*Je m'appelle Jack, et j'ai onze ans.*'

He stuck his tongue out at himself in the mirror, but it didn't make him smile.

'It's so kind of you to make the time, Mrs Henley.'

Mr Finistaire met them under the portico at the front of the house.

Jack's mum made a big fuss, smoothing down her dress – her best dress – and patting her hair into shape, before taking the hand he was patiently holding out to her.

Jack rolled his eyes. The drive over had been bad enough, with royal waves at astonished friends whom they passed in the high street, accompanied by asides like: 'I bet Mrs Jordan never thought she'd see me in a Bentley.'

Once they had left the village, his mum fidgeted nervously with her handbag, which she eventually opened.

Oh no, thought Jack – but yes: out came the lipstick and the vanity mirror, despite the fact that she'd spent at least forty minutes in the bathroom before Sefton arrived.

Jack had glanced at the chauffeur, hoping he wouldn't notice what was going on behind him. Sefton sat as impassive as an Easter Island statue, barely moving a muscle as he steered the car smoothly along the empty road.

'Are we nearly there?'

Jack had to smile at being asked that by his mum after all the years he'd spent driving her mad with the very same question. 'Another five minutes, Mum,' he'd said, trying to suppress the fear that it was going to be the worst afternoon of his life.

Mr Finistaire did his very best to put her at ease, ushering them through the front doors and letting the size and grandeur of the place sink in.

'I can't believe it. It's so . . . it's so . . .'

'It is a bit overwhelming,' Mr Finistaire agreed. 'I've lived here most of my life, but I still have to pinch myself sometimes. Mind you, it takes an awful lot of cleaning to keep it looking like this.'

He laughed his friendly laugh, and Jack could see his mum relaxing, even as she echoed the laughter with a slightly false peal of her own.

'And as for the maintenance . . . you can't imagine. Happily not your problem. I'll give you the grand tour later, but first come and have a nice cup of tea.'

He ushered them into the morning room, where Mrs Grout had set out a magnificent array of cakes and sandwiches, scones and teacakes. There were also two teapots.

'I sometimes prefer China tea,' Mr Finistaire said.

'Oh, so do I.'

No you don't, thought Jack.

'Splendid . . .' Mr Finistaire poured a very pale-looking liquid into a cup for her. There was a pause. Jack's mum looked at it, and Jack could see she was wishing she could change her mind.

'A slice of lemon?' Mr Finistaire pushed a bowl of thinly sliced lemon with a pair of silver tongs across the table towards her. 'Just freshens it up a bit, I find,' he said, pouring a second cup for himself.

Jack's mum reached for the tongs, which unhelpfully gathered three slices of lemon. One of the slices slipped out and fell on the tablecloth.

Mr Finistaire raised his hand to cut short any apologies. 'I do that all the time.' Then, lowering his voice to a conspiratorial whisper, he said: 'Actually, I normally just use my fingers.'

His expression was so comic that Jack's mum had to put her hand over her mouth to suppress a giggle.

Mr Finistaire bunched up his shoulders and let his eyebrows ripple. Jack looked up at the grim portrait of Sir Archibald. At least they weren't having tea with him.

Rescued from disaster at the outset, the tea party went very well. Mr Finistaire brushed aside Jack's mum's attempts to apologize for the damage inflicted upon the car – 'All forgotten, I assure you' – and went on to say some very nice things indeed about Jack.

'A very special boy – a good, hard worker – never complains, just gets on with it. And such a fine touch with plants and flowers, I really do think he may have a future there. Amazing how life works out, isn't it? A casually propelled pebble, and a green-fingered genius is revealed!'

Jack could see that his mum was having difficulty believing this, but Mr Finistaire was bringing her round by the sheer force of his personality.

'As soon as we've had tea, I'll show you what Jack helped with last night. A very delicate operation, as I said on the phone. The Lady of the Moon – that's what we call her – needs the most sensitive handling. Jack was terrific.'

Ten minutes later, Mr Finistaire got to his feet. Jack wolfed down his last slice of delicious sponge cake, and watched his mum brush an imaginary crumb off her lap.

Down the familiar corridor they went, though Jack noticed that Mr Finistaire didn't stop to show off the tapestry. Better to focus on what they were meant to have been doing, he thought, looking down at his hands and trying to imagine them delving into the soft soil to ease the orchid's roots free.

When they stepped through into the first of the walled enclosures, Jack noticed that something had changed.

Mr Finistaire caught his look of puzzlement. 'Yes, we've had to take Sefton's net down. We've got a marquee coming for the special gathering next week. An awful lot of people coming. Mrs Grout will be rushed off her feet.'

Jack looked at where the wicket had been, at the three stump holes and the dozens of marks where Sefton's express deliveries had landed on the grass.

They passed into the second walled garden and made their way between the yews.

'Be prepared to be amazed,' Mr Finistaire said as he unlocked the glasshouse door.

Jack was expecting his mum to be amazed. What he wasn't expecting was that *he* would be amazed too. But he was. For there, just a few metres away from the door, was the orchid, standing high above them on the raised wooden platform from which the walkway extended into the depths of Mr Finistaire's miniature rainforest. And it had been transplanted into a magnificent urn with two ornate handles – although it would have taken a giant to lift it.

Mr Finistaire gave him a look, registering his surprise with a raised eyebrow and a slight incline of his head, as if to say: *You weren't expecting that, were you?* Then he launched into an extraordinary account of what had happened last night. It was so good that Jack found himself believing it, even though he knew that none of it was true.

'You see, in her natural habitat, the soil is naturally fed by the rest of the forest – leaf mould, and so on.'

Jack's mum nodded, her brow furrowed in concentration.

'But here – in captivity, as it were' – Mr Finistaire laughed – 'the soil doesn't get that. We can feed the soil and we do, but after a while it's exhausted. Hence the need to transplant her into fresh soil, newly fertilized.'

Jack looked at the orchid. It seemed to have grown since yesterday. Perhaps fertilized by all the lies told about it.

Mr Finistaire continued. 'This is a very difficult thing to do – difficult and dangerous. The roots can't tolerate sunlight. Direct sunlight would . . .' He shook his head to show what a catastrophe that would be. 'Of course, we have artificial light. But all the experts say that even that is risky. Everyone agrees that moonlight is the safest – the kindest – sort of light to do it by. Which is what we did, and where Jack came in.'

He beamed. 'The roots are so long,' he went on, stretching out his arms, 'and so fragile, that you need a combination of brawn and delicacy. Well, my chaps have the brawn all right. But you need small hands to reach in and coax the roots out. And then, vitally, to brush away the old soil.'

He broke off and looked down at Jack. His mum looked at him as well, and smiled.

Jack smiled shyly back. He pictured himself brushing the soil from the long, delicate roots – dangling down like the tentacles of an octopus, while Mr Grout and Sefton supported the plant, holding it by the thickest part of the stem.

'And then, of course,' Mr Finistaire went on, 'those freshly cleaned roots had to be positioned – carefully – in the new soil. A very painstaking operation. Which is why, of course, it got so late, Mrs Henley.' He put his hands together and smiled. He looked like a magician who had just performed, effortlessly, a really difficult trick.

Which, in a way, of course, he had.

'Come up and see.'

They all climbed onto the little stage on which the orchid's urn had been placed. At first Jack's mum just looked; then she put her nose up to it. Her eyes closed, and a slightly dreamy look swam across her face.

'It's lovely,' she said eventually. 'Very special.'

She put her hand on Jack's shoulder. Jack just managed to stop himself from twisting free. Although he was pleased that Mr Finistaire had convinced his mum with his fictional account of the previous night, he still felt horribly uncomfortable about the whole subterfuge. Getting all this praise and attention for something he simply hadn't done just seemed wrong. What would his mum think if she ever found out the truth?

Mr Finistaire smiled at the pair of them. 'We're very pleased with him,' he said. 'And you know, I was thinking we might change the conditions under which he comes here.'

Jack's mum looked at him enquiringly.

'Yes, I think he's passed the weeding stage. He's proved himself to be hard-working – and highly talented. I think we can forget the unfortunate accident with the car – you wouldn't know it had ever happened now it's been repaired. And so, from now on, I propose a regular addition to Jack's pocket money for the more advanced work he is so obviously capable of doing. Of course, if you agree . . .'

Jack's mum looked slightly flustered, but said, 'Oh, well, if you really mean it – and Jack's OK with it – yes.'

'Jack?' Mr Finistaire gave him a businesslike look.

'Sure,' Jack said.

'Well, say thank you, Jack,' his mum said, nudging him with her elbow.

Mr Finistaire raised a hand, as though taking Jack's thanks for granted. 'You might like to talk it over with Mr Henley.'

'Oh, I'm sure he'll be fine about it. He always enjoys coming over for the shoots. He'd be ever so pleased for Jack to work for you as well.'

'Just let me know,' said Mr Finistaire.

Then he led them along the walkway to see the pond and the hummingbirds, before, with a last look at the orchid, they went back out into the walled garden.

'Now I've got my guide's hat on, perhaps you'd like the grand tour of the house?'

'I don't want to take up any more of your time,' Jack's mum said, but Mr Finistaire dismissed the notion with a wave of his hand.

'It will be my pleasure.'

They retraced their steps, and as they were

walking along the great corridor, Mr Finistaire stopped outside the map room.

'Jack, why don't you go and browse in there for a few minutes?' Turning to Jack's mum, he said: 'I showed Jack around yesterday, while we were waiting for the moon. He probably won't want to do it all again.'

Rapidly trying to remember something else that hadn't happened, Jack said: 'You'll enjoy it, Mum,' and went into the map room. There were two very important things he wanted to do, and here was his opportunity.

As the footsteps retreated along the parquet floor, he moved over to the shelves and started pulling down the great calf-bound volumes of estate maps. The earliest were the crudest, showing unending woodland divided by the odd track and the stream. But things gradually changed. The cottage appeared, with its track to the bottom of the village. The Great Glade became a feature about the same time, and contour lines began to appear. But nowhere, in any of the maps, was there any trace of the looking-glass lake. It was as if the map-makers had never ventured into that corner of the estate. All they came up with was unbroken woodland.

But someone had once known about it. The artist who designed the tapestry had clearly seen it with his own eyes, or at least been given a very accurate account of it by someone who had. Those who knew had kept it secret, while at the same time announcing it in the most public way possible – in the tapestry.

Jack went to the door and listened. He could still hear Mr Finistaire's voice from further down the corridor. Jack had something he wanted to do when they went upstairs. But in the meantime he turned his attention to the volumes that contained ground plans of the house.

The one he had looked at before was definitely missing. Had Mr Finistaire taken it away for some perfectly innocent reason, or was he deliberately keeping it away from Jack?

Jack pulled down volume after dusty volume, but none of them offered what he was looking for. He didn't know why he was becoming so obsessed with the extension, except that it was strange that such a massive part of the building was treated as though it didn't exist. A banqueting hall would surely be of as much interest as the ballroom? And even if it had been closed up, there must have been a way into it.

But nowhere inside the house had he seen a door that could give access to it. And its main feature from the outside was that it *had* no features. Along the entire wall there wasn't a single window, and certainly no doors that Jack had seen.

He might be on some wild-goose chase, but the thought that there could be some dark mystery at the heart of Charnley and that, in some strange way, it was related to the story depicted in the tapestry, and so to that of Keras and his forebears, nagged away at him.

Was Mr Finistaire protecting a secret within the house just as Jack was trying to guard his secret about Keras's cave and the looking-glass lake? He was determined to find out.

Shutting the last folio and putting it back in its place, he went over to the door again. Surely Mr Finistaire had taken his mum upstairs by now. He slipped out of the map room and looked up and down the great corridor, listening hard.

Nothing.

Jack walked along to the tapestry and stood in front of it. A shaft of afternoon sunlight fell on the foreground, where the two lovers gazed into each other's eyes. He had hardly given them a second glance on previous occasions. But now he looked closely – as closely as he had ever looked at anything. And yes, he was as certain as he could be that this was the pair in the miniature in the locket.

He wished he had it with him to compare it with the tapestry, but the episode with Luke and Dan had shown him the folly of wearing it around his neck. He'd wrapped it in a handkerchief and put it under his mattress at home, but decided to bring it with him on a future visit to Charnley.

In the meantime, he had another interest in the tapestry. He wanted to know what was behind it. The obvious place for a door into the annexe would be along the corridor. The only place it could be was behind the tapestry.

The trouble was, the tapestry was enormous. Laid out flat, it would have been far bigger than the lounge at home. And it was obviously very heavy – not just a big curtain you could push aside. It hung from a lengthy pole high up near the ceiling, and was then secured at regular intervals along both sides, right down to the parquet floor. The wall behind it was virtually sealed off.

Looking up and down the corridor, Jack knelt down to see if there was any gap between the bottom of the tapestry and the floor. There wasn't – at least none big enough to allow him to get a finger underneath. But something flat – something that would slide along the floor – might work.

He started going through his pockets, and found a piece of paper he'd been doodling on in French and had been forced to hide quickly when Mrs Hinton made one of her rare excursions to the back of the classroom. He folded it over two or three times length-wise and then, kneeling down, pushed it under the tapestry.

There was skirting board all along the corridor, and that obviously continued. The folded paper barely went in a centimetre. Jack shuffled along on his knees. Every now and then he had to remove the paper when he came to one of the points where the tapestry was secured.

Each time he withdrew it, it brought out little telltale balls of fluff and dust. He plucked them away with his fingers and hid them in his pocket.

Skirting board . . . skirting board . . . skirting board. Out, and a quick pinch of dust. Under again. Skirting board . . . skirting board . . . skirting board.

Then two things happened. The skirting board abruptly ended – a couple of metres from the end of the tapestry – and at the same time he heard voices. Or rather, Mr Finistaire's voice and his mother's laugh.

He just had time to assure himself that there was a gap in the skirting board – the paper went in five or six centimetres. There wasn't time to discover how wide the gap was, but it was an odds-on certainty that this was the door to the banquet hall. And it had quite clearly been deliberately concealed behind the tapestry.

Jack found his heart beating with the excitement of his discovery. But terrified of being found snooping, he scrambled to his feet, scrunching the paper into a ball and stuffing it into his pocket. His fingers, he noticed, were black with dust, but he didn't have time to worry about that.

Mr Finistaire's voice was getting louder – they must be descending the grand staircase. He might have time to get back to the map room, but didn't want to be seen scuttling guiltily along the corridor. It would be better to go and meet them as they came down the stairs.

'Ah, there you are, Jack,' Mr Finistaire said as they met in the entrance hall. 'I think I've exhausted your mother's patience, and you obviously got bored of waiting. I'm afraid my house is just too big!'

'Oh, it's wonderful,' Jack's mum said. 'I can't thank you enough, Mr Finistaire. You've been so kind.'

For once Jack was grateful as he listened to her gushing on about all the things she had seen.

'You don't need to thank me at all.' Mr Finistaire beamed at her. 'I should rather thank *you*. Jack is a real find, and has a rare talent. As I say, I think we can agree that his period of penance is over; but I would be mortified if he shook the dust of Charnley from his feet and never returned to us. He will come again, won't he?'

'Of course! Any time – any time at all.' Jack's mum turned and smiled at him. 'That's all right with you, isn't it, love?'

Jack dropped his head. He hated that grown-up thing of talking about you as though you weren't there, and then remembering that you were and trying to involve you as an afterthought.

'It's fine, Mum.' *Now can we go, please?*

'Excellent,' said Mr Finistaire. 'I'll get Sefton round with the car, and he'll whisk you back to the village in no time. It really has been a great pleasure.'

Here he made a little bow to Jack's mum, who

simpered in a way that showed she was both pleased and embarrassed at the same time.

'And we'll see you again very shortly, Jack.' Mr Finistaire gave him one of his penetrating looks, as if to signal that there was unfinished business between them.

Jack just wanted to be alone to think about it all – especially his discovery of the secret door behind the tapestry.

CHAPTER 14

Jack was practising long passes with Dan and Luke at break when a foot suddenly shot out and trapped the ball.

It was Harriet.

'What's going on?' she demanded fiercely.

'Going on? We're just having a kick-about.'

'Don't get smart with me,' Harriet said. 'When's my big day? When am I going to get my prize?'

Jack stared at her. The events of the last couple of days had been so overwhelming, he had forgotten all about her stupid prize.

'Don't gawp at me like a goldfish,' she snapped, rolling the tennis ball vehemently under her shoe. 'You go over there all the time,' she said. 'Even your mother gets invited to tea. Driving around in Mr Finistaire's Bentley, waving as though she were royalty.'

Jack sighed. Gossip travelled around the village like wildfire.

'So – when am I going? When's he going to invite me?'

'I don't know,' Jack said, and saw immediately that it was the wrong answer.

The small foot drew back, away from the tennis ball, poised to kick it.

'Don't do that,' he said. 'It's not my fault—'

'I know it's not,' Harriet said, dropping her foot.

Now she looked miserable rather than angry. Jack felt sorry for her.

'He's just forgotten, hasn't he?'

'No. I know he hasn't – it's just that there's a lot going on. He's having some huge party next week – they're putting up a marquee and all that, so there's a lot to organize. But he hasn't forgotten. He mentioned it yesterday.'

Harriet's face lit up. 'He did? Really? What did he say?'

'Oh, just that he was going to let you know this week – before the end of term.'

'Let me know what?'

'What day.'

'Really? You're not just saying that because I've got my foot on your ball?'

Jack glanced down and then looked her in the

eye. 'Really, Miss Moneypenny,' he said in his best/worst Sean Connery accent.

She gave him a brilliant smile, tapped the ball back to him and went back to her friends with an ill-suppressed skip.

'Got a date then, lover boy?'

Dan was at his elbow. Jack whisked the ball away and hit a sweet pass to Luke.

He didn't know how much more of this he could take, but at least the end of term was in sight.

Once again, Jack eluded Luke and Dan at the end of the school day. He felt bad – he missed them, even though Dan's teasing about Harriet was getting on his nerves. But there was just too much going on in his life. He needed space to think, to try to confront all the things that were worrying him.

He cut away off the high street and retraced his steps of the previous week, ending up in the privacy of the churchyard. He sat on a bench and eyed the nearest headstone. He could just make out, through the patina of lichens, the legend: ELISA, WIFE OF THE ABOVE, AGED 69. Her worries were over, he thought grimly. His were most certainly not.

Foremost among them was Mr Finistaire. Or rather what he was up to, and what role he, Jack, was playing. Although Mr Finistaire remained his usual charming, pleasant and intriguing self, there were clearly things he was not telling Jack – like the fact that even when Keras was standing right in front of him, he couldn't see him. That was certainly shocking, but more worrying was the idea that Mr Finistaire had a completely different agenda. Jack had gone along with the line that their mission was to save and protect the unicorn, and to do this, as with tigers in their few remaining habitats, they needed to find out as much as possible about him. Jack trusted Mr Finistaire; he *had* to, after revealing so much to him. It was impossible even to think that his trust could be betrayed. But the seeds of doubt had been sown. He questioned everything – everything about Mr Finistaire; everything about Charnley.

Which brought him back to the mystery annexe. He didn't know why he was obsessing about it so much. It was just an old wing of the ancient house that they didn't need any more. If Mr Finistaire had waved an arm to it on Jack's first visit and said, 'That's the old banqueting hall. It hasn't been used in fifty years,' he wouldn't have given it another thought. But because Mr Finistaire hadn't made any reference to it at all, and because it had clearly been hidden, in so far as you could hide something that big, it had wormed its way into Jack's thought processes.

There was no reason to link the banqueting hall to Keras, just because its door was concealed by the great tapestry with its graphic depiction of the looking-glass lake and Keras's cave. But Jack was still consumed by an anguished curiosity about it – about what it might contain, what it might be used for. He felt a sick unease about what activities might be sheltered from view by those high, blank, windowless walls.

All he wanted was a glimpse of its interior, even if he saw only the dust-covered humps of long-abandoned tables and chairs. It would set his mind at rest, and he could certainly do with some peace of mind.

He got to his feet. Thinking about things only took you so far. Restless and dissatisfied, he started walking rapidly down the hill towards the cottage.

* * *

'Mr Finistaire rang. He wants you to go over there tomorrow. Such a nice man.'

'Don't start getting ideas above your station, woman.' Jack's dad looked up from the table. 'I don't know,' he said, shaking the paper. 'Having tea at the big house, being shown round by Mr Finistaire himself. And you . . .' He looked at Jack. 'I can't believe it. You cause three hundred quid's worth of damage to his car, and next thing you're going over there every other day being groomed for the job of head gardener. You've never done a stroke in ours. I don't know what's going on, I really don't. All I do know is that in a few weeks' time, I'll be stamping across the estate shooing his stupid pheasants into the air so his equally stupid millionaire pals can take pot shots at them.' He retreated huffily behind his paper.

'Mr Finistaire doesn't shoot.' Jack said it without thinking. Immediately he wished he hadn't.

'And you'd know?' Jack's dad lowered the paper once more. 'Listen, son, I've been there, remember. I've seen him. He's got one of the smartest guns money can buy. And believe me, he likes to take a pop. Not that he ever seems to hit anything.'

Because he's not aiming to hit anything, Jack said in his head.

'So what made you think he doesn't shoot?'

Jack looked away. 'It was just something he said. I must have got it wrong.'

'You must have, son. Like I said to your mother, don't go getting ideas. Just because Mr Finistaire's taken a bit of a shine to you doesn't mean you're going to be anything other than what you are.'

'Leave the boy alone. He's doing really well. And Mr Finistaire said—'

'*Mr Finistaire said!* Listen to yourself, woman. One afternoon over there, and it's turned your head. Mr Finistaire may be a decent sort – I'm not saying he's not. But he's on a different planet from us. In a different solar system. He's been very good about Jack, I grant you. But that's all. Don't go building impossible fantasies about what he might do for him later, because it's just a nonsense. And you' – again he swung his head in Jack's direction – 'if I ever think you're getting too big for your boots, I'll stop you going. For your own good.'

'You're jealous,' Jack's mum said. She was about to put a plate of sausages down on the table, but Jack's dad banged his fist down on it, and stood up.

'Jealous? Don't make me laugh.'

He certainly didn't look like laughing. Jack hadn't seen him this angry in ages.

'That's it. I'm going down The Feathers – where people still live in the real world.'

Jack felt awful. He hated it when his mum and dad rowed, but being the cause of it made it ten times worse.

They'd gone into the hall, but he could hear angry voices, and a minute later the front door slammed.

His mum came back into the kitchen with a flush on her face and a tear in her eye.

'Sorry, Mum.'

'There's nothing for you to apologize for. It's not you that begrudges other people the chance to enjoy the good things in life, if only for one afternoon. I had a ride in a posh car and a nice tea, and Mr Finistaire took the time to show me around his lovely house. Why can't I be allowed that – without being accused of losing my grip on reality, and filling your head with nonsense? Tell me that.'

She sat down at the table and raised her apron to her eyes. She didn't cry very often – Jack could only think of three or four times – but he hated it more than anything.

'It's all right, Mum,' he said, without conviction,

reaching out timidly and touching her sleeve.

She suddenly turned and pulled him to her in a great untidy hug. 'Oh, Jack,' she sobbed. 'I work so hard, slaving away to put food on the table, day in, day out, and I have one afternoon off – out of the blue, a treat – when it's me being waited on hand and foot for once – well, I hope he chokes on his beer and serve him right!'

She brushed a tear away. 'Better eat the sausages before they get cold,' she said, putting some on his plate.

But Jack noticed that she didn't take any herself, and suddenly found that he wasn't as hungry as he'd thought he was.

'Ah, yes, Harriet . . .' Mr Finistaire frowned slightly. 'I hadn't forgotten, but thank you for reminding me. There's a lot on at the moment. If it were done, then it were well it were done quickly, as the Bard says.' He smiled, briefly catching Jack's eye. 'Next week – it's the end of the school term, isn't it. What about the day after that – before the gathering. And I think her mother wanted you to be around. Would you join us?'

Jack nodded.

Mr Finistaire was just as friendly and open as he had always been. But somehow Jack felt as if everything had changed – and not just between them. The whole house was buzzing with activity, and Mr Finistaire was obviously having to supervise all the arrangements for the great gathering. Mrs Grout was constantly bustling about, giving orders to the staff recruited for the occasion, and her husband was more in evidence too – driving around in the buggy on errands Jack could only guess at.

'It's the biggest thing we've done in years, and frankly I'm dreading it.' Mr Finistaire smiled at Jack. 'Nothing I can do about it though. It's a tradition. My great-grandfather Archibald started it, and my grandfather carried it on, and so did my father. There are people from families who have been coming for over a hundred years. And of course, I get invited back – see some very splendid castles and palaces, I can tell you.'

He laughed. 'And that's the point really. We show each other things. The most exquisite things we can find – and there' – he waved towards the glasshouse – 'is my trump card: the rarest orchid in the world. And of course we don't just admire these amazing things; we talk seriously about preserving and protecting them. There are some highly influential people – people with the power and the money to get good things done.'

Jack imagined these rich and powerful people queuing dutifully to climb the steps to see the Lady of the Moon, with Mr Finistaire standing by, enjoying their astonishment.

They were sitting at a table under a huge parasol, only a few metres away from the glasshouse. It was as if Mr Finistaire needed to be near his prize exhibit.

Jack took a sip of lemonade, and watched a couple of butterflies playing a lazy hide-and-seek in the nearest flowerbed. There was the murmur of bees going about their business in the lavender bushes. The only discordant noise was the distant buzz of what sounded like a chainsaw, but which, Mr Finistaire explained, was in fact Sefton on his rallying bike – 'He misses his net, I'm afraid.'

It didn't disturb him much. Peace reigned under the parasol, and Jack even began to feel he could relax.

Big mistake.

'We never really got around to talking about your adventure the other night . . .' Mr Finistaire was looking at him across the table, his head cocked to one side.

No, they hadn't, and Jack had hoped they wouldn't, either – while knowing, of course, that they would.

He took another sip of lemonade to buy time. His brain suddenly felt tired again. But he knew that if he was going to lie, or at least conceal the truth, he would have to be at his sharpest to be a match for Mr Finistaire.

'You were gone for quite a long time.'

'I'm sorry,' Jack said lamely.

'Sorry! Don't be sorry. I wouldn't have blamed you if you'd ridden all through the night! I didn't begrudge you a moment of it. It must have been wonderful.'

'It was.'

'Tell me all about it. Where did you go – where did he take you?'

This was the moment of maximum danger, Jack thought. He must keep his guard up, but at the same time he mustn't seem evasive.

'I'm not sure, really. He went so fast, and you have to watch out for branches and things, so it's hard to know where you're going.'

'Of course. Not to mention the sheer thrill of the ride. I do understand.' Mr Finistaire caught Jack's eye and smiled.

Jack dropped his gaze, and looked stupidly at the slice of lemon resting on the ice-cubes in the bottom of his glass.

'Did you recognize anywhere you went?' There was a slightly pleading note to Mr Finistaire's voice. 'Did you go up on the ridge?'

Jack shook his head. At least, he thought, they weren't doing this over the map with the sticky-back spots on, though he was quite certain that any details he did give would be recorded back in the map room.

'So, did you go in the opposite direction? In a new direction?'

Jack picked up his glass and drained it. It was a desperate measure because now it was gone, it was gone. *Think, think*, he urged himself. *You've got to say something – something convincing*.

'It wasn't somewhere we'd been before. I'm sure of that.'

'In which direction?'

'Don't know – away from the house, I think.' Jack felt he had to say something, but regretted giving even that much away.

'And did you stop?'

'Stop?'

Yes, we stopped. Keras took me to the looking-glass lake, and I waited outside his cave, and he gave me the locket. With Mr Finistaire's mild eye on him, it would have been the easiest thing to say. But he knew he would never forgive himself if he said it, and he was glad he'd resisted the temptation to bring the locket with him. He knew that under close questioning he'd have done something stupid, like put his hand in his pocket to feel it.

'Why would we stop?'

'Why indeed? I just thought . . . the time you were away. You might have stopped somewhere.' Mr Finistaire looked at Jack, his eyebrows slightly raised.

'We did stop. I remember now.'

Fool, you stupid, stupid fool, Jack thought. What was it Dad always said? *If you're in a hole, stop digging.*

'There was a tree. A big tree, blown down by a storm. Years ago probably.'

'And you stopped by the tree?'

'Yes,' Jack said miserably.

'I expect you were glad of the rest.'

'I was.'

'And did you dismount?'

Jack thought, but he was beyond extricating himself, and just went on doggedly, saying the first thing that came into his head. 'Yes . . . I got off onto the trunk.'

'What kind of tree was it? Can you remember?'

'It was an ash.'

'You could make that out, could you?'

'I think it was an ash.'

'Well, the moon was very bright. I do remember we lost a big ash a number of years ago. So you explored the fallen ash. And then you came back?'

Yes, Jack thought wearily, *we came back. And you couldn't see him, could you?*

But he knew Mr Finistaire wouldn't admit to that.

'You seemed very knocked up. You seemed troubled by your side. Did you have a fall?'

Of course – Mr Finistaire wouldn't have seen Keras's horn glancing off his ribcage.

'No, I didn't fall. I got a bit of a whack from a branch.'

Jack's hand stole towards his rib and gave the affected area a tentative rub. The bruise was quite dramatic, but the sharp pain had been replaced by a dull ache.

'I'm fine now,' he said. 'I'm so glad you let me stay.'

'Don't mention it. It was the only sensible thing to do. You really were all in. And now,' Mr Finistaire said, 'you can repay me by helping to plan some diversions for our prize-winning artist.'

Jack was surprised – and relieved – that the interrogation seemed to be over. But at the same time he felt bad about not telling the truth. He was sure Mr Finistaire knew he was holding things back – and that he was disappointed in him.

But, he realized, that was how it had to be now. Mr Finistaire had his agenda, whatever that might be, and he, Jack, had his. He had to find out more about the annexe. It might just be full of discarded furniture under dustsheets, but somehow he didn't think so. He was determined to find out, one way or the other, even though he had no idea how.

Obviously the one thing he couldn't do was show any interest in it. Had things been different, he might have found a good moment to ask about it. But that was now out of the question.

As they passed through the kitchen, he noticed that a vast array of pans had been lifted down from their hooks, and all sorts of other things had been brought out of their cupboards.

'The delights of mass catering,' Mr Finistaire said. 'Poor Mrs Grout – she's cleaning every last ladle we possess! I should have had young Harriet over before now. It's going to be mayhem next week. But come on – let's go and plan out what we're going to do with her. She seemed a nice little girl. I want her to enjoy herself.'

They passed the map room. Jack was glad he wasn't asked to try and plot the route of his most recent ride on the estate map, though he had no doubt that Mr Finistaire would be poring over it with his little coloured dots before too long.

Nor did they linger by the tapestry. Jack couldn't help looking up to the top corner, and there, sure enough, was the cave and the tree, just as he had seen them with his own eyes. The tree, he noted, was in much better shape – vibrant with leaves, in contrast to the leafless, lifeless thing of the present.

And of course, behind the tapestry there lay the mystery of the banquet hall. If only he had X-ray vision that could penetrate the ancient stitches and reveal the door he was certain he'd found the previous day . . .

Mr Finistaire led the way into the morning room. He ushered Jack to a seat and produced a notebook from his pocket.

'Harriet's big day,' he said, writing on a blank page with an expensive-looking fountain pen. 'What do you think? The grand tour for starters? She struck me as a bright girl. I wouldn't want to bore her.'

'She's the cleverest in the class,' said Jack, happy to have something positive and uncomplicated to contribute. 'She loves history and art, and all that.'

'Good,' Mr Finistaire said, writing in his notebook.

It *was* good, Jack agreed. The longer Harriet was tied up with Mr Finistaire, the better. He didn't know how he was going to exploit it, but if the two of them cancelled each other out, it would give him the chance to probe more deeply into Charnley's secrets.

'I have to say,' Mr Finistaire said, looking up, 'your mother took a keen interest in the house. A very nice woman. I enjoyed meeting her.'

Well, he didn't have *to say it*, Jack thought.

'Back to Harriet . . . A walk round the gardens, I think, leading to the glasshouse. I can't imagine her not being impressed by the Lady of the Moon, can you?'

'No,' Jack said.

'Perhaps she'd like to do a picture of it? I was thinking of getting her a box of paints as part of her prize.'

'She'd love that,' Jack said, thinking that painting it would certainly keep her occupied for a while.

That seemed to be Mr Finistaire's idea as well: 'Yes, that would take up some time, and I could ask her to let me have her picture to go with the lovely unicorn painting.'

'She might want to take it home.'

'Ah, but she couldn't, you see. Too precious, too rare. I had to swear your mother to secrecy. If the news got out, I'd have to have a small army of security men patrolling the grounds day and night. Not what we want at Charnley! But if Harriet would be happy to do a picture to add to my collection, then I would be delighted.'

The fountain pen glided over the page of the notebook, then lifted with a flourish. 'Splendid. That should take us up to lunch, don't you think?'

'It should do,' Jack agreed.

'And then after lunch, a ride in the buggy – up the ridge? What sort of a girl is she – outdoor type?'

'She likes riding,' Jack said. 'She's got her own pony.'

'Lucky girl. Well, you're the only one who does any riding around here, aren't you? And I don't think we'll be inviting her to share in *that* little secret.' Mr Finistaire gave a short laugh.

Jack began to feel slightly sorry for Harriet, having her day out planned so as to cause minimum inconvenience.

'Do you like her?'

The question caught him off-guard.

Mr Finistaire pounced on his hesitation. 'So you don't – particularly?'

'She's all right,' Jack said.

'She sounds as if she can be a bit – how shall I say? – pleased with herself.'

'A bit . . .'

Mr Finistaire smiled understandingly.

'I think it's her mother,' Jack explained. 'She seems to expect a lot. She was very nice to me when I went over – Harriet, I mean. Took me round the stables, showed me her pony.'

Then, before he even realized he was going to say it, he went on: 'Maybe I could do the same here – show her around a bit. If that would be helpful?'

'Very helpful – thank you, Jack. But I don't want to lumber you with someone you don't get on with. Or who thought she was better than you.'

'Oh no – she's not like that really. Just at school, she's a bit . . .'

'I understand,' Mr Finistaire said. 'So it's the mother we have to watch out for? Hm. I was thinking of inviting her over to tea to round the day off.'

'I'm sure she'd love that – especially as the whole village knows about my mum coming over.'

'I hope she enjoyed it.'

'Oh, she did. She loved it.'

'I'm glad. A very nice woman, as I said.'

'I'm sure Harriet's mum's nice too,' Jack said. 'When you get to know her.'

'Well, I certainly don't propose to do that,' Mr Finistaire replied; 'but it might be a kindness to invite her.'

He sighed, then looked at his notebook again. 'Tea at four, and then *exeunt omnes*?'

Jack didn't know what that meant, but he saw Mr Finistaire draw a line under the word *Tea* in his notebook, so it was obvious that that would be the end of Harriet's outing.

'Thank you, Jack. Harriet will have a lovely day, and I will invite her mother for tea, so honour will be satisfied, and all manner of thing shall be well.'

Mr Finistaire put the notepad down on the table.

'And now,' he said, 'I really do have rather a lot on my plate, so if you don't mind, I'm going to send you home.' He smiled, but when he pulled off his glasses to polish them on his napkin, Jack saw the strain around his eyes.

The glasses went back on. 'Come on. Let's go and find Sefton – he can take you back in the Land Rover. I think we'll try and keep the profile down a bit.'

They went out through the kitchen and into the stable yard where the Land Rover was parked. Sefton was nowhere to be seen. Mr Finistaire went off in search of him, giving Jack a moment to himself.

He looked up at the great blank wall of the annexe, looming over the yard. There was something about its blankness that seemed to deflect your gaze, made you look away to find something more interesting. Even one window would have drawn the eye, but the monotony of unbroken brick contrived to make it virtually invisible.

Jack looked carefully at the entire length of the wall, just in case he'd missed anything – a tiny door perhaps . . . But there was nothing.

Maybe there was access from the gatehouse. Was

there a door under the archway? The two big gates were open and hooked back, so he couldn't see. But it was quite possible that there was a door concealed behind one of the gates.

He had just taken a step or two in the direction of the gatehouse when Mr Finistaire reappeared with Sefton. Jack veered aside to make it look as if he was making a bee-line for the Land Rover, and was ready by the passenger door when the chauffeur strode up. He was dressed more casually than usual, but his chilly demeanour remained the same, and Jack felt his spirits fall at the prospect of another silent drive back to the village.

He climbed up into the passenger seat, and Sefton took his place behind the steering wheel. Mr Finistaire raised a hand in farewell, and then, with a throaty roar, the Land Rover trundled off over the uneven surface of the stable yard.

Much as Jack wanted to stare to his right as they went under the archway, he knew it would tell him nothing – and would risk alerting Sefton to the fact that he was more interested in things that didn't concern him than he should be.

He did, however, steal a glance as they bounced round the side of the house. It was only a glimpse, but it was enough to confirm that the exterior wall of the annexe was as blank as the one dominating the stable yard. There was no sign of a door.

Sefton stared straight ahead, as usual, locked in his own world. It was clear he wasn't interested in conversation. Which suited Jack fine.

He liked the Land Rover. In fact, he preferred it to the Bentley, wonderful though that was. The Land Rover was a working vehicle. Boys at school whose fathers were farmers drove around in Land Rovers. And you were higher up, so you could see over hedgerows, over walls.

The drive doubled back on itself for the climb up to the village road, and Charnley lay below them to the left. Jack had an unimpeded view of the house, and looked down intently, searching for the annexe and any clue as to its purpose.

It was the first chance he'd really had, and with a jolt of excitement he saw that there was something: a flash of reflected sun from the roof. The view immediately vanished behind a screen of trees, but he was certain of what he had seen – a skylight of some sort set in the roof. He didn't know why that excited him so much. After all, it gave no clue as to what the space was used for now. But it did offer proof that the annexe had been built with a purpose and had once, at any rate, played its part in the life of Charnley in its glory days. Jack felt even more determined to penetrate its defences and discover its secret for himself.

CHAPTER 15

'About my visit . . .'

Jack spun round. It was Harriet. Having spent the time since their last encounter effortlessly ignoring him, here she was, suddenly, at his side.

'What about it?' he asked, looking into her intense face.

'Well,' she said, 'you're going to be there, aren't you?'

'Yes . . .' Jack wondered why they were going over it again.

'The thing is,' she went on, 'how are you going to get there?' She dropped her gaze and looked at the ground.

Ah, thought Jack. *I get it*. 'Oh, don't worry about that. You'll have the Bentley all to yourself.'

'Really?' Suddenly she was smiling at him.

He nodded back. 'Of course: it's your big day.'

'Oh wow. That's great.' Then her brow furrowed slightly. 'But how *are* you going to get there?'

Jack had decided he would go on foot through the woods, but stopped himself from saying so just in time.

'Oh, they can send the Land Rover over for me. I'll probably have to be at work long before you get there. What time is Sefton picking you up?'

'Sefton?'

'That's what the chauffeur's called.'

'Sefton. That's an odd name.' Harriet looked at him. 'For a gardening boy, you do seem to know a lot.'

Jack considered telling her about his recent 'promotion' but thought better of it. Life was complicated enough without going into his supposed position at Charnley.

'The car's coming at ten thirty, Mr Finistaire said. And my mother's to come and get me – and have a cup of tea there – at four o'clock.'

Five and a half hours to discover the secret of the annexe, Jack thought. Well, it gave him a fighting chance.

Jack sat on his bed with the locket open in his hand, gazing at the lovers and the unicorn. He did this at least once a day, and it still delighted him that the dull silver casing could contain a picture of such freshness and beauty. It was even more thrilling to let the two locks of hair lie in his palm, as light as a feather yet heavy with mystery.

On the face of it, the couple had been happy: they were obviously rich and occupied a high position in society – not to mention being blessed by the unicorn which, as Jack could testify, was the most special thing in the world. And yet now their story was shrouded in mystery, with only the faintest memory of a tragic ending passed down by word of mouth by generations of village women, ending with Mr Finistaire's nanny.

He wanted to find out more – more about the lovers, more about the artist – but he had no idea how to begin. Mr Finistaire would be the obvious person to ask, but just as obviously, he was the last person Jack could ask. At least until his doubts about the annexe had been resolved.

He replaced the locks of hair and closed the locket, wrapped it up in his handkerchief and shoved it well under his mattress again. He would, he decided, take it with him on Harriet's day out, just in case there was an opportunity to hold it up beside the tapestry and compare the two portraits.

Harriet's big day looked like being a big day for him as well. He would have to prepare his mum and dad for it.

However, he would have to tread carefully. The row over his mum's visit to Charnley had quickly blown over after his dad's night at the pub and his moaning about how his head felt the next day.

But it had been a warning. Jack would have to make it clear that he was still going over to the big house to work, even though the terms of his engagement had changed. He would use the big gathering Mr Finistaire was preparing for as the reason why he would need to be there early in the morning.

He heard his mum come in, and suddenly felt hungry for his tea.

Finally it came. The last day of school. There had been moments during that last week of term when Jack thought time had slowed to a standstill. He could see that Harriet was feeling it too. Her bright talk in her circle of friends sounded brittle and increased in volume as the weary hours ticked away.

At assembly Miss Hubbard made a speech congratulating everybody on another successful year and wishing those who were moving on in September all the best at their new schools.

One of these was Harriet, whose achievement in winning the art prize was apparently one of the highlights of the year. 'It's nice,' Miss Hubbard couldn't help adding, 'to have a pupil of ours going over to Charnley for the right reasons.'

A lot of heads turned towards Jack, who felt his face growing hot.

Dan whispered: 'That's put you in your place, lover boy.'

Jack tried to kick him, but it's difficult to kick someone standing beside you. He had to wait till break, when he chased Dan all round the playground until he collapsed, pleading for mercy and saying he didn't mean it. Jack got him in a half-nelson, but his heart wasn't in it.

'That wasn't very nice.'

It was Harriet, who as usual appeared as if by magic by his side as he was walking back into school.

'Well, he annoyed me.'

'I don't mean Dan. Miss Hubbard. Making an example of you like that – on your last day. Quite unnecessary. See you tomorrow!' And she slipped back into the crowd once more.

Then they were into the last hour, which they spent taking their pictures down from the wall, discovering long-lost socks in their games lockers and killing time until the final bell of the school year rang.

There was the usual scrum in the playground, and Jack watched Harriet climbing into the four-by-four beside her mother, who was as unsmiling as ever. He hoped she wasn't going to change her mind at the last moment – both for Harriet's sake, and because he was relying on Harriet being at Charnley. Not that he had any intention of telling her anything.

'Walk down, then?'

Dan had obviously seen Jack watching Harriet, but for once he managed not to comment on it. Luke was standing beside him.

'Come on, then,' Jack said, shifting his bag over his shoulder.

So the three of them set off down the hill away from the school for the last time.

'What are we going to do?' Dan said. 'Shall we have a feast in the cottage?'

'Wicked,' said Luke. 'Can we, Jack?'

Jack looked from one to the other. Suddenly he

knew exactly what he wanted to do. He wanted to be alone.

'Jack?' Luke was looking at him, concern in his eyes.

'I've got stuff to do.' Jack felt bad, but he just had too much going through his head to be distracted. 'I'm sorry,' he said. 'Next week . . . We've got all the summer holidays.'

'Oh, Jack!'

But he was gone, walking purposefully home.

He let himself in and raced upstairs to change out of his school uniform. Then he raided the fridge for a cold sausage before letting himself out the back door and setting off down the lane for the woods.

That was where he wanted to be. That's where he *needed* to be. He felt that things were happening. He didn't know what, exactly, and he didn't know what he could do about them. But he couldn't just sit at home. He was drawn irresistibly towards the woods.

He followed the familiar path past the stricken oak and the derelict cottage – how glad he was he'd turned down an end-of-term feast with Dan and Luke. He just wasn't in the mood.

He pushed on deeper into the woods. He didn't have a plan; he was simply following his instincts.

But now he found that he was heading towards the Great Glade, and accepted that this had been his intention all along. This was the most likely place to meet Keras.

Something buzzed up in front of him and tried to settle on his cheek. He batted it away. Sweat trickled into his eyes, and he had to stop to dab it with his handkerchief. When he got to the stream, he knelt down and splashed water onto his face. It was surprisingly cold. Then he cupped his hands and drank.

He was just about to continue into the woods when something made him pause. He stood still, his ears straining. Insects hummed and buzzed, the wood pigeons cooed at each other. But there was another noise in the mix. At first he couldn't identify it, though instinctively he disliked it. Then the breeze changed direction. It sounded like a chainsaw.

It was a horrible noise at the best of times. Now, it filled him with dread. He didn't know why – after all, the woods needed to be managed, and trees sometimes had to be cut down. There were piles of neatly stacked logs all over the place. But today it alarmed him.

Still, at least it was a long way off.

The massed ranks of beech boles gradually thinned as he approached the glade. He slipped stealthily from tree to tree. Great shafts of sunlight speared down through the beach leaves, and instinctively he stepped out of their spotlight.

It was just as well he did. He had almost reached the glade when he heard something that made him freeze. It was a human voice. He flattened himself against the nearest trunk and then peered out cautiously.

His pulse started racing. Mr Grout and Sefton were standing on the soft turf only a few metres away from him.

Mr Grout was talking, and Jack strained to hear.

'Ever since that blasted kid came trespassing, laying his confounded snares, he's been completely off his chump. Always daft as a brush, but I've never seen him like this before. *Jack this*, *Jack that* – thinks the sun shines out of the boy's backside. I'd show him what I think of him given half a chance. But no, the boy's untouchable. Even has you driving him and his ma around the village like bloomin' royalty.' Mr Grout cleared his throat and spat.

Jack found that he was trembling. Though nothing the gamekeeper had said surprised him – he knew Jack had been the one laying the snares, and had almost certainly found the rucksack Jack had left in the woods the night he met Keras – it was still a shock to hear the man express his anger and resentment so forcefully. The fact that Sefton remained silent was of course no surprise. But what were the two of them doing together in the Great Glade?

Jack was about to peer round the side of the tree again when Mr Grout continued.

'As for the other night – what a caper! Getting my missus up in the middle of the night to make up a bed for that blasted boy – dragged out of bed to wait on the son of one of my beaters! It's an outrage. What the hell were they doing out in the woods at that time? All to do with this damn quest he keeps on about—' Mr Grout broke off and spat again.

'I sometimes think he's mental, I really do. Next thing we know we'll have the men in white coats turning up to take him off to the funny farm. And now he's sent us off into the wilds to practise catching this creature he's sure exists but can't tell us anything about. It's lunacy. I've a good mind to tell him to shove it, I really have.'

Jack tried to absorb what he had heard, while listening intently for more. But Mr Grout had had his say, and if Sefton replied, it was too softly for Jack to hear.

The silence began to stretch out. Whatever the two men were doing, they were doing it very quietly. Jack burned with curiosity. He just *had* to look.

What he saw when he darted his head round the tree trunk made him gasp. His skin went prickly with terror.

Sefton had walked away from Mr Grout up the Great Glade, and slung over his shoulder was the cricket net.

Jack looked on in horror as the chauffeur unburdened himself of the net and made his preparations. These were unmistakable – and sure enough, he was soon whirling the net into the air with his long, powerful arms. He looked like the gladiator Jack had seen in a book about ancient Rome. But he was not practising in order to entangle another fighter in the net's coils – it was Keras he was after!

With a graceful movement, Sefton swung his arm and the net flew away. It seemed to hover in the air for a moment, before falling with a sickening finality, spread wide over the grass of the glade.

Jack imagined it falling over Keras, saw the

beautiful creature snagged and snared, his horn sticking through, his hooves getting entangled as he tried to shake his way free. He felt sick, but had to go on watching.

The two men – the one tall and lithe, the other short and compact – were now inspecting the net, judging its spread, assessing its likely effectiveness. Sefton stood there, impassive as usual, but Mr Grout was shaking his head and waving his stick about animatedly. He said something – it must have been along the lines of *Try again*, because Sefton gathered up the net and strode back up the glade.

Once more he cradled the net in his left arm while grasping one corner with his right hand. Once more he wheeled and released it – and once more the dreadful net spread out in the sunlight like the shadowing wing of an immense bird of prey.

Jack shivered.

'Getting better,' Mr Grout shouted grudgingly, adding, as Sefton went across to retrieve the net, 'What I wouldn't give to go after that dratted boy with this. Hunt him down and tan his hide.' He laughed at the thought. It was an unpleasant sound. ''Stead of which we're pitching at empty space like a couple of loons.' The gamekeeper spat once more.

Sefton was speaking, but again Jack couldn't make out what he was saying.

Mr Grout shrugged. 'That's as maybe,' he said. 'He loves to keep you in the dark. Then it's *Do this; do that* – six impossible things before breakfast.' He kept on grumbling, but Jack lost the words as the gamekeeper bent down to roll up the net.

He had seen and heard enough; he couldn't bear to watch any more as Mr Finistaire's henchmen prepared to capture Keras. He would never have believed it had he not seen it with his own eyes. How could he have been so trusting? How could he have given so much away, putting Keras in such terrible danger? It was so clear now. Jack had brought the great prize to Mr Finistaire – betrayed the most precious relationship he'd ever had – and, for all his apparent charm and sympathy and interest, Mr Finistaire had simply used him to get the thing he most desired in the world: the unicorn.

He hated Mr Finistaire; he hated himself. But most of all, he hated what was about to happen to Keras. But what could he do to stop it?

Jack stopped for a moment and leaned against a tree. His breath was coming in great painful gulps; the bruise on his ribs was beginning to ache, and he felt a terrible knot of dread clenching in his stomach.

He was no match for Sefton and Mr Grout, so there was no way he could physically prevent any harm coming to Keras. The only hope was warning him. But how?

He had only the vaguest idea where the looking-glass lake and the cave were. What chance did he have of finding them and then explaining to Keras what was happening?

Far away across Mr Finistaire's vast wood, the chainsaws whined dismally. The noise rose and fell like a dreary wind on a stormy night. It made him want to turn and bolt for home, but he wasn't going to be hounded off the estate by the chainsaws' derisive fanfare. He would go and find out what was happening. He was pretty sure it did not bode well for Keras.

Giving the Great Glade a wide berth, he headed as best he could towards the din.

The path – if you could call it that – led up a steep incline, and he suddenly lost his footing. He went down with a jarring thump, and cursed his carelessness. He'd instinctively turned away to save his damaged side, but that had resulted in an untidy sprawl, which left him with his face close to the ground.

There was a stabbing pain in his side, and Jack felt a wave of self-pity threatening to engulf him. He fought against it, and started to haul himself to his feet.

But then he stopped. Something had caught his eye less than a metre from where he had fallen. He scrambled over and gazed down as though he'd found a rare coin or piece of jewellery. But it was much more precious than that. What he was looking at was a faint indentation in the baked soil: a cloven hoof-print. Right in front of his eyes was proof that Keras had been there, right there. He was on the unicorn's trail.

Jack's self-pity evaporated instantly, burned off by the thrill of this chance discovery. He scrambled up, the pain in his side completely forgotten. He was on the right track. If he could find Keras, there was still time to warn him, to save him.

The hoof-print was pointing in the direction Jack was going – towards the unknown quarter of the estate, and the droning chainsaws. These had gradually been getting louder, he realized; which meant he was getting closer to them.

How he hated the noise they made; how he hated what they were doing. It was now obvious that they were not merely engaged in everyday forestry: they were trying to cut their way through the woods towards Keras, intending to flush him out of his sanctuary.

Jack felt a bolt of anger explode in his brain. He stood up, his fists bunched, wanting to shout out in fury.

Deeper and deeper into the woods he went. He'd lost all sense of time, but the sun, when he glimpsed it through the leaves, was lower in the sky. The chainsaws were much louder, and when he stopped to listen, he could hear the crack of tree trunks falling. Jack crept forward towards the noise. He could hear shouts now – and the dull low growl of diggers, obviously employed to shove the felled trees aside.

There was a loud cry of warning. Jack glanced up and saw a treetop waving drunkenly, and then, with a terrible tearing sound, it came crashing down. There was a ragged cheer. Jack crouched down and crept forward.

At last he could see and not just hear. About a dozen men were milling around, some wielding chainsaws, others lugging the lopped branches away, while two JCBs shunted the trunks aside, making a crude track through the woods. The trail of destruction seemed endless, reaching back across the estate towards Charnley. It was quite obvious where it was destined to end up.

It was too much for Jack. He'd seen enough to confirm his darkest fears. All his renewed energy drained out of him. What could he do against the might of this invading army? What chance did he have of finding Keras when the woods were alive with tramping men and roaring machines? And even if he *did* find him, what help could he be? He'd hardly be bringing news, would he? These were Keras's woods, this was his domain. He wouldn't need to be told it was being invaded – especially by the person most responsible for it happening.

Perhaps he should go in the other direction. But again, what good could he do? Even if he stormed over to Charnley, he'd just be a sweat-stained boy from the village – a beater's boy, as Mr Grout had put it – dwarfed by the towering portico, pleading with the man who owned everything as far as the eye could see.

Jack slipped away, defeated. This should never have happened: two worlds that should never have come anywhere near each other had collided, here in the depths of Mr Finistaire's woods. And all he could do was look on, powerless to intervene, while the horror unfolded before him.

And he had brought all this about himself. That was what added to his torment, making it unbearable. It was all his fault. He ought to be punished for it; but he couldn't think of a punishment severe enough.

He felt tears stinging his eyes as he retraced his steps through the woods. He was half running, desperate to distance himself from the chainsaw carnage behind him. Perhaps that was the answer – to keep on running – not to go home, not to say goodbye to anybody; just to vanish.

But that wouldn't solve anything. Jack could see that. And running away was the cowardly option. Though he hated the thought of it, he would have to continue to play his part in the drama – go over to Charnley for Harriet's big day and hope, just hope, that he could do something useful; something that might make the situation less totally awful.

He drove himself on. If he was going to play his part tomorrow, he had to be home in good time and get his parents on side. He had brought this catastrophe down on Keras; the least he could do was to keep his head.

Oh, Keras! Would he ever see the unicorn again? The thought that he might not was too painful to contemplate. Instead he went over their meetings – the rides through the woods, the sensation of speed and freedom and power. He wouldn't have been surprised if Keras had suddenly left the ground and carried on sailing upwards, above the woods, above the village, above Charnley, leaving all the problems and worries of ordinary life far below them.

Jack came down to earth as a bramble snagged on his jeans. It was darker now, and cooler. To his great relief, he realized that the chainsaws had fallen silent. An expectant hush fell through the woods. It was like the eve of a great battle – though his role in it was likely to be marginal at best.

How was he going to keep up the pretence at Charnley? How could he look Mr Finistaire in the eye? And how was he going to deal with Harriet while finding a way to unlock the mysteries of the windowless annexe and at the same time protecting Keras? It seemed such an impossible task. He stood with his eyes closed, letting the last rays of the sun bathe his face.

Perhaps he could sink down by the path and lie there, motionless, gradually becoming absorbed into the landscape. Birds would settle on his head; rabbits – the rabbits he'd once set out to snare – would play happily around the mound made by his feet. Seeds would blow into his shirt and, in the fullness of time, he would become nothing more than a grassy hump, dotted with wild flowers.

He felt the chill as the sun slipped down behind the beech trees. It was time to go home.

CHAPTER 16

The following morning Jack stood looking up at the old oak. Brilliant sunshine bathed the surrounding trees in dancing light, but even on the brightest day, the ancient veteran of the woods held a darkness all its own. It was like a dying star, Jack thought, a black hole from which no light could escape. Its days of growth and hope had long gone. Now it simply was. It existed, a monument to the passing of time.

What was a day to it? Even a day like the one that stretched ahead of him would come to an end eventually, to join all the other days fading into a forgotten past. The thought gave him a moment of comfort, a slight spur to his determination. He placed his hand on the scarred bark, hard as granite, and then set off through the woods.

It seemed no time since he had been facing in the other direction, dragging himself home after the horrors of Mr Grout's invasion of the woods. It had been late when he got back, and his mum was anxious. It had been painful, listening to her reproaches as she waited for the microwave to warm up his meal. And she had been very upset when he told her he had another long day at Charnley ahead of him.

Jack had sat miserably hunched over his shepherd's pie thinking she was going to stop him going. Then his dad came in from the lounge, his forehead creased with a forbidding frown.

But all he said was: 'Leave the lad. He's got to stand on his own two feet. And if Finistaire's found a use for him, that's all to the good.' Then, to Jack: 'Has he started paying you yet?'

Jack had to admit he hadn't.

'Well, make sure he does, or I'll have to have words. Now, help your mother with the clearing up, and get off to bed.'

He'd had a restless night, sleeping only fitfully, disturbed by the owls calling from the woods in the small hours. When he did drop off, he was tormented by dreams, vague but terrifying, involving speed, pursuit, and some sort of catastrophe at the end as he fell.

He had put on his working trousers, slipping the

locket into the side pocket with the zip. Then, after a hurried breakfast, and an even more hurried goodbye to his mum, he had set off.

Normally, in the woods, Jack felt calm. But now he was nervy, super-alert. Something was in the air. The encounter between Sefton and Mr Grout, the chainsaw army advancing through the wood, Mr Finistaire's plans for his great summer gathering – everything was coming to a head. And this was the day.

His route to the house took him past Mr Grout's domain. It was a hateful place, with its dismal enclosures and the stupid doomed game birds pecking away in the shadows of the firs. His instinct was to give it a wide berth, but as he looked down on it, his eye was caught by the hut.

Grim, functional and shuttered, it was the last place he would want to go near. But perhaps it might contain some clues as to what Mr Finistaire's plan was – and how much progress they had made . . . It was too good an opportunity to miss.

Very reluctantly, and looking about him in every direction, Jack broke cover.

He became less sure it was a good idea with every step he took, but he was committed now, and pushed on, listening hard for any danger signals. The silence here was of a different quality, as though the surrounding fir trees muffled the natural noises of the wood. But the strange quiet made him even more nervous.

He crept down the slope. At the bottom he picked his way through the runs. The birds pecked listlessly, breaking off to take a few steps in their funny clockwork way, their tail feathers waggling ridiculously. Jack felt sorry for them: pampered captivity followed by a day of terror and slaughter as the beaters drove them up into the air for the first and last proper flight of their lives.

But he didn't have time to worry about a few dumb game birds. He had to stay focused on the hut. It would probably be locked, Jack told himself as he approached it. Then he wouldn't have to go in, but at least he'd have tried.

He reached the door and stood outside, listening intently. Not a sound. Jack crouched down to peer through the keyhole. It was hard to make anything out. The shutter over the window was closed, but one or two shafts of light got in. As his eyes adjusted, Jack could see a chair at an angle to a simple desk, on which stood a bottle and a couple of glasses. But it was what was behind the desk that caught his attention. Pinned to the wall above the table was a map. Although he couldn't make out any details, he felt sure that it was a map of the estate.

He stood up, took a deep breath, and put his hand on the doorknob. He turned it very slowly, and then pushed. He had expected the door to be locked, but it wasn't. He swung it open and stepped inside.

The hut was a surprisingly lived-in space: a coat hung from a hook, a pair of heavy boots had been thrown down in a corner. There was a wood stove with a battered old kettle on it, and a cardboard box piled high with empty whisky bottles. Along one wall was a camp-bed with a dirty-looking blanket and a couple of cushions for pillows. It looked as though Mr Grout sometimes spent the night here. The thought spooked him, and he looked back in terror, half expecting the gamekeeper to be standing in the doorway. But there was no one there. Jack went over to the desk. There was half a loaf and a plate smeared with butter and some sort of sandwich spread. Next to the whisky bottle sat an overflowing ashtray. The smell of stale tobacco smoke lingered horribly, and tickled the back of his throat.

But it was the map on the wall that drew his

attention. He was right: it was an estate map. And to his horror, it was dotted with the same colour-coded spots Mr Finistaire had used on the one in the map room. Every journey he had made through the woods, either alone or with Keras, was faithfully recorded with either red or yellow dots. And, even more ominously, there was a trail of white dots leading towards the far side of the estate where the looking-glass lake and Keras's cave lay. The dots petered out, but Jack was certain the chainsaw gang had been following them.

He felt dreadful. This was more evidence that his stupidity had led to Keras being placed in such terrible danger. He felt even worse when he pulled open the desk's one drawer and saw the battered old rucksack, his torch, the gardening gloves and a couple of the skewers and the wire from his snare. If they'd been placed in plastic bags they would have looked exactly like items taken from a crime scene. Just as Jack had thought, Mr Grout had known about him all along.

He felt a sudden surge of panic. He had to get out of that horrible hut, away from everything associated with the gamekeeper and his oppressive world.

As he turned to escape, he saw something that

made him freeze. Propped in a corner behind the door was a double-barrelled shotgun. It stood there, so matter-of-fact – beautiful in a functional sort of way. The gunmetal gleamed dully. He wanted to touch it, to pick it up, feel the weight of it. But instead he made his way to the door, keeping his eye on it as he did so.

It was then that he heard a sound from outside. Mr Grout? One of Mr Grout's men? Sefton?

He mustn't be found in the hut – or anywhere near it. He slipped out of the door and round the side, his heart thumping so violently it seemed to drown out any other sounds.

He headed for the safety of the firs, thankful that the groundcover of pine needles muffled his footsteps. Only another twenty metres to go . . . He looked back over his shoulder, but there was no sign of life. He was nearly there. Nearly safe.

He made it up the slope and into the fir plantation. He stumbled on for a few metres and then flung himself against a tree to get his breath back.

Something – some tiny disturbance in the air – made him spin round.

'Well, well, if it ain't Master Jack. You're up bright

and early.' Mr Grout was looking at him from a distance of about five metres.

Jack stared at the red whiskery face under the cap. The eyes seemed to drill into his, and the mouth was set in a wolfish grin that revealed discoloured teeth.

Jack was suddenly aware that his own mouth was gaping open in surprise. 'Mr Grout,' he managed to say. 'You gave me a shock.'

'I dare says I did, young man. But then, I'm surprised myself to find you creeping about the estate at this time in the morning.'

'I'm – I've got to go—'

'I know where you've got to go, my lad. Decided you'd do without the lift today, did you?'

'Yes,' Jack said. 'I thought I'd walk through the woods. Mr Finistaire said—'

'I know what Mr Finistaire said. But I wasn't aware he said anything about you snooping around my neck of the woods. Or have you developed an interest in game birds, along with your interest in gardening?'

Jack could tell the gamekeeper was mocking him, but it was just possible he hadn't seen him coming out of the hut.

'I – it seemed . . . I think I got a bit lost. I'm sorry. I don't think I disturbed your birds.'

Mr Grout's grin cracked open a little at this and he gave a short laugh like a bark. 'Well, at least you're thinking like a gamekeeper.' The grin faded from his face, and he took a step forward.

Jack retreated a step, but found his way blocked by the tree.

'Nowhere to go, is there, young man?' the gamekeeper said, coming up to him. 'There's just the two of us, all on our ownsome, out here in the woods.'

Mr Grout's face was horribly close, and Jack struggled not to turn his head away to avoid his breath, which was sickly with the stench of stale tobacco. He was very frightened, and didn't want to provoke the angry little man any further.

He thought of the shotgun leaning against the wall of the hut not thirty metres away. Who would hear the shot? No one. Mr Grout could have him buried in a shallow grave in no time, and who'd be any the wiser?

He found himself looking at the network of veins running across Mr Grout's face. His nose, Jack noticed, was almost purple, and stray hairs grew out of it. There was thick stubble around his mouth and chin: Mr Grout obviously hadn't shaved for a day or two.

'I know I ain't a picture,' the man said disconcertingly. 'But that ain't the issue, is it?'

Jack lowered his eyes.

'The issue, young man, is you – prowling around the estate as though you owned the place. Oh yes – don't think I don't know, because I do. Nearly had you that first time, didn't I? And I would have done in my younger days. Very quick across country I was, back then. Plenty of stamina. I'd have caught you, my boy – and I'd 'ave given you something to remember me by.'

Jack was uncomfortably aware of the bone-handled stick in his hand.

'Yes, back in the day, you got caught, you got a hiding. Teachers, policemen – and gamekeepers. That's how it was: everyone knew where they stood, and took the punishment they deserved without running off bleating about it. But now—' Mr Grout broke off, looking fiercely at Jack. 'I don't know. Spare the rod and spoil the child, I was always taught. And it worked, I can tell you. But it's all changed. Kids these days – none of them got any respect.'

He raised his stick. Jack cowered, convinced he was going to feel the weight of it.

There was a heavy swish as the stick came swinging down. But the blow Jack was expecting didn't come.

Mr Grout laughed unpleasantly. 'Don't think I wouldn't – if it was down to me. But it ain't. You're protected. A protected species, you might say. *Boy Trespasser: preserve at all costs*. Pah!' He cleared his throat and spat vehemently. 'You lead a charmed life, young man. Driven around the parish in the Bentley, despite the damage you done to the coachwork. Picked up here, dropped back there. Taken in to tea and consultations in the big house. Oh yes, very nice. And for the moment, you're safe. I can't lay a finger on you. Out of bounds. Off limits. But let me tell you this, my boy . . .' And here Mr Grout thrust his face close to Jack's. 'Things change. Things don't last for ever. And when they do change, then we'll see what's what. Then we'll see . . .' He paused for effect, glowering at Jack.

'And in the meantime, young shaver, let me tell you this. You may have the run of the estate – and there may be very good reasons why you should – but this is my patch, and you do not have the right to come poking your nose in here. Understood?' For emphasis, he stuck a bony finger into Jack's chest.

'Yes,' he gasped. 'I'm sorry. I won't—'

'You'd better not, young man. You'd better not.'

Mr Grout took a step back. 'It so happens that I'm on my way to the big house like you. Got one or two things to report' – here he half closed his eyes meaningfully – 'so, I'm thinking we may as well go together. I've got the buggy at the top. Come on.'

Jack hated the idea, but he saw he didn't have any choice. 'Thank you,' he said, as respectfully as he could.

Mr Grout flashed him a look, but seemed satisfied that Jack was genuinely trying to be polite.

They walked up to the escarpment, the silence broken only by Mr Grout's tuneless whistling. Jack felt like a prisoner being taken into custody. But he had to accept that, unpleasant as it had been, he'd got off lightly.

And he was still in the game. But the stakes were higher than ever.

Suddenly there was a loud crackle, and Mr Grout was fumbling in one of the pouch-like pockets of his jacket. He pulled out a radio handset, and said, 'Yes?' At the same time, he walked quickly ahead of Jack so that he was out of earshot.

Jack strained to hear what was being said, but caught nothing. Mr Grout listened impassively, and then said, 'Copy that,' and put the handset back in his pocket. 'Very interesting,' he said, his mouth pursed in a little grimace of satisfaction.

They carried on up the slope. Mr Grout's whistling was just as tuneless, but sounded more jaunty now. Jack found it very irritating. He also fretted about the news that had put Mr Grout in such a good mood. It must have come from his men, away on the other side of the estate, and any news that came from that quarter could only be bad for Keras.

They left the fir plantation behind them and entered the natural woodland that covered the escarpment. The sun was up, and the hint of early morning chill had gone. At the top they got into the buggy and were soon rolling down the bumpy track. Normally Jack would have enjoyed the drive, but not today. He remembered a film in which a condemned man was taken to be executed in a rickety little cart. Although Jack didn't have his hands roped together behind his back, and was being driven through a wood and not a jeering crowd, that's exactly how he felt.

As the trees thinned to their right, he looked down at Charnley. For a moment his sense of dread lifted. The great house looked so magnificent and at the same time so peaceful. A huge marquee now filled the first of the two walled gardens, and in the corner of the outer garden the glasshouse glittered in the morning sunlight. No doubt Mr Finistaire would greet him with his usual friendliness. Everything would seem the same. Even though it wasn't.

'Nice view.' Mr Grout said it without looking at him, but then turned his head to add: 'Enjoy it while you can, young man.'

Jack didn't have time to ponder the significance of the remark, because he could see the Bentley coming round the bend below them, gliding majestically towards the house.

'That'll be the young lass,' Mr Grout muttered. 'Just what we need.'

Jack glanced at him. The gamekeeper was frowning and his jaw was set hard.

'Better get you down there, pronto. Don't want her eating up all the jelly, do we? Jelly! As though my missus hasn't got enough to do with a party of seventy plus to cater for.'

Mr Grout accelerated, which meant that they

bounced around in the buggy like corks. Jack clung on to stop himself being flung out, and was relieved when they got off the uneven track and onto the flatter meadow leading to the gatehouse. They sped under the archway and pulled up in the middle of the stable yard.

'Out you get,' Mr Grout said, leaping out himself.

With a quick glance at the blank wall of the annexe, Jack followed him to the gateway into the kitchen yard.

As they reached it, Mr Finistaire emerged from the kitchen door, and standing beside him was Harriet.

'Perfect timing!' cried Mr Finistaire.

Jack thought he looked relieved. He certainly seemed pleased to see him.

'Good morning, Jack. Mr Grout found you coming through the woods, did he?'

'I found him snooping around my hut,' said Mr Grout darkly.

'Snooping, Grout?' Mr Finistaire looked at Jack. There was a twinkle in his eye. 'Natural curiosity of the genus *Boy*, Grout. In you go and get Mrs G to make you a coffee.'

Instead of doing as he was told, the gamekeeper

went up to his employer and whispered something in his ear.

'Thank you, Grout. Wait for me in the kitchen.'

With a parting look at Jack that was anything but friendly, Mr Grout disappeared inside.

'Well, here we are,' said Mr Finistaire. 'And you've got a splendid day for it, my dear.'

Harriet gave him her brightest-girl-in-the-class smile.

Jack looked at her properly for the first time. She really had gone for it: an immaculate sky-blue dress with little white socks sticking out of her best shoes. And goodness knows how much time she and her mum had spent on her hair. It was as though she'd been invited to a garden party at Buckingham Palace.

From Harriet's glance down at him, Jack realized he must look a total mess. His shirt was untucked, and he could feel sweat drying on his neck. *Well*, he thought, *I* am *meant to be the gardener's boy*.

'Hello, Harriet,' he said. 'Did you enjoy the drive?'

'Oh yes,' she gushed. 'What a lovely car – it's sooo comfortable.'

She said this, Jack noticed, not to him, but to Mr Finistaire.

'One of life's little pleasures, my dear. I'm always pleased when I have to go somewhere in it. But the buggy's fun too, isn't it, Jack? We'll give you a ride in that later, perhaps,' he said to Harriet. 'Now, though, I thought we'd start with a tour of the gardens, before the heat becomes overwhelming.'

'Oh, I'd love that,' Harriet said, coming down the steps.

Mr Finistaire stayed where he was, hesitating for a moment. 'Jack,' he said, 'would you kindly show Harriet around, and' – here he reached into his pocket and produced a key – 'introduce her to our prize exhibit in the glasshouse. I just need to have a word with Mr Grout.'

Harriet looked disappointed.

'Don't worry, my dear; you're in good hands. I shall be along in a minute. Off you go.' He handed Jack the key and went back into the kitchen.

'Through here,' Jack said, and led the way through the gateway into the first walled garden.

This was where the marquee had been erected, and it took up most of the space. One of the flaps was open, and they walked through, past trestle tables resting on their sides and great stacks of folding chairs.

'What's going on?' Harriet asked. 'Is he giving a party?'

'You could say that – more a grand reception,' Jack said. 'Lots of people coming from all over the world. It's a tradition. They all get together at somebody's house and show off their best things.'

'And what's Mr Finistaire's best thing?'

'I'll show you.'

They made their way down the side of the marquee and through the next gateway into the second garden.

'Oh, what lovely topiary!' Harriet said, admiring the yew trees. 'Gosh, this must take a lot of upkeep. Is this where you work?'

'All over,' Jack said vaguely. The less said about his imaginary gardening the better. 'Come on.'

They walked down the avenue of beautifully shaped yews and over to the glasshouse. Jack fumbled with the key and then slid the door open. 'It's hot,' he warned, ushering Harriet inside.

'So it is,' she said, fanning her hand in front of her face. And then she looked up and saw the orchid. 'Oh my goodness! It's amazing. It's so big. Can I . . . ?' She ran up the wooden steps to the platform where the huge urn stood. 'It's beautiful,' she murmured in a hushed voice.

Jack climbed up beside her.

'I've never seen anything so perfect.'

For once, Jack thought, *she's found something more interesting than herself*.

'It's worth a fortune,' he said. 'Thousands and thousands of pounds. So you're not to tell anyone. He had it shipped from the rainforest. It's incredibly rare – probably the only one in Europe.'

'And that's what all those people are coming to see?'

Jack nodded. He was enjoying being the guide. 'The Lady of the Moon, she's called. When we transplanted her—' He stopped. That hadn't happened, remember? It was a lie.

'*We?*' Harriet's eyes were wide. 'You mean you were involved? Tell me.'

So he did. Every last made-up detail.

'Wow, Jack – that's incredible,' she said when he'd patted down the last bit of soil and rubbed the dirt off his hands. 'And they let you do all that? Weren't you terrified?'

'Not one whit. Performed as though he'd spent his entire life potting priceless plants. The most naturally green-fingered boy in existence!'

They both swung round. Mr Finistaire had come

into the glasshouse and was standing in the lobby looking up at them, smiling.

To Jack's disappointment, Harriet's whole mien changed. She put her hands together in front of her dress and gave Mr Finistaire a big-eyed look. 'I've never seen anything like it,' she cooed.

'You won't have, my dear. If there's a rarer plant anywhere in the world, it hasn't been discovered yet. But don't let me distract you. Pay your respects to her. Like all beauties, she loves to be looked at. Get as close as you like – just don't touch her.'

Harriet turned back to the orchid and made a great show of admiring the lucent goblets of the flowers, the elegant strength of the stem. She breathed in deeply, her eyes closed, and when she finally turned away, she had a rapt expression on her face, as though she'd just got up from kneeling at an altar. 'It's wonderful,' she sighed. 'You must be incredibly proud to own it.'

'I don't own her, my dear. I paid for her, but that doesn't mean I'm the owner. I'm just a humble custodian. Our motto is: preserve the precious, the imperilled, the unique, the irreplaceable.'

Here he caught Jack's eye. It was almost as if

nothing had changed; as if they were still working together with a common purpose.

Then Mr Finistaire's mobile phone began to ring. 'I'm sorry: I have to take this . . . Yes?' he said sharply, the phone to his ear. Then he walked out of the glasshouse.

Something was up. Jack wondered what it was, but he didn't have a good feeling about it.

Harriet had gone back to the orchid. 'How much did you say it was worth?'

A lot more than your dad could afford, Jack thought, but he only said: 'I don't know. You couldn't put a price on it. A fortune, anyway.'

Mr Finistaire came back in. He looked distracted. 'Something's come up,' he said, pushing his hand through his hair; 'something I have to attend to. I'm sorry, my dear; but Jack will look after you. There'll be lemonade and other good things in the kitchen. I'll catch up with you later, but now I must fly.'

And with that he was gone.

CHAPTER 17

Jack looked at Harriet, shrugged his shoulders and smiled. Like the story of his part in the re-potting of the orchid, the smile was a fake. He had intended to use the time Mr Finistaire took showing Harriet round the house to investigate the annexe, but obviously the day was subject to sudden changes and he couldn't rely on that happening. This might be the only opportunity he got. It wasn't perfect, but if he could keep Harriet on side, it might work. He would have to go for it anyway.

'Come on,' he said. 'Let's do some exploring.'

'Can't I see round the rest of this?' Harriet asked, looking into the depths of the glasshouse beyond the Lady of the Moon. 'It's fantastic.'

'We can come back.'

'But I want to stay here,' Harriet said, looking determined.

Jack thought hard. This was turning into a nightmare.

Then he remembered. 'Actually,' he said, 'you've got a surprise coming.'

'What?' she said.

'Can't tell you – but you'll love it. And it'll happen here.'

'Please tell me. I won't let on, honest. Whatever it is, I shall look as surprised as anything.'

'OK,' Jack said. 'As long as you promise to do what I want to do next.'

She looked at him suspiciously. He gave her his most innocent smile.

'As long as it's not a trick of some sort.'

'Not at all – just a thing I've wanted to do for a while.'

'All right then. Now, tell me about my surprise.'

'Mr Finistaire is going to ask you to do a picture' – Jack paused for effect – 'of the orchid.'

'Really? You're not teasing me? But I haven't brought my paints.'

'I don't think that'll be a problem: you have won a *painting* prize, remember.'

Harriet's eyes sparkled. 'Oh, Jack – that's wonderful! When? When will I do it?'

'Oh, later,' Jack said, off-hand. 'Now come on.' He was halfway down the wooden steps, the key in his hand.

Harriet took a last lingering look at the orchid and followed him down to the door. 'Wow, that's awesome,' she said in a breathy whisper. 'Thanks for telling me.'

'That's all right.'

'So where are we going now?' she asked.

'The stable block,' Jack said.

'Stable block? Boring. I see enough of stables every day of my life. There must be somewhere more interesting than that.'

'They're massive. Really. I've always wanted to explore them. It won't take a minute. And besides, you promised.'

They were now walking back up the aisle of yews.

'Shouldn't you be busy?' Harriet looked at him. 'I mean, doing garden stuff?'

'Oh, I will be. Don't worry. I'm not going to hang around all day. Mr Finistaire just wanted me to show you around a bit to begin with. He'll take over when he's finished with whatever it is that called him away.'

Jack felt the pull of dread in his stomach, but he had to hide what he was feeling. 'Come on – let's go this way this time.'

They had reached the second garden, and Jack led

the way to the side of the marquee that was next to the wall.

'Why?' asked Harriet. 'There's hardly any room with all those ropes.'

'More fun,' Jack said, leaping over the first rope. His intention was to keep out of sight for as long as possible, but he had to make Harriet think it was a game. He jumped over the second rope and, turning his head, saw that Harriet was following him, though she was not exactly throwing herself into it.

'I think it's stupid,' she said. 'If I fall over, I'll ruin my dress. It doesn't matter for you.'

Ignoring the put-down, Jack went back to her and, lowering his voice, said: 'Come on, Moneypenny. This is the Bad Guys' HQ, and we're trying to find a way in without being seen.'

'I don't want to be Moneypenny. She just stays in the office all the time.'

'OK: you're the beautiful – and brilliant – CIA agent they've teamed me up with.'

'What's my name?'

Jack wanted to grab her by the arm and drag her by force – with his hand over her mouth, if necessary. 'Harriet Hopeful.'

'I didn't know they had Harriets in America.'

'They do. It's a very special name.' Putting on his James Bond accent, he whispered, 'There's a goon with a submachine gun inside the marquee, so we have to be very quiet. Come on, Agent Hopeful.'

Agent Hopeful sighed, but decided to humour him.

'Now,' he said as they came to the end of the marquee, 'we just have to get across the kitchen yard—'

'What about the lemonade? Mr Finistaire said there'd be lemonade in the kitchen. I'm thirsty.'

'It'll spoil the game. We can have a drink after we've explored. There's a mystery room I want to get into.' He hadn't meant to tell her that, but he could see that it had caught her imagination.

'But are we allowed . . . ?'

'Of course we are. Come on. Follow me.'

Jack led her through the archway into the kitchen yard. Hearing voices from inside the kitchen, he made a bee-line for the corner and waved for Harriet to follow him. Reluctantly she did so.

'This is silly,' she said, but at least she kept her voice down.

'Come on, Agent Hopeful. The future of mankind

depends on us.' His hold on the accent, never very strong, was giving way under the pressure.

Harriet frowned at him, but then suppressed a giggle. Perhaps she was all right after all.

'Now,' Jack said and, crouching down, ran as quietly as he could under the kitchen windows, and waited at the far corner of the yard. He was relieved to see Harriet following him.

Only a few metres to the gateway into the stable yard . . . Jack suspected that all the men would be busy with Mr Grout. They just had to get out through the kitchen gateway without Mrs Grout seeing them.

'Come on!' he whispered, and made a dash for the gate.

He looked back, but Harriet hadn't moved. She pointed to her shoes and shook her head.

Jack rolled his eyes. Girls! *Take them off*, he mimed, keeping an eye on the kitchen window. He could see Mrs Grout moving around with a big pan. He waited until she turned her back, and then put his hand up to beckon Harriet on. She had taken off her shoes, and sped across the cobbles to join him.

'Well done, Agent Hopeful,' he said, with genuine admiration.

'Ruined my socks,' Harriet said. 'Mum'll kill me.'

'A pair of socks. A small sacrifice to save civilization.' He gave her his clenched Sean Connery smile. Anything to keep her sweet. 'Right – over there,' he said, pointing across the empty yard. The buggy, he noticed, had gone, which was both good and bad. Good because Mr Grout, and probably Mr Finistaire, were almost certainly a fair distance away. As for the bad, he couldn't bear to think about it.

Harriet put her shoes back on.

'Off we go,' he said. And they headed across the yard towards the stable block. Jack walked as casually as he could, but he knew that at any moment someone might see them and tell them to stop. He just hoped that the stable block would give access to the gatehouse, and that he could get into the annexe from there.

The door was ajar, and Jack pushed it open and let Harriet through.

She looked around at the row of empty stalls. Piles of greying hay spilled out of the feeding baskets. 'I wonder how many stable boys they had,' she said, idly touching an old harness that was hanging from a hook.

'Lots,' Jack said. 'They used to have dozens of servants.'

'I wonder what goes on up there.' Harriet had moved down the stalls and was standing at the bottom of an open staircase.

It was exactly what Jack had been hoping for, but he wasn't sure he wanted Harriet exploring the secret wing. He'd always planned to go it alone.

But before he could think of a way to stop her, she started to climb the stairs.

'Come on,' she said, looking down at him. 'You said you wanted to explore.'

At the top there was a small landing with a door leading off it and a window looking out onto the yard. Jack peered through the filthy pane; there was still nobody about.

Harriet was inspecting the door. It had an old-fashioned latch next to a big keyhole. You could see from the cobwebs across the corners that it hadn't been opened for years.

She pressed her thumb down on the latch and shoved. The door remained shut. 'Locked,' she said.

Jack wasn't surprised. If ever a door looked locked, it was this one. Perhaps the key was hanging conveniently from a nail . . .

Harriet shook her head. She'd had the same thought. She bent to the keyhole, and then turned back to Jack with a purposeful expression in her eye.

Jack looked too. The keyhole was dark. The key was in the lock.

'We could push it through and—' Harriet broke off, looking around. Not finding what she wanted, she ran down the staircase.

A moment later she was back brandishing an old colour supplement with an unrecognizably young member of the royal family on the cover. Throwing herself onto her knees by the door, she slid the magazine underneath. Then she pulled something out of her hair and poked it into the lock. 'Ta-dah!' she said as she pulled back the magazine. There, resting across the royal features, was the key.

'Brilliant, Agent Hopeful,' Jack said, genuinely impressed.

Harriet picked up the key, weighing it in her hand. Then she passed it to Jack. 'Go on, James. This is your show,' she said in a passable American accent.

It was funny, but Jack didn't feel like laughing. And despite Harriet's smile, he could see the tension in her eyes. Perhaps she sensed that this was more than just a game.

Jack put the key in the lock. It was very stiff, but by using an uncomfortable amount of force, he managed to turn it. He paused and looked at Harriet, to check that she was still up for it. She tilted her head slightly, to show that she was, and Jack pressed down on the latch and pushed the door open.

The room they found themselves in was disappointing. Apart from an old chest and a couple of rickety chairs, it was empty. The floorboards were bare. Dusty cobwebs hung in the corners. There were two windows, one overlooking the yard, the other commanding the approach to the gatehouse. Jack peered out, but again there was nothing to see.

Then he turned his attention to the far end of the room. There was another door, similar to the one they'd just come through, and he went over to it, Harriet at his side.

This door was also locked. He peered through the keyhole, but there was no key in it.

Harriet went and fetched the key from the other door. 'Worth a try,' she said, then, 'What are we looking for? It's not exactly exciting, is it? No one's been in here for ages.'

'I want to see what's through here,' Jack said, taking the key from her.

He had difficulty getting it into the lock and thought for a moment that it was not going to fit. Then he realized that his hand was trembling. He steadied himself and tried again. With a look at Harriet, he applied pressure to it, and watched incredulously as his hand rotated.

He paused. He had got what he wanted – access to the annexe. He hoped that the lack of excitement would continue; that they'd find an old storeroom filled with discarded furniture. But somehow he doubted it.

Harriet had picked up on his mood, and was studying his face. 'Go on,' she said.

'Sure?' Jack checked.

She nodded.

There was no James Bond jokiness now. Swallowing hard, Jack pressed down the latch and pushed the door open.

They found themselves in a space which was half room, half landing. There were windows to both sides of the block, and two doors. One was full sized, and from its position Jack guessed it led to a flight of stairs giving access to the ground floor. The other door was smaller, and reached by a couple of wooden steps.

Jack tried the larger door first. It was locked, and a glance at the keyhole told him that the key they had would not fit. His disappointment must have shown in his face.

'Try the other one,' Harriet whispered.

'It's probably just an empty old attic,' Jack replied. He noticed they were both whispering.

He approached the steps and tried the doorknob. The door was unlocked, and he cautiously pulled it open . . .

He gave an involuntary cry and slammed it shut again.

'What is it?' Harriet asked. 'Let me see.'

But Jack stood with his back to the door, barring the way. 'You can't,' he gasped. His palms were slippery with sweat. He felt winded, and had to fight for breath. 'You don't want to see . . . it's too terrible.'

He slumped down on the step and put his head in his hands. Hot tears fell through his fingers onto the dusty floor.

He wished he was dead.

CHAPTER 18

He didn't know how long he sat on the step with his back to the little door. It was probably only a minute or so, but it seemed like an eternity as he desperately tried to take in what he had seen. It was almost beyond comprehension, and the horror he felt made him press his palms into his eyes until they ached.

Even his worst fears about what he might find in the secret wing – vague but disturbing as they had been – were nothing compared to the reality. How could Mr Finistaire – so warm, so friendly, so seemingly *genuine* – how could he have smiled and smiled, chatting and making plans to protect Keras, knowing what lay behind the tapestry, sealed off from the rest of the house and never mentioned – a terrible, toxic and terrifying secret?

Jack saw things so much more clearly now. The grand gathering Mr Finistaire was preparing for – all the important people from around the world that he had invited – they weren't coming to look at a rare orchid in the hothouse. That was just a sideshow.

He had been duped, outwitted, outplayed. He groaned aloud.

He felt Harriet's hand on his shoulder. She had stood there silently letting him recover, suppressing her impatience to look through the door and share the awful secret. 'What is it? It can't be *that* bad.'

Jack shook his head at the impossibility of describing how bad it was.

'I don't know what's going on, Jack. I wish you'd tell me.'

'I can't,' he said, barely able to get the words out. 'You wouldn't believe me if I did.'

'Try me,' she said fiercely.

She stood in front of him with her hands set determinedly on her hips. He saw that her dress was dusty, and her hair-do had begun to disintegrate. What could they do, a couple of kids? It was hopeless.

'Don't give up,' Harriet said. 'Whatever it is, you can always do something. And I'll help, if you let me.'

Before Jack could answer there was a noise outside, a rumble of engines. They both rushed to the window. Roaring round the bend came the Land Rover. It was towing a horsebox.

Behind it came a pick-up, and behind that, Sefton on his motorbike.

'What are they doing?' Harriet said. 'That's far too fast if they've got a horse in there!'

Jack knew with sickening certainty what the horsebox contained. 'Oh no,' he said. 'Oh please God, no . . .'

The Land Rover slewed round to get a better angle as it approached the gateway. As it did so, Sefton revved his bike and shot past it. They heard the bike clatter into the stable yard, and crossed to the other window.

Sefton got off his bike, and the Land Rover drew up. Mr Grout emerged, and waved instructions to the men from the other vehicle. There was a scraping noise. They were obviously shutting the big gates.

But there was another sound. From inside the horsebox came a succession of splintering blows.

'Hurry!' Mr Grout shouted. Then he leaped back into the Land Rover and backed it so that the rear of the horsebox was under the archway.

It was exactly as Jack had thought – there was a door there. Right below where they were standing.

The horsebox was now rocking wildly, and the men were standing back, well clear of it.

'What are they doing?' Harriet exclaimed. 'They can't treat a horse like that. They've terrified it.' She turned her face to Jack. It was flushed with anger. 'Stop it!' she shouted through the glass.

'Don't!' said Jack. The last thing he wanted was Harriet drawing attention to them.

'I'm not standing by while they mistreat an animal like that,' she said, moving across to the door.

'Harriet, please. You don't understand.'

'I understand cruelty to animals. And so does the RSPCA. Does Mr Finistaire have any idea what's going on?'

Jack sighed miserably. He glanced out into the yard again. Sefton was striding towards the archway. The noise from the horsebox intensified, and then there was another bang as the doors slammed open.

There was a terrible whinny, escalating into a sort of scream, and a dreadful drumming of reluctant hooves. And then, suddenly, the noise was coming from directly below them. There must be some sort of stable down there, Jack thought.

There was a great bellow of fury, and then a lot

more kicking, accompanied by a groundswell of grunting and cursing.

'Listen to that,' Harriet said, breathing hard. 'We've got to stop them.'

The sounds from beneath the floor were truly awful. Jack wondered what was going on. It would be dangerous, shut in a confined space with Keras, especially if you couldn't see him – though he supposed there would be the outline of the net. He experienced a fleeting admiration for Sefton's bravery in amongst the disgust he felt for what he was doing.

'Come on.' Harriet's eyes were wide with purpose. 'If *you* won't, I'll go on my own.'

Jack knew she was right. Keras *had* to be rescued. He just couldn't see how. He glanced down into the yard to buy himself a moment's thinking space. What he saw made him leap away from the window.

'What is it?'

'Mr Finistaire. Just coming through the kitchen yard.'

'Right. I'm going to speak to him. He's in charge, and he's got to stop it.'

Jack let Harriet go ahead, but they had only got halfway across the next room when they heard the ominous sound of boots coming up the stairs from the stables.

Someone must have spotted us, Jack thought.

Harriet reacted faster. 'The key – quick!' She raced past him, yanked the key out of the keyhole of the second door, and flew across to the door at the top of the stable stairs. She just managed to lock the door as two pairs of boots thumped onto the landing.

The latch rattled and a heavy hand shook the handle. They heard a curse, followed by a weighty blow from a boot.

'What d'you think – kick it in?' said a voice.

'Nah – we'd only have to fit a new one. They can't go anywhere, can they?' came the reply. 'Someone can get them from the house.'

The boots retreated down the stairs again.

'I'll head them off,' Jack said. 'You stay here.'

'What do you mean?'

'Please . . . You'll be all right. No one's going to hurt you.'

'They're hurting that horse downstairs.'

'Just do as I say. Trust me.'

Harriet looked at him fiercely. 'A nice day out I'm having, I must say.'

Jack thought she was going to cry, but she fought back the tears.

'All right then – you go,' she said. 'I just wish you'd tell me what's going on.'

'I can't. Not now. But I will. Honest.'

There was a sudden commotion from below, and the sound of a heavy impact.

Jack had to find Mr Finistaire and confront him. He *had* to force himself to face the horror behind the little door.

But when he came to it, he felt paralysed. It was only a particularly awful sound from downstairs that forced him to reach for the doorknob. He pulled the door open and went through.

It was no less shocking than the first time. It was worse, in fact, because he could now take more of it in.

He was standing in a gallery that ran along two walls of a substantial hall. There was a spiral staircase connecting the gallery to the floor of the hall, down the centre of which ran a long table with twenty or so high-backed chairs set on either side of it.

But it wasn't the hall's furniture that caught the eye. It was what was hanging on the walls. On almost every available space there was a trophy – a hunting trophy: the heads of stags with their branching antlers, boars with their tusks, tigers with their huge teeth bared, and a whole host of other animals, some of which Jack didn't even recognize.

But far, far worse than that was what hung in pride of place above the main entrance: it was the head of a unicorn. The shock when he'd first seen it was like being hit by lightning. To find a unicorn's head on display in Mr Finistaire's home, after all the conversations they'd had about preserving and protecting Keras . . .

Even now, Jack struggled to believe his eyes, but as he looked more closely, he realized that this unicorn was older and grander than Keras. The horn was longer, as was the beard. It had a truly regal bearing. Unlike the other mounted heads, with their dull glassy eyes, the unicorn's eyes, even in death, seemed to glare furiously at the indignity done to it.

Jack felt sick. It was as if every certainty, everything he had faith in, had been centrifugally ripped from his being. How could Mr Finistaire have behaved the way he had, knowing that this chamber of horrors lay just behind the tapestry?

Jack clung to the balustrade, drained of strength.

To his left hung the head of one of Keras's forebears, and behind the wall to his right, Keras himself was engaged in a life-or-death struggle with Sefton and Mr Grout. Jack's head spun as he listened to the blows and bangs, the curses and the high-pitched whinnies.

Then the door of the hall opened.

'Jack!' It was Mr Finistaire. He looked up, wild-eyed. 'Jack,' he said again, moving rapidly towards the spiral staircase.

Jack watched in horror as he climbed the stairs, unable to move, unable to speak.

'Jack, my dear boy, listen to me, please. I can explain . . .' Mr Finistaire had reached the gallery, and was advancing towards him. Jack couldn't read the expression on his face, but he found that he was moving away, backing towards the gallery door.

But Mr Finistaire was soon upon him. 'I'm not going to hurt you, Jack.' Although the voice was strained, it was gentle. 'Please look at me, Jack.'

Reluctantly Jack raised his head. Mr Finistaire's face was drawn. His eyes looked desperate, pleading.

'Come with me. I want to show you something.'

The appeal in his eyes was so strong that Jack found himself compelled to follow as he was led along the gallery to the spiral staircase.

As they descended, they came closer to the unicorn head. There was a metal plaque fixed to the wall below it.

'Look,' said Mr Finistaire, pointing to it.

Inscribed on the plaque were the words: *Charnley, 1897.*

'He was shot by my grandfather. It's terrible, I know – truly, truly terrible.'

'But you're going to do the same to Keras,' Jack said.

'No, Jack – never. How could you think that? I would never do that. Everything I've done has been aimed at saving him.'

'Then why . . . ?' Jack nodded his head at the far wall.

'It's all gone wrong. The timing was wrong. But they found him, and the opportunity was too good to miss. We might never have had another chance. But they bungled it. He was meant to be sedated. Then we could have found out more about him; made plans to protect him. My friends coming next week are some of the most powerful people in the world. I was going to appeal to them for help – but I needed proof that he existed.'

'But you can't even see him,' Jack protested.

'Ah, so you noticed . . .' Mr Finistaire sighed.

'What makes you think any of your rich friends could either?'

'Nothing,' Mr Finistaire said sadly. 'But there's no doubting his physical reality. Touch is almost as good as sight.'

'So you were going to keep him sedated and let a whole lot of strangers feel him?'

'Put like that it sounds terrible. But I really was acting with the best of intentions, Jack, I do assure you.' Mr Finistaire looked so crestfallen, Jack almost felt sorry for him.

But before he could think of anything to say, the battle on the other side of the wall seemed to reach a crescendo.

Then something extraordinary happened. Plaster began to fly all over the place, as though someone were hacking at the wall with a pickaxe. And, smashing through like an icebreaker forcing its way through a frozen sea, Keras's horn appeared, rapidly followed by his head, half masked by the web of the cricket net.

'Keras!' Jack wanted to run down the stairs to him, but Mr Finistaire was blocking the way.

Keras shook the plaster out of his eyes, and then swept the hall with an imperious glare. Suddenly the great head froze. Jack wanted to shout out, but the look on Keras's face seemed to paralyse him. The unicorn was staring fixedly ahead, taking in Jack and Mr Finistaire and, right next to them, the mounted head of one of his own family.

Jack couldn't bear it – couldn't bear the look of outrage and judgement. At last he managed to move his mouth: 'It's not . . . it wasn't me!' he shouted out in desperation, pushing past Mr Finistaire.

But before he could reach the floor of the hall, Keras threw back his head with a terrible bellow. At the same time, the net around him was yanked ferociously, and he disappeared again.

There were more sounds of combat. Jack launched himself down the hall.

'Jack, stop!' Mr Finistaire shouted from the staircase.

Jack ignored him, but before he could reach the far wall, there was a wild cry of pain, and suddenly another head plunged through the plaster.

It was Sefton.

Jack was close enough to the cropped head to see a powerful vein throbbing violently at his temple.

Then there was a terrific thump, and the chauffeur shot forward so that his shoulders made the hole in the wall wider. He gave a dull grunt, glanced up at Mr Finistaire with a look of appeal, and then his eyes closed and he slipped backwards through the wall, falling with a thud on the other side.

Jack rushed over and looked through the gap. Sefton was lying motionless on the floor of a grim, dungeon-like space. Jack barely registered the feeding trough along one wall and the tangle of netting on the floor. The most important thing was that the door to the gateway was open. Keras was nowhere to be seen.

Jack flung himself at the hole and squirmed through, using Sefton to break his fall. Jack felt no sympathy for him, and was on his feet in an instant. He dashed over to the door, where Harriet was standing, open-mouthed.

'Did I just see what I thought I saw?'

'Yes,' Jack said. 'You let him out?'

'I had to. It was too cruel.'

'Well done. Where's he gone?'

Harriet pointed in the direction of the kitchen garden.

Jack saw why. Mr Grout and his men had

barricaded the far end of the stable yard with an old trailer and some wheelie bins.

'Quick,' he said, and led the dash to the garden gateway.

'He's amazing – I can't believe it. Why didn't you tell me?' Harriet cried, trying to keep up with him.

'I – I couldn't,' he gasped. 'I'll tell you about it later. I just need to see him now.'

They darted through the kitchen yard. Mrs Grout was standing in the doorway in her apron, her eyes screwed up in an expression of outraged disbelief.

'Hey, you – stop!' she shouted, but they ran straight past her into the first walled garden.

Their way was blocked by the marquee, but there was no mystery about where Keras was. They could hear chairs being kicked over and the crash of crockery. Then there was a loud rip.

They pushed through the tent flaps and found a scene of devastation. At the far end there was a gaping tear in the canvas.

They sprinted down through the wreckage of strewn chairs and toppled flower arrangements. Somewhere ahead of them, Mr Grout was shouting orders, marshalling his men.

They raced into the second walled garden. Jack

could hear Keras's hoof-beats, but he was blocked from sight by the yew trees. Jack glimpsed Mr Grout's men spreading out from the far doorway, holding hoes and rakes like some makeshift peasant army. Keras was trapped.

'Oi, you kids!' Mrs Grout had followed them and was brandishing a frying pan. Mr Finistaire came panting up to her and gently pulled her arm down.

'That'll do, thank you, Mrs Grout,' he said firmly. 'Jack, wait,' he called out.

But Jack wouldn't wait. He had to find Keras, try to make him understand that he had played no part in any of it.

'Look!' Harriet pointed to a set of hoof-prints in one of the flowerbeds. 'This way.'

But before they cleared the avenue of yews, they heard a tremendous crash and a splintering of glass.

Mr Grout's furious voice rang out: 'You idiots! Get him out of there.'

Jack and Harriet sprinted across the grass to the glasshouse. The door had been smashed in, and there was a great commotion from inside.

Mr Grout's men were running in the same direction.

'Grab those bloody kids!' Mr Grout yelled, but they were too quick.

Ducking under flailing arms, they charged on, leaping over the shards of glass.

Once in the glasshouse, they stopped immediately. The great urn that had held the Lady of the Moon lay shattered on the floor, and the orchid had been stamped into a mess of flowers and mangled roots.

Feet crunched on the broken glass behind them. 'My orchid!' Jack heard Mr Finistaire wail.

Then he felt a hand on his shoulder. It was Mr Grout. 'You'll pay for this, you—'

'Leave him alone, you brute,' shouted Harriet, and she kicked him hard on the shin. 'Come on, Jack,' she said, pulling him up the stairs.

They ran along the walkway, over the pond, and down into the jungly depths beyond.

Keras was rampaging somewhere ahead of them, leaving a trail of devastation in his wake. Jack and Harriet ran after him, ducking under creepers, stepping over the gigantic leaves that had been trampled to the ground.

It was hot, and Jack had to keep brushing the sweat away from his eyes. *Keras, wait. It's me!*

But although he could see the leaves moving violently ahead of him, he was never quite close enough to catch sight of the unicorn.

And then there was another almighty crash.

'He's broken out,' Harriet said, clutching Jack's arm. 'He's made it. He's free!'

They came to the far wall. There was glass everywhere, and they picked their way gingerly through the hole Keras had made.

They stood blinking in the sunlight.

'There he is!' Harriet said, looking out across the fields. 'Isn't he the most magnificent creature in the whole world?'

Jack felt her hand grip on his arm, and he wiped the sweat out of his eyes.

'Look – he's saying goodbye!' Harriet waved with her free hand, and Jack heard a trumpeting neigh ringing out across the paddock. He could see little puffs of dust as Keras galloped away across the parched earth.

But of Keras himself he could see nothing. Nothing at all.

'What's wrong, Jack?' Harriet peered into his face. 'Jack? It's all right – he's escaped – he's free. We did it!'

Jack felt the tears scalding his cheeks. He reached into his pocket for his handkerchief, and his fingers fumbled with the locket chain. He pulled out the locket and pressed it clumsily into Harriet's hand.

'*You* did it.' He closed Harriet's fingers over the locket.

'What's this?'

'It's your prize. This was meant to be your special day, remember? Your prize day? Well, this is your prize. He'd want you to have it.'

He narrowed his eyes and saw the last faint puff of dust. But stare as he might, there was no unicorn that he could see.

Jack let out a terrible cry, and started running and stumbling towards the first belt of trees. *Keras! Keras! Come back . . . Come back.*

He knew it was hopeless, but he didn't care. He had lost the most precious thing he had ever known, and he had no hope that anything could ever restore it to him.

CHAPTER 19

Ignoring Harriet's cries, Jack staggered into the trees at the far end of the paddock. It was a relief to get out of the sun; to escape the pandemonium that Keras had left in his wake.

But as he lurched from tree to tree, Jack realized that there was no relief; no relief from the terrible pain he felt at losing Keras. Though 'losing' wasn't the right word: he had been judged, found wanting, and rejected.

How could he have been so foolish as to seek punishment for his stupidity in revealing Keras's secret? This was a more terrible punishment than anything Mr Grout could have dished out with his bone-handled stick.

Jack felt the merciless stiletto of a stitch stabbing into him, forcing him to stop, doubling him up in agony with his hands stapled to his stomach. Fighting for breath, he tried to find a position to ease the pain, but nothing worked.

The pain of the stitch was a relief in a way because it distracted him from the pain of his loss, but it was still no protection against the dreadful flashback to the moment when Keras saw him standing next to Mr Finistaire, just below the head of the ancient unicorn. It was like being caught by an old-fashioned flash-bulb. And there, in the developing tray of his memory, the image was captured for all time. His mind's eye flinched away, but there was no escaping it. It must have looked as awful as it felt – absolute proof that he had been working with Mr Finistaire to bring about the same end for Keras as that suffered by his ancestor.

But it was so unfair! He had been doing everything he could to foil Mr Finistaire's plan. Surely Keras could have seen that; surely he could have allowed Jack to explain himself. But instead of giving him the benefit of the doubt, Keras had kicked his way out of Mr Finistaire's garden, out through the glasshouse wall, and off into invisibility, leaving Jack aching with sorrow and a burning sensation of injustice.

If only he could find Keras; if only he could track him down. But there was no chance of that. If the unicorn didn't want to be found, he wouldn't be.

True, Mr Grout and Sefton had captured him, but that was more like an army hunting down a fugitive. Jack was on his own.

There was nothing for it but to pick his way home through the empty woods. And if he paused along the way to cry because the pain was too great to bear, then at least he would cry alone, in the barren privacy of his own grief.

The next few days were the worst of Jack's life. His misery was like a sickness. He moped around, hardly able to move. He lay in bed in the mornings until his mum lost patience with him and shouted at him to get up. But when he did, he annoyed her even more.

'Why don't you go out with your friends,' she demanded, 'instead of hanging around the house all day, getting under my feet?'

He groaned at the thought of Dan and Luke asking him questions, trying to get the story of Harriet's big day out of him. It was bad enough trying to deal with his parents. For once, even his dad seemed interested, and badgered him from the moment the story – or versions of it – broke the next day.

It was an established fact that something had happened, something dramatic. Mr Finistaire had cancelled his great gathering, had had the marquee taken down and the shutters fastened over Charnley's dozens of windows. Some said that he was planning to leave the country, possibly for good. But rumours as to Mr Finistaire's intentions were nothing compared to the stories about the events that had forced him to change his plans so dramatically. Those villagers who had been brought in for the great gathering came back with tales of the greenhouse being smashed in some cascading cataclysm, though no two stories agreed on what had caused the damage.

'So what did happen?' Jack's dad asked, dropping the paper by the side of his plate when he came in for lunch. 'And why didn't you tell us yesterday, when you came back from Charnley? I felt a right Charlie at work – me with a boy on the estate, not knowing what they were talking about.'

Jack shifted uneasily on his chair. Talk? The way he'd felt yesterday? He stared at his plate. Never had Spam, boiled potatoes and beetroot swimming in its own thin, vinegary blood seemed less appetizing.

'Well? I've got to have something to tell the lads. To listen to them, it was little short of an alien invasion.'

'I don't know, Dad. I was in a different place,' he replied, adding bitterly, 'I didn't see.'

'Even if you didn't see, you must have heard. You were there, for Pete's sake. From what I heard it was pandemonium.'

'But who's going to take time to explain what's going on to an eleven-year-old?'

Jack looked gratefully at his mum, but he could see that she was just as curious.

'But you must have seen something – afterwards,' his dad went on. 'Stan Shipton says the glasshouse was smashed up like a bomb had hit it. And as for your precious orchid . . .'

'That's so sad,' Jack's mum said. 'It was beautiful, wasn't it, Jack?'

Jack had a flashback of the pale flowers and slender stem stamped into a mess amidst the broken glass.

'Well, I wouldn't know about that,' Jack's dad said with emphasis. 'But it seems like old Finistaire shouldn't have "liberated" it from the rainforest in the first place, so perhaps it's no bad thing it's gone.'

'You wouldn't have said that if you'd seen it,' Jack's mum said wistfully.

'Well, not having been invited over to inspect it . . .'

Jack was hoping that the orchid would prove sufficient distraction to let him off the hook. But he was soon disappointed.

'So?' His dad slapped the palm of his hand down on his paper, challenging Jack to respond. 'Stan said there was a wild animal went mad up there. You must have heard something.'

Jack took a deep breath. It was almost too painful for him to think about, but he realized he would have to come up with some line if he was ever to get any peace. But what could he say? What could have done the same amount of damage as a maddened Keras?

He felt his mind go completely blank. As he looked around in desperation, his eyes fell on his dad's newspaper, folded to the sports page as usual. A ferocious-looking man with a rugby ball under his arm was breaking through a tackle under the headline: LEEDS RHINOS CHARGE TO WEMBLEY.

Praying his dad wouldn't look down at the paper, Jack took the plunge: 'It was a rhino, Dad. A rhinoceros.'

'A rhinoceros! You've got to be joking.'

Jack could see the doubt on his mother's face as well.

'It's a secret, Dad. It wasn't meant to be there. I mean, not legally. Like the orchid. It's endangered, and Mr Finistaire was trying to save it. But it went mad, and he had to—'

'They had to shoot it, did they? No wonder they're trying to keep a lid on it. Makes sense. And they're big brutes, rhinos. Easily capable of destroying a glasshouse.'

Jack stole a look at his dad, who was stroking his chin, running through the story, probing it for improbabilities.

Eventually he nodded, and when he spoke, Jack could tell that his curiosity had been satisfied. 'Your mum and I just wanted to know. I can see why it's hush-hush, so you better not tell anyone else, will you?'

Jack shook his head.

'Good lad,' his dad said, getting down to his lunch again. When he'd finished, he left the table, folding the paper without looking at it and tapping his palm with it. 'Who'd've thought it, eh? A bloomin' rhinoceros at Charnley.' A moment or two later they heard him call out 'Ta-ra,' and then the front door closed.

Jack's mum looked at him. 'Well done, love. I'm glad you told him – otherwise he'd have gone on and on about it. Mind you, it's a blessing you were elsewhere. Imagine having you brought back in bits, trampled to death by a rhinoceros.' Then, looking at his untouched plate, she added: 'Not hungry, love? Don't worry. Leave it. I know beetroot's not your favourite. I'm going into town to do some shopping. I'll get sausages for tea.'

She cleared the table. Jack sat and watched her. He knew he should offer to help, but he felt too drained to lift a finger.

Maybe it was his failure even to get up from his chair that prompted it, but after she'd taken the potato bowl over to the sink, his mum turned to him.

'Jack, I understand that's it's been a big blow – not going to Charnley any more and all that, but you've got to put it behind you. It was great, but now it's over and you have to move on. I know it's disappointing, but you must pick yourself up. I can't have you moping around the house all summer, especially if you're not even going to help clear the table. It'll drive me round the bend. Now, assuming you don't want to come into town with me . . . ?'

Jack squirmed.

'OK, that's fine. But I expect you to do the washing up, and there's a great heap of clothes in your room that needs sorting out for the shop – school stuff, gardening stuff – and I want it in neat piles when I get back. All right?'

'Yes, Mum,' Jack said listlessly.

'I mean it, Jack: you are going to have to pull yourself together. You need to get out. Arrange to see your friends. You've hardly seen them this holiday – Luke, and what's the other one called?'

'Dan.'

'Dan, that's right. I don't mind what you do – within reason – provided you do something.'

She bustled around finding shopping bags and her car keys, before leaning over and giving him a peck on the cheek. And then she was gone, leaving Jack on his own in the cottage.

He listened as the car engine coughed into life, but he remained motionless in his chair.

How long he would have stayed sitting there at the kitchen table he couldn't have said. He had no plans for the day. He had no energy. No interest in anything. He was simply relieved at being left alone.

But although this meant that he didn't have to fend off questions with more painfully improvised lies, it left him all the more vulnerable to his own thoughts and interrogation.

It had all been his fault. The whole tragic catastrophe. He played the memory tape of events over and over again, each time writhing with the agony of having led Mr Finistaire to Keras and exposing the unicorn to the cruelty and indignity of capture. The echoes of the terrible sounds coming from the stable in the annexe made him clench his fists in pain and rage. And the image of Keras's head crashing through the wall, and his eyes, wide with terror, staring at him as he stood on the metal stairs below the mounted head made him almost choke with self-loathing.

The thought that this was the last he would ever see of Keras – that because of his betrayal, he had been deprived of the power to see him – cast a pall over every waking minute. If he was distracted, it was only for a moment; and then the full force of his loss came crashing back to overwhelm him. He couldn't imagine escaping from it, ever.

And so he sat at the kitchen table, looking vacantly at the calendar hanging on the wall opposite him. His life seemed as empty as the little blank squares that neither his mum nor his dad ever wrote anything in. Empty and pointless. He leaned slowly forward and let his head rest on the table top.

The clock ticked. The tap dripped into the washing-up bowl. The clock ticked faster than the tap dripped. He gradually became absorbed in the two sounds, counting the half-dozen ticks between each little splash.

He was so absorbed that when a new noise burst in, it took him a moment to realize what it was: the telephone. He listened to it for a while, rehearsing the two possible responses: *He's at work*; *she's out shopping*. Then he pushed his chair back and went into the hall. 'Hello,' he said emptily.

There was a slight pause, and he heard the person on the other end of the line take in a breath.

'Oh, Jack, it's you. I'm so glad. I'd been preparing to face one of your parents.'

Jack froze. Although he kept holding the receiver to his ear, he seemed incapable of doing anything more. The voice in his ear was quite unmistakable. It was Mr Finistaire.

'Jack?'

This time it was Jack's turn to draw in a breath. But it took a lot of effort to get out the single syllable: 'Yes?'

However, this was all Mr Finistaire needed.

'Dear boy. I am so, so sorry. I know what you must have felt and what you still feel now. I'm shattered too. It was a horror, an unspeakable calamity, and I don't know whether I'll ever recover from it.'

You? Jack thought. *What about* me?

As on so many occasions in the past, Mr Finistaire seemed to read his unspoken thought.

'I know it's terrible for you too. I do understand that. But at least he's free – and you are free to see him again.'

As if, thought Jack; but Mr Finistaire did not pick up on it this time.

'As I tried to explain at the time, it was never meant to happen like that. I think – I hope – you know me well enough to realize that I wholly dissociate myself from my ancestors' appalling behaviour. It would no more have occurred to me to harm Keras than it would to harm you, or that charming, if rather self-regarding girl, Harriet. Everything I did was designed to atone for bad deeds done in the past, and to preserve Keras into a long and secure future.'

Jack drew breath, but this time Mr Finistaire was on to his thought-process. 'I know, that must have seemed a very odd way of going about it, and I won't try to make excuses. I have to take full responsibility for what happened, even though it came out so badly because of a combination of bad luck, bad timing and, I have to say, an excess of zeal on the part of that extraordinary – and very brave – young man, Sefton.'

There was a pause. Jack waited for Mr Finistaire to continue.

'I'm not going to keep you long, Jack. This episode has been painful for us both. But I did not want us to part company without an explanation – and an apology – from me. What I did, what I authorized, was well intentioned. I hope you can believe that. Whether you can ever forgive me, only time will tell. However tragically it all ended, I owe you an enormous debt. The last few weeks have been the most exciting, the most fulfilled of my entire existence, and you were the person who brought that blessing into my life. I thank you now, and will continue to give thanks for what you did.'

Mr Finistaire broke off, and Jack thought he detected the slightest check at the other end of the phone.

'It is a sad time, Jack, and I am off to lick my wounds in a distant country where I shall be well looked after, and where, hopefully, I may find balm for my wounds. One of the things – one of the many things – I have reproached myself with is my foolish reluctance to take you into my confidence. If I had shared the full story with you, it might have ended differently, less disastrously.'

Here Mr Finistaire paused again, and Jack heard a definite sigh.

'However, what's done is done – or rather undone, and we have to live with the consequences. As part of the healing process I may, when I am calm enough to think straight once more – write an account of everything – everything I know about Keras and the unicorns of Charnley. It occurs to me that if I wrote it in a series of letters, the task would be less onerous. And there is only one person I could send those letters to, isn't there, Jack? I would have to send them to you – for your eyes only, of course.'

There was another pause. Then Mr Finistaire said: 'Goodbye, Jack. It has been a privilege to have known you and shared these experiences with you.'

Then the line went dead.

Jack stood with the receiver in his hand for what seemed an age, before gently slotting it back in its rest. Even after he'd done that, he stood rooted to the spot for a long time. His head was so heavy with thoughts, he was surprised it didn't weigh him down and anchor him to the floor. He knew what Mr Finistaire meant about the time it would take before they could make sense out of what happened. But of course *he* would have the advantage of staying with one of his rich and powerful friends and being waited on hand and foot. Jack had to stay in the village, a brief crow's flight from the scene of the disaster, with reminders of how badly everything had gone wrong confronting him on all sides.

He finally forced himself to move. He felt like a diver with lead boots to keep him on the sea-bed, but he eventually made it to the sink, and started to do the washing up.

A few days later, the phone rang again. Again, Jack was on his own, as it was one of the days his mum worked in the charity shop.

She had gone off with a big bag of his old clothes, leaving Jack to his own devices once more.

'Hello,' said the voice, a much smaller voice than Mr Finistaire's.

'Who's that?'

'Harriet!'

There was a silence.

'Jack? It's me, Harriet.'

'How did you get this number?'

'The phone book. There aren't that many Henleys in the village.'

There was another silence.

'Jack – are you all right?'

'Yeah,' he said listlessly.

'You're not, are you? I know you're not. Look,' Harriet continued, 'I've got to see you.'

'What for?'

'I can't tell you over the phone.'

People were always saying that in books and films – Jack never understood why.

'But it's important,' she went on breathlessly. 'Can you meet me in the woods?'

'Where?'

'At the ruined cottage.'

The ruined cottage. How did she know about that?

'You've been to the woods?'

'Yes.'

'And you've—' He couldn't say it. The thought of Harriet riding Keras set off an explosion of feelings in him.

'Yes.' Although she said it very quietly, she couldn't keep the excitement out of her voice.

Jack couldn't speak. He felt his throat constricting, as though someone were tightening a rope around it.

'Jack . . . ? Say something. Please. I know what you're feeling . . .'

No – no you don't. No one knows what I'm feeling; no one could ever know!

Jack held the receiver away from him. Harriet's voice became a distant squeak in his hand. He hated her. He wanted to put the phone down and be left to his misery, not tormented with the thought of her enjoying what he had lost.

'Jack! *Jack!*'

Little squawks from the end of his arm. Slowly he brought the receiver closer. He looked at it stupidly, as though he'd forgotten what it was for.

'Are you still there, Jack?'

A great warm tear splashed onto his wrist. 'I'm still here,' he whispered hoarsely.

'Good,' said Harriet. 'Meet me at the cottage at three this afternoon. All right? Jack – did you hear me? Will you be there? It's important. Jack?'

'Yes,' he said, and put the phone down.

Then the dam inside him burst, and he crouched in the hall, letting the tears rain down on the tatty old carpet until he could cry no more.

The rest of the time passed. Jack did nothing. It didn't matter where he did nothing. Sometimes he did it in the kitchen, sometimes in the lounge, sometimes upstairs. Wherever he was, he did nothing.

But even though he was staring vacantly out of the window, or tracing the cracks in his bedroom ceiling or the pattern in the carpet in front of the fireplace, something was going on inside.

Jack didn't know what it was at first, but he didn't like it. It was disturbing. It made him feel uncomfortable. It was, he sensed, what made him move from room to room; what made him switch his empty stare from one boring thing to the next.

After a restless hour he finally recognized it. It was hope.

He was back in the kitchen, and when he realized what it was, he put his head in his hands and groaned. Ever since the terrible day at Charnley he had resigned himself to his fate: never to see Keras again, never to be in contact with him, never to hear of him.

It was unbearable, but the extraordinary thing about the unbearable was that you had to bear it; you had to accept it – and find a way of living with it. All the love and yearning he felt for Keras had to be suppressed, all the feelings of limitless happiness that Keras had released in him had to be driven out, stamped down, buried deep. He had to anaesthetize himself. It would mean deadening his life, but it would dull the acute pain. It was the only way.

But now, with Harriet's phone call, the anaesthetic was wearing off. Jack felt as if bandages had been ripped off an open wound. Hope – the crazy, delusional, futile hope that he might be forgiven, that he might see Keras again – twisted in his mind like a knife.

He knew that if he allowed hope the smallest foothold, he would be exposing himself to the terrible dangers of disappointment – to the risk of being hurled back down into a pit from which there could be no escape.

He got up and paced around the kitchen. The clock seemed to have packed up. Each tick was begrudged, each tock a calculated insult. Hours, minutes, meant nothing. He was here, in the house. He wasn't there in the wood waiting to hear first-hand news of Keras. And however painful that might be, that's what he wanted, more than anything in the world.

He walked out of the kitchen, across the hall, and went into the lounge once more. Sunlight fought its way through the dusty lace curtains and formed an inviting square on the carpet.

He lay down in it and shut his eyes, willing himself to be still, willing himself to empty his mind completely.

CHAPTER 20

At last the grudging kitchen clock ticked and tocked its way to half past two. Even though he knew he was going to be early, Jack leaped up and got ready to leave the house. He felt super-charged. He had to be out, in the woods, active at last. However much pain the next couple of hours would almost certainly bring, it was better to go out and face it than sit like a zombie at home.

Jack let himself out through the gate onto the lane at the back of the cottage. It took an effort of will not to run. He looked about him. The sun was still high, and there was hardly a cloud to be seen. Yes, it was good to get out. He just had to fight down the hope, ignore the expectation. He was merely going to see Harriet, who would tell him something about Keras. He would meet her, listen to what she had to tell him, and come back. That was the deal. Nothing more.

He kicked at a stone and watched it rattle down

the lane ahead of him. It reminded him of that other stone he had kicked only a few weeks earlier; the stone that had turned his life upside down. Well, it was the right way up again now, and he wished with his whole heart that it wasn't.

He pushed through the gate. Its warning against trespassing looked even more feeble now. It was as though the estate's defences were down. Keras had kicked his way to freedom, sending Mr Finistaire into exile, and overthrowing Mr Grout and all he stood for.

Jack came to the old oak tree, and looked again into its wrecked branches. It had given him some comfort on the morning of his last day at Charnley. It offered none now.

He moved on along the familiar paths. Everything was as it had been, but it was all different. *He* was different. He felt like a stranger in the place where he had always felt most at home.

A wood pigeon suddenly flapped into flight, bursting clumsily through the foliage. It startled him as it never would have done before. He walked on uneasily, and eventually came to the derelict cottage.

There was no chance of Harriet being there yet, he knew that. So he decided to go inside. The door had long since been wrenched from its hinges. He picked his way through the litter in the hallway and went into the front room. He looked up through the hole where the ceiling had fallen in. Had more plaster come down since he was last there? He wasn't sure.

He thought about climbing the rickety stairs, but couldn't be bothered. He knew he was just killing time.

And then he heard it: the sound he wanted to hear most in the world – the sound of hooves on the flagstone path.

Catching the cry in his throat, he darted out through the door and round the side of the cottage.

'Jack!'

He stopped dead. There was Harriet sitting astride Seth, looking faintly ridiculous in her jodhpurs and riding hat.

She saw the disappointment in his face. 'Oh, Jack, I'm sorry. I should have warned you. It's the only way I can get here. Not that I'm meant to be here at all. Mum thinks I'm in the water meadows.'

She jumped down and stood looking slightly flushed in front of him. 'How are you, Jack? Has it been awful?'

Jack looked away. He couldn't trust himself to speak.

He felt her hand on his arm. His instinct was to shrug it off, but he didn't. He knew she was trying to help. It wouldn't be fair to take out his feelings on her.

She took off her helmet and shook out her hair. 'I felt so sorry for you. I couldn't bear it when you just ran off – you looked so . . . I wanted to come after you, but . . .'

'What happened? Afterwards, I mean,' Jack asked huskily.

'Oh, utter pandemonium. People running around like madmen, Mr Finistaire absolutely frantic. It was quite funny in a way. But frightening too. They certainly didn't want me around.'

'But your mum was meant to be coming for tea.'

'Well, that didn't happen. No way. Mr Finistaire rang her up and said there'd been an accident and he was sending me straight home.'

'And then what?'

'Well, he sent me straight home, of course. He managed to sound calm on the phone, but he was in a frightful state really – absolutely devastated. He said how sorry he was and that it wasn't supposed to be like that, and everything had been done with the best possible intentions, and that all he could ask of me was that I keep my mouth shut and not tell tales that would have every reporter and television crew in the world descending on the village and Charnley.'

'So who drove you home? It can't have been Sefton. The last I saw he was out cold on the floor of that horrible stable place.'

'No, it wasn't. It was one of the other men.'

'And what did you say to your mum?'

'I didn't know what to say really – just that there'd been an accident and one of the men had got hurt.'

'Was that enough?'

'No. She wanted to know all the details. I had to make something up.'

'What did you say?'

'I said that a marquee pole had smashed the roof of the glasshouse and one of the men had got cut very badly. It wasn't much good, but it was the best I could do. What did *you* say?'

'Rhinoceros. Run mad.'

'A rhinoceros?' Harriet looked at him. Suddenly there was a spark of laughter in her eyes.

To his astonishment, Jack felt his mouth forming

the strange shape of a smile. 'Better than a marquee pole,' he said.

And they both burst into laughter.

'A rhinoceros! Jack, you're amazing,' said Harriet. 'Let's hope our parents never meet. It could be embarrassing if they compared notes.'

They laughed again, but then stopped, suddenly serious.

After a pause, Jack said: 'So you've seen him?'

'Yes. I had to. I just had to try.'

Harriet pulled the reins over her pony's head. 'Come on, Seth, you old softie,' she said, looping the reins expertly around one of the garden's few remaining fence posts. She pulled a carrot out of her pocket and held it up on her flattened palm. 'Good boy,' she said as it disappeared. 'Jack and I are just going for a little walk. We won't be long.'

'Where did it happen?' Jack asked as they headed away from the cottage.

'Over on our side of the woods . . .' Harriet nodded her head. 'It was as though he was waiting for me.'

Jack nodded, remembering his own meetings with Keras.

'One minute Seth and I were ambling along this bridleway, and the next – there he was!'

'How was Seth? It must have been a bit of a shock for him.'

'Seth was fine. It was me who was shocked – even though it was what I was hoping for.'

'So what happened?'

'Well, Seth and Keras sort of said hello, and then – I don't know how, but I just knew he wanted me to go with him, so I got off Seth, and then, next minute, I was up on Keras and – oh, Jack, it was amazing.'

Jack looked away into the undergrowth. He remembered the speed, the sense of power and freedom, the excitement – underpinned by a deep sense of security, the knowledge that he was safe.

'Where did you go?'

'I don't know, really. There was this great open bit—'

'The Great Glade – that's what it's called.'

'We galloped down the Great Glade. I never knew riding could be like that. It was like being in the Grand National – and winning it!' Harriet's eyes flashed. 'He's magnificent, isn't he?'

Jack nodded. 'Then what?'

'Well, we slowed down after that, and went

through some very dense woodland. But you could see where Mr Grout and his men had been at work, cutting down trees, clearing a path. It was like logging in the rainforest. Horrible.'

Jack nodded again.

'Eventually we came to a clearing. They'd made a real mess with the chainsaws – trees down all over the place. And in the middle of the clearing the ground was all churned up, and there were tyre marks – and hoof-prints. That was where they caught him. Keras walked round it very cautiously. It was as though he were reliving it all. It gave me the shivers. All those men and that terrible net, forcing him into the horsebox.'

'What happened next?'

'It was a bit weird. He stood there for a while. It was as though he'd forgotten I was on his back. I didn't know what to do. So I got down to have a look at the marks more closely. I suppose I just wanted to be face to face with him. Because I—'

Here she broke off, rummaged in her jodhpur pocket and brought out the locket. 'It was so kind of you to give me this, Jack. But obviously it was Keras's gift and I thought – well, I just wanted him to see that I had it; if he wanted it back he could take it. It's so beautiful.' She opened it. 'And so romantic! I've spent hours looking at it, and trying to work out what the initials are.'

'Any luck?'

'No – they're terribly old-fashioned. But there must be a way of tracing who they were – tracking down their story. I've got a cousin who's reading History at Oxford. I bet she'd help us.' She smiled at him.

'What did Keras do?' Jack asked.

'Nothing. He stared at it for a moment, as though working out how it had come to me. And then he gave my hand a little nudge with the end of his horn, as if to say: *You keep it; that's OK.* Then he looked at me. Right in the eye. Right down the length of his horn. It was frightening. But I knew I had to be brave. I somehow knew that he wanted to know more . . . about you.'

'About me?'

'About you, Jack. About everything you'd done, and how it wasn't your fault, and how you'd been determined to find out about the secret room and everything. You never told me what was in there, by the way.'

'I will,' Jack said. But not now. This was more

important. He felt his heart beginning to thump. Harriet had tried to tell Keras his side of the story. He felt humbled by her generosity.

'What did he do? Did he . . .?'

'Understand? Yes, I'm sure he did. I told him. I said, "It wasn't Jack's fault; none of it was." And I swung my arm round, meaning the ambush and the capture and everything.'

'And?'

'He just kept staring at me . . . and then he nodded his head very slowly, and his horn came right down almost to the ground, and then went up again. It was very solemn . . .' Harriet's voice trailed away. She wasn't looking at Jack any more, but over his shoulder, and her mouth was open.

Jack felt his whole body go cold with fear. Keras was behind him – instinctively he knew that. And every fibre of his being urged him to turn round. But if he did, and he couldn't see him, he felt he would die.

He heard the snap of a twig as Keras approached.

Harriet reached out her hands and took Jack's.

Keras was now right behind him. Jack could feel his legs going weak. Harriet squeezed his hand, and then there was warm sweet breath on the back of his neck.

'I think you can turn round now, Jack,' Harriet said, and gently pulled him round by the arm.

Jack wanted to close his eyes, but told himself not to be a coward. He didn't know whether to look up or down.

He looked up, and the first thing he saw was the pearly horn, high above his head. Then he stepped back to take in the full picture – the massive white head with its straggly beard, the deep, solemn eyes, the powerful legs with their cloven hooves.

'Oh, Keras,' he whispered. 'I'm so sorry. It was all my—'

But Keras didn't let him finish. He gave a loud whinny, and stamped impatiently. With a flick of his head he indicated that it was over and done with, forgotten, forgiven.

Jack stood before him, unable to move.

Keras gave a snort, and lowered his head. The beautiful wand of his horn rested on Jack's chest and then prodded him.

Jack stepped back.

'I think he wants you to ride him,' Harriet said softly.

Keras nodded his head vigorously.

'Come on, I'll give you a leg up.'

She led him to Keras's side and clasped her hands together for his foot. 'One, two, three – up!'

And suddenly Jack was on Keras's back once more. To feel his legs astride those strong shoulders and bury his hands in the coarse white mane was sheer bliss. It was the thing he had most longed for, the thing he'd thought he would never experience again. He wanted to give a great whoop of joy. He felt Keras poised to start. The slightest sign from him that he was ready to go, and they would be off.

Jack looked down.

Harriet grinned up at him. 'Off you go,' she said. She looked very small and rather prim in her riding gear.

'No,' he said. 'You come too.' He leaned down, extending his arm to her.

'Are you sure?'

'Sure I'm sure,' he said, in his best Sean Connery voice, pulling her up.

It was a bit of a scramble, and for a moment he thought they would both fall off. But they regained their balance, and Harriet put her arms around him.

Then Keras gave a whinny and set off along the

path. Soon his hooves were thundering, and they were flying – flying through the trees towards the heart of the wood.

'Look – you've finally got some colour back in your cheeks.'

Jack's mum glanced up from the ironing board. He went up to her and gave her a big hug. He was still breathless from the ride, and so exhilarated that if he didn't do something energetic straight away, he felt he would simply explode with happiness.

'Careful, love – mind the iron.'

Jack released her and headed for the kitchen door.

'Where are you going now?'

'Going to see if Dan and Luke want to come and kick a ball about on the rec.'

'All right, love. Enjoy yourself. Tea'll be about seven.'

'Hand ball!' Luke shouted.

'No it wasn't,' said Dan.

'It was, wasn't it, Jack?'

Jack didn't care. He glided onto the ball, left both of them for dead and aimed a shot through the rusty old metal goal posts.

‘What’s the point of kicking it that hard with no net?’ exclaimed Dan. ‘You can go and fetch it.’

Jack kept running after the ball, running and running. He didn’t mind that the goal didn’t have a net. He wouldn’t mind if he never saw a net again for the rest of his life.

ACKNOWLEDGEMENTS

I want to thank a number of people who have helped and supported me during the writing and preparing for publication of [illegible].

Firstly I should thank [illegible] my editor at [illegible], for putting me [illegible] Fletcher, and then David [illegible] [illegible] Simon Flinch was my [illegible] [illegible] [illegible] [illegible] [illegible] [illegible] Hannah [illegible] [illegible] and the [illegible] [illegible] shaped as a result [illegible] [illegible] [illegible] whenever [illegible] [illegible] up at the [illegible] [illegible] Richard Collingridge pinned above my desk a [illegible] inspiration.

I would also like to thank [illegible] the [illegible] team: Hilda Johnson, [illegible] person or on the phone; Sophie Nelson, my copy-editor, who crossed the 't' and dotted the 'i' in 'meticulous' like no other copy-editor in my experience; while Bella Pearson and Natalie Doherty undertook the painstaking job of proof-reading.

Bill Hamilton, my agent, has been a tower of strength throughout, and I would also like to thank Charlie Brotherstone, also of AM Heath & Co for bulletins relating to a subject dear to an author's heart, money.

Meanwhile, my own PA, Olivia Stanton, has worked valiantly to keep on top of the paperwork that can pile up behind a writer's back.

I would also like to thank the Royal Literary Fund for a very timely grant, and in particular, the RLF's Eileen Gunn for her kind help with my successful application.

Finally I would like to thank Michael, Naomi and Albertine for their gratifying impatience to read Dad's next book. I hope the wait was worth it!

SR
Banbury, 2013

ACKNOWLEDGEMENTS

I want to thank a number of people who have helped and supported me during the writing and preparation for publication of *Keras*.

Firstly, I should thank Carey Smith, my editor at Ebury Press, for putting me in touch with David Fickling, and then David himself for commissioning me. Susan Hitch was my first reader, whose eagerly awaited feedback provided a constant spur to keep going. Crucially, too, she came up with the name 'Keras' for my central character. Once the first draft was submitted, Hannah Featherstone assumed the editorial reins, and the story became sharper and better shaped as a result. I normally enjoy the revision process, but whenever I flagged, I only had to look up at the magical cover image created by Richard Collingridge pinned above my desk: a true inspiration.

I would also like to thank the rest of the DFB team: Tilda Johnson, unfailingly cheering either in